SECOND ACTS
BOOK ONE: MADISON'S CALL

J. R. Pickens

BookLocker
Trenton, Georgia

Paperback ISBN: 978-1-64719-916-6
Ebook ISBN: 978-1-64719-917-3

Published by BookLocker.com, Inc., Trenton, Georgia.

The characters and events in this book are fictitious. Any similarity to real persons, living or dead, is coincidental and not intended by the author.

Library of Congress Cataloging in Publication Data
Pickens, J.R.
Second Acts - Book One: Madison's Call by J.R. Pickens
Library of Congress Control Number: 2021922854
Fiction | Christian | Contemporary

Printed on acid-free paper.

Booklocker.com, Inc. 2022

Dedication

God's Word asks, "Who can find a virtuous wife?
For her worth *is* far above rubies."

This is certainly true of my wife, to whom I dedicate
this work. Not only is she a constant source of
encouragement, but she has endured countless hours
of staring at the back of my head while I sat at the
keyboard, tapping merrily away.

I am greatly blessed by my family, and by the people
God has put in my life. They have, without being
aware of it, provided confirmation that I was on the
right path while writing this book.

CHAPTER ONE

It was late summer, the weekend before Labor Day. On this oven-hot, Illinois summer afternoon the air hung thick, close, and humid. Madison Newman lived with her parents in an older suburban neighborhood, moderately upscale, with lush, old-growth trees.

Yard work had been completed in the cool of the early morning. Now, the only sounds in the neighborhood were children playing and dogs barking. Lunch was a distant memory, and the sun had begun its slow crawl toward the western horizon. Backyard barbeques sent lazy plumes of aromatic smoke skyward.

Maddie played in Frankie Patterson's front yard along with Frankie's best friend, Buddy. A Jack Russell Terrier, Buddy had been a gift to Frankie on his twelfth birthday. Eight months later, they were inseparable. The pup was lightning fast, chasing the tennis ball that Frankie and Maddie took turns throwing.

The two kids had been friends and neighbors for all of Madison's twelve years. Together, they waged a losing battle against Buddy. They tried to wear him out by throwing the saliva-sodden tennis ball again and again.

Buddy had recently learned that if he didn't want to give back the tennis ball, there was nothing these small humans could do about it. He was faster than either of them. The two kids chased Buddy, laughing, and calling out to the capering puppy.

"Buddy! Give me the ball, boy," Frankie called. Nothing doing.

"Give me the ball. BUDDY!" Maddie shouted.

The kids collapsed on the lawn in front of Frankie's house, laughing as Buddy ran circles around them, still teasing them with the ball.

***

Phil Sandoval drove his Range Rover through the neighborhood at a cautious twenty miles per hour. He'd lived there with his wife and two kids for seventeen years. The four of them had been out to the lake earlier in the day. They'd met up with Phil's brother and his family for a picnic.

Phil looked forward to catching a game on TV, and maybe having a couple of beers. Although his brother had beer up at the lake, Phil had abstained. He was driving, and he wanted to be a good example to his kids.

Despite Phil's careful driving, he couldn't stop in time when a small dog darted out into the road right in front of the Rover. Phil slammed on the brakes as his wife, Sylvia, screamed. The car came to a stop, but it was too late.

Phil put the car in park and turned off the engine. He reluctantly opened the driver's door and eased out of the car, dreading what he would find. There was a small dog, not yet fully grown, lying motionless on the tarmac. It wasn't gory, but there was no mistake. The dog was dead.

***

Frankie stood in the road, frozen in disbelief. He and Maddie had been chasing Buddy when the dog raced into the street. It felt like the car had come out of nowhere. Frankie looked at the man who stepped out of the car, the man who had just killed his best friend. He wanted to scream and rage, but all that escaped his lips was a small cry.

The boy dropped to his knees in the road and cradled Buddy's body. Frankie held his best friend close, sobbing, and rocking back and forth. He said Buddy's name over and over, as though by repetition he could undo everything the car had done.

Madison hurt for her friend's loss. She adored Frankie. He was the brother she never had. They sometimes fought and tormented each other, but they were closer to each other than any of their other school friends. Maddie felt sick to her stomach watching Frankie absorb the reality of Buddy's violent death.

She looked around. The accident had started to attract attention in the quiet neighborhood. The couple from the corner house, Tony and Connie Sanderson, had stepped outside and was heading over to see what was going on.

Helga Miller, a friendly neighbor that sometimes stopped by and visited with Maddie's mother, dashed toward them from her back yard gate wearing paint-splattered clothing. Helga took one look at Frankie holding his dead dog, glanced at Maddie, and whispered, "Oh, dear God." She ran off toward the Patterson's house.

Madison felt a strange tug. She'd felt it before. It came from deep inside of her. It felt like a thousand slender threads knitted within her, now pulling at her, urging her on, demanding something of her.

This time it wanted her to do something for Frankie, for Buddy. It was a frightening sensation, but also exhilarating. The first time it had happened it had come suddenly, scaring her. Now all that mattered to her was taking away Frankie's hurt.

Maddie wiped away her own tears and knelt next to Frankie in the middle of the street. She put her arm around her friend's shoulder and said, "Don't cry anymore, Frankie. It's going to be okay."

Frankie gave her a look of profound misery, a terrible, aching look that said nothing in the world was ever going to be okay. Not ever.

Madison sat down in the street next to Frankie, and gently took the dead terrier from her friend. He let go and buried his face in his hands. As she took the small dog, blood seeped from the dog's mouth, staining the girl's clothing.

She settled Buddy into her arms when his lifeless head lolled back, limp and hanging. She looked around at the people gathered. The man who had been driving stood still, his hand over his mouth. The man's wife stood next to him, digging her nails into his arm. She was crying. Their children were in the car, looking frightened.

She noticed Tony Sanderson as he stepped forward. His face was pale. "Maddie, I don't think you should hold him like that."

Maddie swallowed hard. This wasn't easy, especially now, when people were watching. But she couldn't resist the feeling that urged her onward. She supported Buddy's head, holding him like a baby.

"He'll be okay," she said firmly. She believed it even more firmly.

She rocked the dog and talked to him. "Buddy, it's not time yet. You have so many balls to chase. We love you. Frankie loves you." She leaned forward, head down, hovering close to the dog's still form. She whispered quietly, so no one would hear, "God, please, for Frankie's sake. Bring him back."

Frankie's mother, Diane, came running up to the scene in the middle of the street. Helga trailed behind. They were just in time to see little Buddy kick, and then squirm in Maddie's embrace, clearly wanting to be released. Buddy began licking and pawing the girl's face. His tail wagged furiously, keeping time to an impossibly rapid beat.

Diane was surprised to hear a woman scream when the dog began to move. The woman had been standing, holding a man's arm tightly as they both stood in front of a Range Rover parked in the middle of the street.

Frankie's mom tried to make sense of the situation. The woman let go of the man's arm and backed away. "I'll see you at home, Phil," she said.

"Sylvia, don't go," the man pleaded. "I have to talk to the boy's mother."

The woman's voice cracked, and she started crying. "I can't! I'm going home." She turned and hurried away.

Diane turned her attention to her son as she heard him shout, "Buddy!" She saw her son's little terrier wriggling free from Maddie's grasp and bolting toward the boy, leaping on him, and covering his face with enthusiastic licks.

All she had heard from Helga were the words "Frankie" and "accident" and she had raced out the door, not waiting for the full story.

"Frankie! Are you all right?"

Her boy laughed and tried to hug his little dog. The terrier yapped joyfully, and then sprinted off after a squirrel.

"Frankie!" Diane screamed again. What was going on?

"What, Mom?" Frankie looked up at her quickly. He seemed surprised by her tone of voice.

"What happened? Are you okay?" Diane asked. Now that he was looking at her, she could see he'd been crying.

The man who had been standing beside the Rover stepped forward. "Excuse me, Ma'am. My name is Phil. I live a couple blocks over. I'm afraid I hit your dog. It ran out in front of me, and I couldn't stop in time."

Diane looked down the street a few houses to see Buddy dashing through the grass. He stopped to lift his leg against a tree, and then ran off. It didn't seem the dog had ever had a bad day in his entire, short life.

Diane said, "As you can see, that dog is one big bundle of energy."

They watched him for a few moments. "I don't doubt for a minute he ran in front of you, but he doesn't appear any worse for wear," Diane observed.

"No. No, he doesn't," replied Phil, sounding thoughtful. "I swear I thought he was…" Diane looked at Phil when he stopped. The man paused, swallowed, and glanced down at her son, who was listening to their conversation. "Well, I thought he'd been hurt pretty bad."

"He seems okay now. I appreciate you stopping to let us know, Phil. Some people might not stop," Diane said.

"You're welcome." Phil pulled out his wallet and fished around for a card. He found one and passed it to Diane. "If the dog needs to see the vet, please let me take care of the expense. I feel so bad."

He looked at Frankie. "I'm sorry about your dog, Son. I hope he's okay."

Frankie grinned. "He's okay now, Mister. Maddie fixed him."

Phil gave a nervous little laugh. "Yes. Well, I do apologize and I'm glad the dog seems okay now. You have a good rest of your weekend. I've got to catch up with my wife." The man wasted no time in heading back to his vehicle and driving off, albeit slowly.

Connie and Tony stood in their front yard as Helga approached them. She had plenty of painting to finish before the day was over, but she had seen their faces. Something serious had occurred.

"What happened?" she asked her neighbors as she waved bye to Diane, who had said something about having dinner in oven.

"I'm not really sure," Tony answered. He looked like he was a complete loss for words.

Helga looked to Connie for answers. Her neighbor looked shaken up. "I would have sworn the boy's dog was dead," Connie said. "Madison took the dog from Frankie. I *know* the dog was dead. It looked like his neck was broken. Then he woke up."

"Maybe he was knocked unconscious," Tony offered. "After a few minutes he woke up. I mean, he couldn't have been dead. He's alive now, isn't he?"

It was difficult to credit that thought as an actual possibility. Helga saw the couple turning it over in their mind. What exactly did they believe happened here?

Helga knew what she had seen. The dog looked like a hundred unfortunate pets she had seen lying by the side of some road or another, hit and left. Dead.

But if that dog had been dead, then the next logical leap was that a twelve-year-old girl had brought him back to life, which was impossible. Obviously, the dog had been stunned, nothing more.

On a brilliant summer afternoon, a few neighbors who had witnessed a miracle abandoned what they'd seen with their own eyes in favor of that which allowed them to remain rational.

***

That night, Diane Patterson told her husband, "First thing tomorrow I want you to get Buddy a collar and a leash."

"Buddy hates the leash. You know that."

"You didn't see your son this afternoon. I don't care what the dog likes or doesn't like. Are you going to be the one to tell Frankie that his dog is dead because you didn't want to get him a leash? That almost happened today, Alan."

"Okay. I'll get him a leash."

"Get him a chip, too. That dog runs, Alan."

"I promise. I'll get him a chip."

CHAPTER TWO

Evelyn Newman sorted clothes from the laundry basket. It had already been a long day. She'd been up early to fix the family breakfast, and then they had gone to church. Afterwards, they'd swung by a couple of stores for some last-minute, back-to-school shopping for Madison.

Once they got back home, she checked on dinner – a pork roast that had been on sale at Schnuck's. She'd put it in the crock pot before they left for church. It wouldn't be ready for another three hours, so she decided to get a jump on the laundry.

"Maddie!" Evelyn called.

"What, Mom?"

"Bring me your dirty clothes basket, Sweetie."

Madison dutifully brought her clothes hamper, and the two sorted through it together.

Evelyn quickly discovered the clothes Maddie had been wearing yesterday when she'd held Buddy.

"Maddie, what did you get into? Your t-shirt and shorts…these are a mess."

"It was Buddy. He got hit by a car yesterday, but he's okay. It's only Buddy's blood."

Evelyn made a face and held the t-shirt away from her. "Buddy got hit? You weren't in the street, were you?"

"No, Mom. Just Buddy. He ran into the street and got hit. He was really still for a while, and then he was okay."

Madison didn't purposely try to keep what she'd done from her mother, but she didn't know how to explain what happened. How could she tell her mom exactly what had taken place without scaring her, or having to answer questions for which she had no answer?

"How's Frankie? Is he okay?"

"Frankie's fine," Madison replied.

"Okay, but I don't want you playing in the street, young lady. Do you understand?"

"But I wasn't!" Madison protested.

"Okay, see that you don't."

They finished sorting the clothes and, after Evelyn put a load in the washer, she pulled her phone out of her back pocket and called Diane, Frankie's mother.

Diane answered on the second ring, "Hey, Evie. What's up?"

"I'm sorry I didn't call sooner. Maddie just told me about what happened yesterday. Is Frankie all right?"

"Oh, the accident. Yes, he's fine. It's that dog of his. Buddy ran out in the road and got hit. The dog's fine, but it sure scared the kids."

"You wouldn't know it from Maddie," Evelyn said. "She never said a word about it. Are you sure the dog is okay? Maddie ruined the t-shirt she had on."

Diane paused. "Listen, do you have time to come over for a while?"

Evelyn glanced at her phone to check the time. "Sure. I'll see you in a little bit."

She clicked off and called out to her daughter, "Maddie. I'm going over to the Patterson's. Do you want to come along?"

Madison came running into the kitchen. "Yes! Let's go."

Her mom held out her hand. "Not so fast. Go put on some shoes, then tell Dad where we're going. And tell him dinner's at six. Got that?"

"Yep. Shoes. Dad. Dinner."

Madison was back in few moments, having finished her tasks, and the two went next door. Diane answered the door and Maddie dashed inside. Diane told her, "Frankie's in the back yard with Buddy. You can go back and join them."

Maddie did not need a second invitation.

Evelyn watched through the window as her daughter went into the back yard. Buddy ran to her, leaping and wagging his tail. Madison tried petting the dog, but Buddy was too quick, and too excited to stand still.

"He certainly doesn't look like he was hit by a car," Evelyn observed.

"No. He doesn't." Diane handed her friend a glass of Chardonnay as she watched the kids through the kitchen window. "He never looked injured to me. I went running as soon as I heard there was an accident, but Buddy was the same as ever as far as I could tell. Frankie and Madison were sitting in the street. I was scared they had been hurt, but apparently it was the dog."

"I was sorting through the laundry just before I called you," Evelyn said. "I saw her t-shirt and shorts. I wouldn't have thought a dog that bled that much would be so frisky the next day. That's when she told me what happened. She said Buddy woke up." She took another sip of her wine. "Kids. Go figure."

Diane agreed. "I know, right? I'm freaking out thinking Frankie was hit or something, and they are so unfazed by the whole thing."

"Still…" Diane paused for a moment. "After I calmed down, I asked Frankie what had happened. He said Buddy was hit by a car, and Maddie fixed him. Of course, he was upset at the time. Obviously the dog is okay. Then this man tells me he's the one who hit Buddy. I could tell he thought he'd killed him. He was amazed that Buddy was still running around."

Evelyn shrugged. "We can chalk this one up as a miracle. I'm glad Buddy's okay. The kids are awfully attached to him."

The kitchen door opened and in burst Buddy, followed closely by Frankie and Madison. "Mom! Can we go down to the creek with Buddy and explore?" Frankie asked.

"Yeah, Mom, can we?" Madison chimed in, turning to Evelyn with a big smile on her face.

Evelyn glanced at Diane and saw the answer in her eyes. "I'm okay with it, but you need to be back in an hour, young lady. No being late."

Frankie asked again. "Can we, Mom?"

"Sure, you can, but you two be careful. Before you go, you have to put Buddy's new collar on him and use the leash."

"Awww, mom. Buddy doesn't like th–"

Diane casually commented, "I guess you didn't want to go that badly after all."

"No, I do. I'll get the leash," Frankie muttered.

"Hurry up, you two. Your hour is ticking."

Once the kids were out the door, Diane continued her story. "Anyway, so it must have seemed Buddy was done for. Even Helga, from behind us? Even Helga said she really thought Buddy was dead."

"He was knocked out?"

"Yes. He must have been. More luck than miracle," Diane concluded. Then she added, "Connie said Madison was a little trouper. She comforted Frankie and told him he was going to be okay. She even held Buddy and talked to him until he woke up."

"Are you serious? Oh my gosh, that's so sweet," Evelyn gushed. Her little daughter was something else.

***

The kids left the house and headed toward the park. Buddy struggled against the leash, unaccustomed to being reined in. They were off to the grove of trees on the eastern side of the park. Beyond the grove was a ravine through which a small creek meandered. When they reached the park, Frankie bent down and unhooked his leash. Buddy immediately raced off toward the ravine.

The creek was nothing special. The water was seldom more than knee deep, and no more than a few yards wide. But for Frankie and Maddie, it was the ideal location for all manner of adventures.

Today, however, Frankie wasn't looking for adventure. He wanted to talk.

Maddie and Frankie walked along the edge of the creek, poking things with their walking sticks – branches they picked up along the way – and watched Buddy scour the landscape for something interesting.

Frankie said, "I didn't say thanks."

Madison looked at him with a question in her eyes.

"For Buddy. For saving Buddy."

She was quiet for a minute, seemingly weighing something in her mind. "You're welcome," she finally said.

They walked in silence for a few minutes more before Frankie asked the question that had been eating at him since last night. "Was Buddy really...you know?"

Maddie bit her lower lip and nodded. She avoided looking in his eyes.

"How did you make him okay again?"

"I didn't do anything, Frankie. I tried to make him comfortable. I didn't want him to be afraid when he came back." Maddie seemed to be stumbling over her words, like she didn't know how to explain to her friend what had happened.

Frankie said, "Even that lady knew. She told my mom you did something."

Maddie shrugged. "She doesn't know."

"Did you ever do it before?"

Maddie nodded. "Yeah."

"This is freaking awesome! It's like you have a superpower."

"No. It's not," Maddie insisted. "You can't say anything, Frankie."

"What? Are you kidding?"

"No, please. I won't be your friend anymore!"

"I was kidding, Maddie," Frankie said, feeling bad for teasing his closest friend. "I won't tell anyone."

"Promise?" Madison asked, eyeing him warily.

"I promise," Frankie answered.

Even as he smiled, Frankie's heart hitched a little. Ever so slightly, but it was there. A part of his mind was worried for his friend. With a special gift like that, Maddie would never be completely normal. She'd ever fit in.

But it was too soon to worry about all that. Right now they had a little time to play, and that thought overshadowed everything else.

"Race you to the creek!" Frankie yelled, taking off after Buddy.

***

Later that night, Maddie's mom came to her room to say goodnight.

Evelyn smoothed down Maddie's bedcovers as she said, "Mrs. Patterson told me what you did, Maddie."

Madison's heart skipped a beat. "She did?"

"You don't have to be so shy. I think it was very nice what you did for Frankie."

She felt her heart brightening a little. "So, it was okay? What I did?"

Evelyn bent down and kissed Madison's forehead. "Of course. It's always good to act out of love and compassion. I'm proud of you, Sweetie."

***

Long after the lights were out, Madison thought about what her mom had said. She thought she'd be in trouble, but her mom said she'd done a good thing. Maybe she didn't have to keep it secret after all.

Then she remembered the people who had gathered after Buddy died. She'd seen their faces. They'd been scared, as if what she had done was wrong. Madison concluded it was better if she didn't say anything to anyone, at least for a while.

CHAPTER THREE

We don't let go easily. We've developed medical science to the point where, even when the body is ready to give up, we can keep a person alive almost indefinitely.

Convalescent Home. Senior Care Facility. Retirement Community. They have many names, but to different degrees they were made for one thing — to make our sunset years as comfortable as possible until we pass from this life into eternity.

On this particular Thursday afternoon, the Newman family found themselves in such a place. They were visiting Madison's grandmother. It was likely the last visit they'd ever make.

Thomas Newman had recently gotten a call from his brother, Donald. Mom was getting worse. She'd had another cardiac event. Minor. Seemingly minor. He needed to come soon.

The elder Mrs. Newman had suffered a heart attack over a year earlier. When it appeared she was well enough to be released from the hospital, she had experienced a major stroke. She was as sharp as ever, but it took months of therapy before she regained the use of her right hand and the ability to speak. She never regained her mobility.

Thomas and Evelyn lived in Oracle, Illinois. Mom lived in Michigan, as did Tom's brother, Donald. It fell to Donald to care for their mother as she got older. When she'd had the heart attack, there really wasn't any other choice. It was impossible for Tom to drop everything. He couldn't possibly travel five hundred miles to Grand Rapids every week.

Following her stroke, Donald had been unable to take care of his mother by himself. He just wasn't equipped to manage such a care-intensive task. Her doctor had suggested a long-term care center in Auburn Hills. With great reluctance, Donald had put his mom in a convalescent home.

Tom visited when he could, but over time his visits had grown less frequent. When he did make the trip, there was always conflict. He tried to compensate for his absence by being critical. He wasn't satisfied with the facility. He felt his mother wasn't receiving the care she needed. Tom took all of his frustrations out on his brother to ease the guilt he felt in his heart.

He always sent a check on time every month, but sending money to Donald didn't salve Thomas' conscience. He couldn't shake the pervasive feeling that he'd abandoned his mother, discarded her to the care of his brother when it became inconvenient for him to be involved.

"Are you going to be okay?" Evelyn asked her husband as they navigated the worn linoleum hallway toward his mother's room.

When she didn't get an answer, she shook her husband's arm. "Tom!" He turned to her and she asked again, "Are you going to be okay?"

He looked like a lost little boy for a moment, but then he smiled and replied, "Yes. I'll be okay. It's just…you know."

She returned his smile, taking his hand in hers and squeezing it gently. "I know."

They continued down the hallway, counting off the room numbers from the doors they passed. They dodged attendants, food carts, and residents parked in the hallway in their wheelchairs.

Tom exchanged tight smiles with some of the patients and nodded politely. The place smelled faintly of urine and too much disinfectant.

Madison followed along behind them. She stopped to look at one of the bulletin boards hanging on the hallway. The birthday board. Each birthday included the person's name, date, and a photograph. Marilyn Sheridan, eighty-seven. Dorothy Hendriksen, seventy-nine. William Brady, ninety-one.

The next bulletin board listed a calendar of events. Today, two fellows from the local Rotary Club were singing old time hymns in the cafeteria. A small flyer said the men had been coming every Thursday for the past seven years, and that they were a guitar/banjo duo who gave a bluegrass spin to the classics. Madison could faintly hear them playing now, even though the cafeteria was on the other side of the building.

"I think your family's waiting for you, Honey."

Madison looked around to see a grey-haired woman sitting on a walker seat. She pointed down the hall where Madison saw her parents standing at the door to one of the rooms. Her mom gestured for her to come along.

Madison turned to the woman. "Thank you, Ma'am."

"You're welcome, Dear. You have a blessed day," the woman replied.

***

Evelyn entered the room first, followed by Madison, and then Tom. The television was on, and the curtains were pulled back from the windows for some daylight.

"Tommy! Am I imagining things?" his mother exclaimed.

Thomas crossed the room to his mother's side and bent down to kiss her forehead. "Mom, I'm sorry it's been so long."

"You're here now, Tommy. Thank you for coming. Oh, Evie! You come over here and give me a hug. It's so good to see you kids."

"It's good to see you, too, Mom," Evelyn said, her heart tightening at the sight of the frail woman lying in bed watching television. She looked old, tired, and very weak. Evelyn blinked back tears.

"And who is *this* lovely young lady?" Tom's mother smiled widely as Madison approached. "This can't be my little Maddie, can it? My, how you've grown! How old are you now?"

Madison hugged her grandmother gently. "I'll be fourteen next month, Grandma."

Her grandmother shook her head a tiny bit, not having the mobility to move much beyond that. "Goodness, where does the time go?"

Thomas asked, "How are you feeling, Mom?"

They talked for a while, trivial chit-chat mostly, and then Tom gave Evelyn a look.

She turned to Madison and said, "We're going to be talking grown up stuff for a while, Maddie." She pulled her wallet out of her purse and gave her daughter a few dollar bills. "Why don't you go out to the lounge and get yourself a snack and watch some television?"

"Thanks, Mom." Madison took the money.

"Stay around the lounge area, and don't go wandering off. Wait for us, okay?"

"I'll be fine."

Truth be told, Madison was glad to go. Eager even. She loved her grandmother, but it was boring sitting and listening to the adults go on and on. Not that she'd ever express those thoughts out loud. Besides, she wanted to hear those guys playing music in the cafeteria.

Maddie began the walk around the facility to the other side of the building. It wasn't a large building, but there were no shortcuts. There was one hallway that ran around the interior of the building. If you started at one place and you kept walking, you'd end up right back where you'd started.

She strolled down the hallway, examining the posters on the bulletin boards and the photographs. One board had drawings done by the residents. Some of them were quite good. She glanced at the medical equipment on carts and wondered what the different machines did.

Maddie knew the rooms were called suites, but they were quite small. There was just enough room for a bed and a couple of chairs. A television was mounted on the wall. The bathroom was shared by the person in the adjoining room. Extras seemed to be few and far between, but the people caring for the patients seemed to be doing their absolute best.

Madison continued her walk down the hallway, reading the room numbers as she went.

Krantz. Room one twenty-two.

Ostlund. Room one twenty-three.

Barajas. Room one twenty-four.

Parker. Room one twenty-five.

Madison gasped and stopped short at Parker's room. She stood at the door, not daring to move, while her heart pounded in her chest.

***

Two summers ago, Madison's family went up to the lake with Frankie and his parents for a cookout and swimming. She and Frankie went exploring along the shoreline. They eventually ran out of beach and came upon a tumble of boulders that had fallen from the cliff rising out of the far end of the lake.

Frankie scrambled up the nearest rock and leaped into the lake. It couldn't have been more than three feet above the surface, but he popped up from the water, laughing, "C'mon, Maddie. This is great!"

He swam for the shore as Madison climbed the boulder and jumped, shrieking as she dropped into the water.

The first few jumps were fun, but then they climbed higher. First to the next boulder up, and then higher to the next one. What began as a small hop into the lake had turned into something potentially dangerous. Each tried to outdo the other by jumping from a progressively higher spot. It was great fun, but now the fun was leavened with generous dollop of fear.

"Geronimo!" Frankie shouted as he jumped from higher than ever before.

When he came up for air, Madison shouted, "That was awesome! Do it again!" She didn't believe he would jump from so high a place. He must have been sixteen feet up the side of the cliff.

"Why don't *you* do it?" Frankie taunted. "Is it too high for you?"

"Hardly," she sneered. "I just don't feel like it."

"Sounds to me like you're too scared," Frankie said.

"Am not!" Madison countered. That last jump she made *had* scared her. It scared her a lot, but she wasn't about to admit it to Frankie.

"Maddie, look at that!" Frankie pointed farther down from where they were standing, and up the cliff. Poking out of the cliff side was the tip of a granite slab, jutting out over the water. It was an easy climb, but it had to be more than twice the height they'd been jumping so far.

"It's perfect. Are you going first?" Frankie asked.

She looked up the cliff, up to where the edge of the granite hung out over the water. Her eyes traced the path she'd need to take in order to reach that foothold. Twenty feet. Thirty. It may as well have been a mile. Her stomach knotted.

"Uh-uh," she said. "No way, Jose."

"I figured you were too chicken," Frankie told her.

Madison glowered at Frankie. "I'm not chicken!"

Frankie took a different approach. "C'mon, Maddie. Please? One of us has to do it."

"What do you mean one of us?" Madison asked.

Frankie was silent for a long minute. Finally he broke and said, "I'm afraid to go that high."

"What?!" she shouted. "You called me chicken, and you're afraid to do it yourself?"

"I'm SORRY, okay?" he implored. "It's just…that would be so awesome. You gotta jump, Maddie."

She didn't answer, but she swam over to the base of the trail that went up to the granite slab. Madison got out of the water and began to climb the ill-defined path that eventually brought her to the edge of the cliff overlooking the lake.

Madison looked down and saw Frankie, treading water, watching her, and shouting encouragement, "All right, Maddie! You can do it!"

Maddie felt hysterical laughter bubbling up inside of her. She couldn't believe she was actually going to jump. She waved cheerfully to Frankie, but inside she was terrified. Madison gulped air, and her trembling legs threatened to give out on her.

Her heart hammered in anticipation of what was to come as she stepped off the granite slab into empty air.

***

That's what she felt now as she stood outside of room one twenty-five. Madison had been taken completely off guard. She was frightened by the urging that welled up within her, but exhilaration drove her forward.

Her heart raced at the sense of being directed, of having to relinquish control. It was scary stuff. Maddie felt herself trembling, but she stepped out of her sandals and walked into room one twenty-five.

The curtains were closed to block the sunlight, and the television was on. Madison's eyes adapted quickly to the partial darkness. Still, when Mrs. Parker spoke, it took her by surprise.

"Are you lost, little one?"

"Oh, hi! No, I'm not lost. Mom wanted me out of the room so they could talk about grown up stuff. But that's okay."

Madison looked around the room, and her eyes locked in on the whiteboard mounted on the wall with the patient's personal information.

"Are you Andrea Parker?" Madison asked.

"That's me. What's *your* name?"

Madison walked over to the side of Andrea's bed and stuck out her hand. "I'm Madison Newman. I'm pleased to meet you, Mrs. Parker."

"Well, I'll be. I'm pleased to meet you, Miss Madison Newman. You're certainly a polite one, aren't you?"

Maddie turned her attention back to the whiteboard. "May I visit with you for a while?"

"Are you sure you won't get in trouble with your folks? I don't want them worrying about you."

"I'll be fine. They're busy talking to my grandma."

"Then I'm pleased to visit with you, young lady. The weeks pass by pretty slow around here. My son and his family often come on Sunday afternoon."

Madison consulted the whiteboard and saw his name under Emergency Contact. "Is that Bradley?"

Andrea smiled. "Yes. Bradley is my oldest son."

She turned away from the whiteboard. "You must be very sick."

"That's true enough. I think the doctors have probably given up on me."

"Does Bradley come and see you often?"

"No. He's a busy man. He has a family, too. Two boys and a girl. I swear the boys look just like him. They try to make it out to visit me at least once a week. If I'm feeling good, we go out back, to the garden. What about you? Do you get to see your grandmother very often?"

"No. We live far away. This is the first time we've come in months. She had a bad heart attack."

Andrea Parker hoped to comfort the curious young girl and asked, "She'll soon be able to go home with you, won't she?"

Madison's response was very matter of fact. "Grandma isn't leaving."

Andrea didn't know what to say to that. The somber girl seemed to understand what she'd implied.

Madison asked, "Where's home for you?"

The woman smiled. "That would be with Bradley and the kids. We had our own place, my husband and me. When he passed, I stayed and took care of it all by myself. There were so many memories tied up in that house. The boys grew up, went to school, and graduated while we lived there. Over the course of twenty years or so, a house takes on a personality all its own."

Maddie smiled and nodded as the woman reminisced aloud.

"Eventually it became too much for me to manage by myself. Bradley and his brothers paid for a gardener, and then later a housekeeper, to help me keep the place up. I knew it was only a matter of time before I had to let the house go. It came sooner than I expected. After breaking my hip, Bradley was worried and moved me in with him and the family."

Madison was back examining the whiteboard.

"What's die analyst?" she asked, pointing at the board.

"That's dialysis, little miss. The hip stole my independence, but the dialysis is stealing my life, bit by bit, until I don't have any more left. My kidneys stopped working. Now a machine has to do the job for me."

"Do you get to go home?" Madison asked.

Andrea shook her head. "Not anymore. I miss my son, but he's grown and is living his own life." She stopped to pluck a tissue from a box on her bedside and dabbed at her eyes. "I'll miss seeing the grandkids grow up. I think that breaks my heart more than anything."

Madison walked over to Andrea's side and took her hand. "It doesn't have to be like that, you know."

Andrea Parker, who had only recently come to a peace about her swiftly approaching death, was ready to grasp at any straw offered. She looked at Madison with a desperate need to believe.

"What do you mean, child?"

CHAPTER FOUR

It was the second week of August, and many of the neighborhood children attended Vacation Bible School at Valley Community Church. The church didn't have a large congregation, as the world measures such things. They had neither an extensive campus of buildings nor an impressive sanctuary.

But what they had was more than adequate for their needs. They had a kitchen, and a dining hall. They had an office, and a small auditorium. God was faithful and met their every need, and a little extra.

There were forty-five children attending VBS this year. Some came because they wanted to hang out with their friends. Some came for the snacks and activities. Some were compelled to attend by parents eager to get a little alone time. And some, a very few, came to discover truth.

Madison was fifteen, and nearly three years had passed since the miraculous healing of a puppy. Her friend Trisha, from school, had invited Madison to join her as a volunteer at VBS. They had just come to the end of a busy afternoon monitoring a group of second graders as they enjoyed singing, crafts, Bible lessons, and snacks. Now the small group of young helpers gathered around listening to a few of the older members sharing stories of how they came to salvation.

It wasn't long before the conversation turned to tent revivals. Many of the older adults recalled being at a revival meeting at one time or another and had fond memories.

"What's a tent revival?" Trisha asked. She and Madison were both going into their sophomore year the following month.

The youth leader, Francine Cady, spoke first. "I can only tell you about the ones I attended. This was back in the '80s when the housing tract behind the church was nothing but acres of empty land. Our pastor got permission to put up a big tent and invited evangelists from all over."

"What? Like a circus tent?" Madison asked.

"Exactly like that," Francine answered. "The tent was huge. The ground had been cleared and fresh hay scattered over the dirt. Rows and rows of benches borrowed from the high school lined the aisles. When the preaching started, every seat was packed. Our parking lot couldn't hold all the cars, and people parked along the highway for a mile in each direction."

Pastor Crane's wife said, "I remember one revival I attended where the preacher laid his hands on people and healed them."

Madison sat up straight. "He really did?" She tried not to sound too interested, but she was completely intrigued.

"Well," Mrs. Crane answered, "I was about your age when it happened. It seemed very real at the time. But yes," she said, nodding, "I believe it was true. There were quite a few people who asked for prayer, and I recall a few of them claimed to be healed."

"So, what exactly is a revival?" Trisha asked.

"Well, the services were very much like a church service," Francine replied. "They had a choir and sang hymns, but the service was very high-energy. The young preachers preached on the Holy Spirit and called for a spiritual awakening across the country, a revival of the spirit. That's why they called it a revival."

Mrs. Crane looked around the room and called out to one of the other older members of the church, "What about you, Mr. Slayton? How did you come to know the Lord?"

Abner Slayton, easily the senior-most member of the church at ninety-seven years of age, looked up from reading his Bible. He smiled and nodded. "It was near the end of the war." He regarded the younger members of the audience and reminded them, "This was World War Two, by the way."

Some of the teenagers laughed.

Mr. Slayton continued, "My ship was in the Pacific, and was assigned to cover the eastern entrance to Leyte Gulf. Our job was to help ward off enemy aircraft. We were surprisingly good at picking them out of the sky, but one enemy pilot still retained some measure of control over his aircraft, and he deliberately struck our ship with his plane."

Mr. Slayton paused and cleared his throat. Madison leaned in closer to listen. "I lost some good friends that day. I was busted up pretty bad, and our ship was out of commission. They sent me to a hospital in the Philippines where there was some lively debate among the doctors about whether or not I was going to lose my leg. In the end, they were able to save it, but it needed a lot of work. When I could tolerate travel, I was sent to the Naval Hospital in San Diego, California."

Madison noticed that Trisha, sitting next to her, had pulled out her phone and was starting to scroll down her Instagram feed. But Madison was fully engaged. She felt like there was something important she needed to know about this man's story.

"The doctors in San Diego were miracle workers and fixed me up pretty good, but they told me I'd walk with difficulty for the rest of my life, likely with the aid of a cane or a crutch. When I could hobble around on my own, they kicked me out. There were boys hurt a lot worse than me, and I was taking up a bed."

"Did you leave the Navy and go home?" one of the boys, Stephen Cully, asked.

"The Navy wasn't finished with me quite yet. I still had a year left on my hitch and there was a war going on. But I did get to go home on a two-week leave. After that, I was to report back to the hospital for a medical clearance and reassignment. It had been almost three years since I'd seen my folks, so I planned to head home, to Iowa."

"You didn't see your parents for three years?" Trisha asked, looking up from her phone. "Was your mom excited that you were coming?"

"I didn't have a chance to tell her. In 1945, a long-distance telephone call was an expensive proposition, and I was a poor sailor trying to hold on to what little cash I had. I'd make it back home before a letter would have a chance of getting to them."

"But how did you get home? California is a long way away," Stephen observed.

Abner Slayton nodded slowly. "Indeed, it is, but back then we looked out for one another. We were mostly all young kids away from home for the first time in our lives. We all had the same goal; stay alive and get back home."

Madison listened as the elderly man talked about getting discharged from the hospital with a small bottle of painkillers, a second-hand cane, and a stern warning to take it easy on the leg.

A couple of VBS helpers got up and left, their parents having arrived to take them home, but Madison, Trisha, and several others remained. Abner continued his story, telling how he talked to pilots, warehousemen, and ground crews, looking for a flight that was headed east and might get him to Iowa. Finally, a forklift operator told Abner he'd just finished loading a transport that was headed to Pennsylvania.

Abner had a faraway look in his eyes as he recounted his story. "I found a transport crew that was flying some parts and equipment to the naval shipyard in Philadelphia. I must have been a sorry sight because their CO gave them permission to drop me off in Iowa."

"I'd call that pretty lucky," Stephen said.

Abner put his hand on the Bible sitting on his lap and said, "I would have thought so at one time. I've since learned it's God who orders our steps. God had an appointment He needed me to keep, so He opened up a seat on that transport."

"What appointment?" Trisha asked. She set her phone down, now fully listening to the story.

"I'll get to that," he said, smiling. "Mind you, this was the first time I'd been out of the hospital since the Japanese plane struck our ship. I'd undergone two operations that might have saved my leg, but I'm sure the doctors never meant me to go traipsing around the airport. Despite the morphine shot they'd given me, my leg began hurting pretty bad."

"But you got on the plane, right?" Madison asked, concerned.

"Yes, well, there was no seat on the plane. It was a transport, and I was cargo. I made myself as comfortable as possible on top of a pallet of something soft. One of the pilots gave me a blanket. The steady thrum of the engines put me to sleep. It wasn't until the copilot shook me awake that I realized I'd slept seven solid hours. My leg had stiffened up on me, and I had a dickens of a time getting off that plane."

"But you were in Iowa, right?" Trish interrupted.

"Yeah, couldn't your parents pick you up from there?" Stephen asked.

"I was still a ways from home," Abner said. "My original plan was to hitch a ride into downtown Cedar Rapids and buy a Greyhound ticket to Mechanicsville, but my leg pained me something terrible. I knew if I didn't stay off of it I'd probably end up back in the hospital. I had my wallet out and was counting my cash, trying to decide if I wanted to part with the money it would take to grab a cab to the Greyhound station. My leg was putting up a very persuasive argument in favor of paying for a ride, but my wallet wasn't quite convinced. The decision was taken out of my hands when a gentleman offered me a lift into town."

Madison leaned back in her seat, listening to Abner's story. Everyone else in the room must have been fully engaged as well, because there were no more interruptions. In her mind, the story unfolded like this...

***

August 1945

The young, limping sailor was grateful for the ride.

Abner eased into the passenger seat of the sedan and grimaced as he settled in. "Thanks, Mister. I really appreciate the ride." He extended his hand, and the man shook it.

"Think nothing of it, Son. I have a boy in the army. He's over in Europe right now. I'd like to think someone would take care of him if he needed a ride. Where are you headed?"

"Downtown. The bus station. I'm headed home for a few days to see my folks."

"I know exactly where it is. I'll have you there in no time." The man watched Abner shift in his seat. "You got hurt pretty bad?"

Abner exhaled slowly, "Yeah, but it won't keep me down for long."

"That's the spirit," the man nodded approvingly. "Where's home?"

"A little place called Fremont Township, just outside of Mechanicsville."

"I'll bet your folks are looking forward to seeing you."

"They don't know I'm coming. I was released from the hospital in California this morning. I hitched a ride on a transport."

The man took a good look at Abner's face. "You're hurting, aren't you, Son?" he asked.

Abner nodded.

"I wish I could help you out, but I'm headed the other way. I have a schedule to keep."

Abner smiled and said, "This ride is a big help, Sir. I really do thank you."

The trip from the airport to downtown Cedar Rapids was swift, and Abner began to think he'd make it home in time for dinner. The early August afternoon was hot and humid, and there was a breeze picking up from a line of thunderheads far to the northeast. Abner rolled the window down for a bit of relief.

The sedan turned left and cruised down the avenue towards the Greyhound station. It had been three years since Abner had last seen the place, but nothing had changed. Bailey's Five and Dime was still on the corner. Next to that sat Maxwell's Diner. Across the street from the diner was Bill's Appliance and Repair.

Before long, Abner's ride dropped him off at the bus station where he wasted no time securing a ticket. The next bus was scheduled in forty minutes. He went into the rest room to freshen up. Digging into his bag, he grabbed a small bottle, shook out a couple of pills, and swallowed them dry. He cupped his hand under the running faucet and drank deeply to wash them down.

The rain arrived before the bus did. The wind had picked up considerably, and the flag in front of the terminal fluttered and snapped in the wind. The rain began full-on as Abner struggled to get on the bus. Drops the size of almonds pummeled the earth, and the highways were awash outside the bus window.

Fierce gusts rocked the big bus as the wipers beat away the rain. Every abrupt movement sent a shock of pain through Abner's leg. He was grateful for the pills, knowing he'd be paying a big price once they wore off.

He looked around at his fellow passengers. Some dozed, some read newspapers or magazines. There was little conversation. It was a somber group, these strangers under the shadow of war, waiting to arrive at their next destination.

There was no bus station. The bus pulled over on Highway Thirty at the intersection of the road that would lead into Mechanicsville, and let him out. Abner would have to hoof it the rest of the way, and he prayed his leg would endure the hike into town.

The main part of the storm had passed, but the road was still wet. Despite the rain, the late afternoon was warm and humid. Abner tested the strength of his leg as he watched the bus disappear into the distance. Resting his weight on his cane, he crossed the highway going north and began to walk.

The going was slow, and Abner took great care not to slip on the wet pavement. His leg throbbed. Leaning heavily on his cane, he tried to keep as much weight off the leg as possible. He was close to town when a car passed him.

It wasn't long before another sedan came up the road. This one slowed, and then stopped once it pulled up even with him. The passenger rolled down his window and asked, "Hey neighbor, can you tell me where I can find the Rose Hill Cemetery?"

Despite the man's claim to being a neighbor, Abner didn't think he'd ever seen him before. Sure, he'd been gone for three years, but things couldn't have changed so much that he wouldn't recognize a resident.

"It's pretty easy," Abner said. "Just continue down this road until you–"

The driver interrupted. "No. Get in. We'll give you a ride into town. There's supposed to be a revival meeting north of the cemetery. Can you show us how to get there?"

Abner smiled at the chance for a ride. "Sure thing." It had started to sprinkle again, and he really needed to give his leg a rest. He was close to home, but it seemed a hundred miles away.

Abner eased into yet another stranger's vehicle, feeling blessed. Here he was in Iowa, with home only a few miles away, when that very morning he'd been in a hospital in San Diego, California. Abner had gotten close to some of his buddies that had been killed on the ship. Their families would never get to see them again, yet he'd be seeing his family within the hour. It was a humbling thought.

As soon as they neared the cemetery, Abner saw the road was lined by cars parked on the dirt shoulder. Up ahead, in the field, an enormous tent stood, and he heard a band playing. There was no place to park.

The driver of the car said, "If you'd like, we can let you off here. We'll have to find a place to park and walk back."

Abner was done in. All he wanted to do was sit down and rest. He was exhausted from traveling, he was hungry, and his leg had turned up the dial on the pain. Exiting the car, he lurched toward the big tent.

In spite of the recent rain, it was still a Midwest summer. Humid and hot. The tent flaps were raised, and a breeze washed over the crowd. Strains of the choir singing, "Standing on the Promise," greeted Abner.

He paused to watch the crowd work their way into the big tent, weaving between the parked cars, men with children in tow, and wives with umbrellas against the chance of more rain. Abner was about to start moving again when the clouds parted, and sunlight poured through the break, creating a brilliant rainbow above the tent where the revival was to take place.

He took that as a good sign. An usher, seeing that he was walking with great difficulty, came and escorted him to an aisle seat.

> *Would you be free from the burden of sin?*
> *There's pow'r in the blood, pow'r in the blood.*
> *Would you o'er evil a victory win?*
> *There's wonderful power in the blood.*

Many in the crowd sang along with the choir. Most exhibited more enthusiasm than skill, but it was heartfelt, and was indeed a joyful noise.

Now that he was off of his leg, Abner no longer felt like he was going to faint, but he remained in terrible pain. He scanned the faces in the crowd, hoping to see a friend, or someone he remembered from school.

Have you been to Jesus for the cleansing pow'r?
Are you washed in the blood of the Lamb?
Are you fully trusting in His grace this hour?
Are you washed in the blood of the Lamb?

Abner found himself on his feet with everyone else, leaning heavily on his cane, singing with deep conviction. It was joy, it was praise, and it was a prayer.

He looked around the crowd and saw many faces streaked with tears. There was enough grief these days to go around. Wartime rationing was in effect. Fathers and sons were gone from home, and bills were due. Abner saw fear in their eyes. He supposed he looked much the same.

"I know why you're here," the preacher said as the song ended, and the people sat down. The choir began singing softly in the background, "Oh, How I Love Jesus."

"Most of you think you know why you're here, but I know the real reason."

He paced back and forth in front of the choir with an easy grace. Smiling, with a microphone in one hand, he made broad gestures with the other. The crowd was drawn to him.

"Some of you might think you're here to pray for a loved one whose absence leaves a hole in your heart. You worry you may never see them again. You fear the war might take them, and you'll never again have the opportunity to tell them how much you love them."

An "amen" was heard among the crowd, and Abner heard a woman begin to sob.

"Brothers and sisters, I am here to tell you God has already heard the prayer in your heart and cries tears with you. You will be comforted, for that comfort is promised by God's word!"

Many people shouted, "Amen!"

"There are those of you who are here tonight because you are broken. You've lost someone close to you. You feel empty, as though there is nothing left to live for in this world. But Jesus knows your suffering and is offering you His hand. The Apostle Paul wrote that we have a 'God of all comfort; Who comforteth us in all our tribulation, that we may be able to comfort them which are in any trouble, by the comfort wherewith we ourselves are comforted of God.' Can I get an amen?"

The response was thunderous.

"I thank God for each and every one of you this evening. In spite of the rain, in spite of the weather, in spite of the war, you are here tonight to raise your voice to God in praise and thanksgiving. Set the worries of this life aside for a while."

Abner took a deep breath, trying to focus on the preaching beyond the pain he felt in his leg as the pastor continued.

"God does not want you mired down by the trials of this world. This world is not our final home. We are only passing through. My desire is that each of you comes to the saving knowledge of Jesus Christ, that you may have life everlasting."

Abner had grown up going to church. He had called out for God's help on the ship that day, but sometimes he wondered whether he was missing something.

"When you have lived out the final number of your days and you are face to face with Almighty God, my desire is that you will hear those sweet words, well done, my good and faithful servant."

"Amen!" the audience cried. Abner's voice was among them.

The revival continued as the preacher proclaimed the Gospel of Salvation. The choir sang, the audience clapped along, and the preacher walked down into the aisles to talk to the people.

Abner wept. He was sick of this life. He was sick of war, and sick of seeing friends die. He wanted more from his time on this earth. He wanted a wife and children. He wanted a family to share life with, but he didn't see how any of that was ever going to happen.

Clouding every thought was the pain in his leg, now so intense he could barely see straight. Abner trembled and feared he might actually lose the leg after all, it hurt so much.

Dear God, he prayed, let me see someone I know so they can take me home. Dear God, hear my prayer.

The preacher held up his hand and the choir stopped singing. "Do you feel it, brothers and sisters? Can you feel the Holy Spirit?"

Abner's dad was a level-headed, no-nonsense type of guy. He had raised his sons to be the same way, so Abner was naturally skeptical. Yet he had to admit he did feel something. It wasn't the breeze coming through the tent. It wasn't the power of suggestion. It was a gentle presence of peace and joy. Others felt it, too.

The people responded to the presence of the Holy Spirit and began to worship spontaneously, praising God, raising their hands high in the air and singing.

Abner opened his eyes to see the preacher standing in front of him. It surprised him, and he very nearly lost his balance. He put a little bit more weight on his left leg and hissed in agony.

"God bless you, Son. It's good to be in the presence of God, isn't it?"

Tears flowed down Abner's cheeks. The preacher was right. In spite of the pain, in spite of his hunger and exhaustion, he felt an indescribable peace settle on his heart. Abner smiled and answered, "Yes indeed. Praise the Lord, preacher."

"You a local boy?"

"Yes, Sir. Grew up here."

"God has a plan for your life, son. Do you believe that?"

"I do." Abner knew it was the right thing to say, although he wasn't convinced that God really had a plan for his life.

"God sent me here. He pointed you out to me, Son. I don't know you and I don't know why, but God has something for you. He didn't tell me what, but He told me you haven't accepted His son, Jesus, as your Lord and Savior. Is that true?"

Abner blushed, ashamed. He wasn't going to lie. "It's true, sir."

"Do you want to accept him now?"

It was medicine to a dying man. "Yes," Abner whispered.

"Do you believe that Jesus died on the cross for the remission of sin?"

"I do."

The preacher continued, "Do you believe he died, was buried, and rose on the third day?"

"Yes."

"By your faith, you are saved. God bless you."

Abner's spirit was elated, but his body was broken. His entire left leg was throbbing like a rotten tooth, and his arm ached from leaning heavily on his cane.

Then the preacher did the most remarkable thing. He spoke to Abner and said, "You won't need that anymore." Then he kicked the cane out from underneath him.

Abner's face was a mask of shock as his arms pin-wheeled, desperately seeking balance. His weight came down heavily on his left leg, and Abner managed to stop himself from falling.

"Hey!" Abner shouted. "What do you think you're...?"

Then he understood.

Abner flexed his leg. He shifted his weight from side to side. He hopped up and down a half dozen times and experienced no pain, no discomfort, and no stiffness. It was complete and total healing. It was exactly as though his leg had never been injured. Ever.

"You healed me!" It started as an exclamation, but soon became a cry. "You healed me!"

The preacher had tears in his eyes. "I didn't heal you, Son. It was our Lord Jesus."

Abner lifted his arms to heaven and cried out, "Thank you, Jesus!" He hugged the preacher, and then he hugged quite a few of the people seated around him.

Then young Abner Slayton did something he thought he'd never do again. He ran the entire two miles to his parents' house.

CHAPTER FIVE

Following the discussion of tent revivals and faith healing, Madison was eager to learn more. She set out on a quest to learn everything she could with a single-minded focus.

She spent hours searching YouTube for clips of old-time tent meetings and videos of healing services. She scoured the Internet for papers and articles on faith healing. Wikipedia was only the start, and she followed all of the reference links.

Having learned the value of index cards when studying for tests, she took a lot of notes. Madison became very familiar with the names Oral Roberts, Kathryn Kuhlman, Benny Hinn, and Aimee Semple McPherson.

Madison was particularly interested in the women. She prayed that she would finally find some answers. At the very least, she hoped her research would help her understand what questions to ask.

Abner Slayton's story had given her a glimmer of hope that she might one day understand her own place in God's plan. She wouldn't be able to speak to these women, but perhaps she could come to some sort of understanding by reading about their lives.

One evening, Madison's mother, Evelyn, eyed the latest stack of books Madison had carried home from the library and asked, "What in the world are you reading this stuff for?"

"Their lives are interesting, Mom," Madison answered. She decided to ask her mother something she'd been wondering about. "Were these people truly chosen by God? If so, I don't understand what happened. Most of their stories don't have a happy ending. Some of them seem pretty obvious fakes. But with others, it's hard to say."

"It seems like a lot of mumbo jumbo, Maddie. I always thought these stories were frauds. Why do you want to read about this?"

Since that day the puppy had been healed, Madison had not spoken to her mom about any other experiences she'd had with her gift. It had remained a secret, and she wasn't ready to divulge it to anyone.

"It turns out a lot of it *is* mumbo jumbo," she replied somewhat evasively. "Most of them were discovered to be frauds. But in some cases, it seems there really were genuine healings."

"But Maddie, what proof can they have the healing was genuine?"

Madison waved a book she was holding about the famed faith-healer, Aimee Semple McPherson. "This book says that, in 1921, Miss McPherson was secretly investigated by the American Medical Association. They went to some of her local revival meetings. Their report said her healings were genuine. One of her biographers *wanted* to expose her as a phony. He searched for evidence of fraud in her faith healing services, and he came up empty handed."

"You've really studied this a lot, haven't you?" Evelyn asked. She was surprised at her daughter's sudden interest in spiritual healing.

"I guess I have," Madison said simply.

"Then tell me, what do you believe? Is faith healing real? Did those people have the power to cure illness?" Evelyn asked.

"Well, as Christians we know that Jesus has power to heal. But as for these people, I don't know. I guess only they know for sure. Well, God knows. I thought I'd find some answers, but…" Madison trailed off.

"Don't get discouraged," her mother said. "What you learned from reading is worth it for its own sake, even if you didn't find the answers you were looking for. I mean, you know more about faith healing than anyone I know."

You have no idea, Madison thought, but she simply smiled and went back to reading.

Before long, Madison wasn't content to simply read about tent meetings and faith healing. She wanted to go and attend an event. This was a matter of some urgency as summer vacation was drawing to a close. Soon, she would be going back to school. If she was going to make it happen, it would have to be in the next few weeks.

It seemed luck was with her. During one of her Internet searches, Madison noticed a website referencing Russell Stillman's Traveling Revival Road Show. She clicked over to the website, and then clicked the events tab. To her delight, they had an event coming up. The only problem was it was in a small town some ninety miles to the south.

Madison knew there would only be one chance to make a successful pitch for her Bible study group to attend this event. She gathered every bit of information she could possibly glean from the website and made up a fact sheet on her tablet.

Next, she sent a group text to her friends in the Bible study group and included the fact sheet. *We should totally go! Show this to your parents and get their permission. Pls reply and LMK if you can go. I need to know ASAP so I can tell Mrs. Cady. If everything is in place already, she'll prob say yes.*

Next, Madison needed to call Trisha. Together they could start texting their friends about the trip and build some positive buzz. If everyone was enthusiastic about going, the adults would make it happen.

Another factor in her favor was that several of the teens in her group had been spellbound by Mr. Slayton's testimony. For many of them, it was their first exposure to the idea of faith healing, and Madison wanted to tap into that interest while it was still fresh in their minds.

Her phone rang. It was Trisha.

Madison answered, "That was fast."

"Yeah. Hey, do you really think we can go?"

"I think so, if we're all together on this. It's a long way, but we haven't gone on a field trip this summer. If enough people want to go, I think it'll happen," Madison guessed. If there's only, like, three or four of us, then probably not."

"I think you're right. We'll have to fill a van, at least."

Madison's phone chirped and she looked at the screen. "Steve's coming."

"Oh, good! That means Brad will probably come."

"That means Hannah, too," Madison added.

Trisha growled, "Meh, don't get me started. She's trying to get–"

"Be nice," Madison cautioned.

Trisha sighed, "I know, but really! Anyway, what's next?"

"I'll start texting people in our Bible study. You text them, too, and be totally enthusiastic. Tell them they'll have a good time. It's the last trip of the summer!"

"It'll be fun. Laters." Trisha ended the call.

Madison started texting her friends. Most replies expressed interest. Some said yes contingent on parent approval. A number of them said they already had plans with their family since it was the last week of summer vacation.

It was still early, but she had too few solid confirmations to count on the trip being a done deal. That is, until she received a group text from Trisha.

Sign up for the trip to see the tent revival and get invited to MY house for a swim party on Friday!

Then Madison got a direct text from Trisha. *That should generate some interest.*

Are you serious? Madison replied.

Sure. I asked my mom and she said I could have some people over.

Madison's phone started chiming right away. A lot of people were interested now. They didn't want to miss a chance to go to a party at Trisha's. She had a big backyard and a big pool.

***

Their campaigning paid off. At the Wednesday night Bible study, the girls were ready to make their case. Madison laid out all the details and the youth group leaders agreed to the trip to see Stillman's revival.

Mrs. Cady passed out the permission slips and reminded them, "Be here at the church at a quarter to nine. We are leaving promptly at nine o'clock. Remember to bring your signed permission slip. If you do not have your signed permission slip, you will not be able to go."

It was official; they were going to the revival meeting. Even more important to some of them, they got to go to Trisha's swim party.

***

Madison got to Trisha's house early to help her set up. Maybe it was because this was the last hurrah of summer before school started, but Trisha's mom put on a lavish spread for her daughter's party.

There were more people than Trisha expected, but that wasn't a problem. The two girls hung out in the backyard by the pool, chatting and watching the guests arrive.

"This party was a great idea. I can't believe how many people wanted to come," Madison said.

"I guess word got out. Mom won't mind as long as things don't get out of hand," Trisha answered.

"By then, it will be too late," Madison said with a laugh.

Trisha rolled her eyes. They both turned to watch Stephen Cully step out of the kitchen door and onto the backyard patio. His friend, Brad, followed close behind.

"Oh, look who it is," Trisha said. "Did I call it or what?"

"That wasn't hard," Madison said. "Those two are always hanging out together."

Much to Madison's surprise, the next person to arrive was Kenny Warner.

"OMG! Look, Maddie."

"I see!" Madison turned around in the foolish hope that Kenny wouldn't notice her if he only saw her back. "Why is he here?" she whispered fiercely to her friend.

"He must have come with Brad. They're in several of the same classes together. Do you not get along?"

"No." Madison tried to act casual. "I'm just surprised to see him, that's all."

"You totally like him! I'll call him over and..."

"No! I am serious, Trish. Please," Madison implored.

Madison had had a crush on Kenny since junior high, and she still didn't know what to do about it. They'd first met when Kenny and his family had moved to Illinois from Virginia. He was in eighth grade when Madison started seventh.

This past summer, she had seen him around more often. In the small town of Oracle, it was inevitable they'd have friends in common. It seemed she was always getting invited to an event where he would be, or go see a movie with a group of friends and would run into him.

She didn't know if he'd noticed her shy glances, or her circumspect inquiries with friends at school. With each chance meeting, she felt their orbits around one another were growing smaller and smaller. Contact was inevitable, but she had no idea how to act around him.

Trish went to greet some friends, and Madison sauntered over to the patio to grab a slice of pizza. She began looking for the ranch dressing when a voice spoke up behind her.

"Can I help you find something?"

"I'm looking for the ranch." She turned to look at the guy who spoke to her and nearly choked. It was Kenny Warner.

"You'll find the ranch over by the chips." He glanced at her pizza and said, "That looks good. What is it?"

Madison cleared her throat a little too loudly. "This is the BBQ chicken and veggie. They have pepperoni and a combo, too."

"Great. I think I'll try a slice. Mind if I join you?" Kenny asked.

Madison wasn't expecting that. Her mind raced through a list of possible answers, but in the end she simply said, "Sure."

"What do you want to drink?" Kenny asked.

"Mountain Dew," she answered hesitantly.

"You got it." And he was gone.

It happened so suddenly that Madison could never quite remember their first conversation together. She wished she'd been prepared so that she could recall what he said and how he looked.

Kenny returned with his own plate and a can of soda for Madison. He set the plate down on the table and was about to sit when he stopped abruptly. "Uh-oh. I'll be right back."

True to his word, he returned promptly with a couple of napkins and a small bowl of ranch from the chip table. "You forgot your ranch," he explained.

Madison grinned widely. "You're right. I did."

Her crush kicked into overdrive with that act of thoughtfulness. He'd noticed something as simple as her forgetting to get ranch dressing, and his kindness put her at ease.

"I'm glad to finally meet you," Kenny said after swallowing a bite of pizza.

"Do you even know my name?" Madison teased.

"Sure, I do," Kenny answered. "Maybe. Marilyn? Madelyn?"

"It's Madison!" She pretended to scold him.

Kenny laughed. "I know. Really, I was kidding."

Madison was relieved. Maybe he *had* noticed her.

"And you're Kenny," she said. "Are you going to the revival with us tomorrow?"

"The revival? What's that?" Kenny asked, finishing off his pizza.

"Oh. I thought you were invited to Trish's party because you were going to the tent meeting with us tomorrow."

"I came with Brad," Kenny explained.

"Hey, is Brad seeing Hannah?" Madison ventured on Trisha's behalf. "She always seems to be hanging out with him."

"Heck no. I'm pretty sure she just wants to hang out with him because he's in a band, but there's already a girl he's interested in." Kenny nodded in the direction of the coolers and Madison glanced in that direction.

Brad and Trisha were each grabbing a drink, chatting easily, clearly enjoying each other's company. The sight made Madison happy. She had somehow caught Kenny's attention, and Trisha was finally getting to hang out with Brad.

"I've heard Brad play," Madison said. "He's really good. He plays with the youth band at our church. Trish and Steve go there, too."

"Yeah, I've heard. Brad asked me to go with him a couple of times and check it out."

"You should come!" Madison urged. "It'll be a lot of fun. Besides," Madison looked directly into his eyes, "I'll be there."

Kenny met her gaze without flinching. "That might be worth it."

"Might?" Madison raised an eyebrow. "Somebody might get pushed into the pool if they're not careful."

"You know, I've heard that about you," Kenny said.

"What? That I push people in pools?"

Kenny snickered. "No, that you spend a lot of time at church. I thought Brad went to church a lot, but he said you're always there when he goes."

"I never thought about it, but I guess I do go a lot. You can still come with us to the revival if you want. You don't have to go to our church."

"What's this revival thing? Brad mentioned it, too."

"It's like a big church service outdoors under a tent and…" Madison trailed off. "To tell you the truth, I've never been to one, either. But I've read a lot about them. I think it's going to be interesting."

"Who's going?" Kenny asked.

"A lot of people from our Summer Bible Study group. Trish is going, and Steve. You interested?" Madison didn't want to press, but she really hoped he'd say yes.

Kenny took a deep breath. "I'm going to have to pass. I promised my dad I'd help him clean out the garage tomorrow. He's been putting it off all summer, and Mom finally put her foot down. He recruited me to help."

Madison nodded, trying not to appear too disappointed. She thought of something to change the subject. "I hear you're trying out for track."

"Yeah." Kenny sat up a little straighter. "I do the mile and some cross country."

"Are you fast?" Madison asked.

"I've got the mile down to the mid fours. That's enough to get noticed in competition. On a good day I can close in on four twenty, so I'm getting there. Pretty sure I'll qualify for the team once school starts."

Madison was happy she had found something he was genuinely interested in. "That's great. When you make the team, I'd like to go to one of the meets!"

"Yeah? Now I'll have to make sure I make it on the team."

"Do you have any brothers or sisters?" Madison asked.

"I have a little sister. Sandra Rene. Sandy."

"Does Sandy look up to her big brother?"

Kenny smiled. "She really does, but she's also a pest sometimes."

"I'm sure you're sweet to her."

"I usually make her cry at least once a day. By accident, I swear!"

"I hope so," Madison said.

"What about you? Do you have any brothers or sisters?"

"Nope, only child."

"That must be peaceful," Kenny commented.

"I guess. I definitely have time to think. Some people think every moment needs to be filled with activity or noise, but they are wonderful times to reflect and learn."

"That sounds very spiritual," Kenny observed.

"Why do you say that?" Madison felt a little defensive. "Because I go to church?"

Kenny raised his hands in mock surrender. "No, not at all, but doesn't the Christian faith promote mindfulness and reverence for sacred things?"

Madison got excited. Was Kenny a believer?

Kenny apologized. "I didn't mean to get all philosophical on you, but what you said is true." He took a last swig of his soda and stood up, turning to her. "Listen, um, do you think it would be okay if I called you or texted sometime?"

Madison was wholly unprepared for his question. "Uh…Yeah, sure."

"If you're not comfortable giving me your number, I understand. I just thought–"

Madison's heart skipped a beat. He was interested in her! "I don't mind. You caught me off guard, that's all. No one has ever asked for my number before."

"Serious?" Kenny asked. "Their loss."

Madison felt herself blush. She pulled out her phone. "What's your number? I'll text you mine."

He told her as she tapped at her phone. *I'm happy to meet you.*

Kenny's phone chirped and he glanced down a second.

Her phone pinged with his reply. *Me too.*

"Hold still a second," Kenny said. He held his phone up to take her picture. Madison squealed in protest, but he was faster and snagged a good shot.

"No fair," Madison pouted.

"I'll erase it if you let me take a better one," Kenny offered.

"Maybe later. Give me a chance to brush my hair."

Madison watched as Brad came out of the kitchen door and onto the patio. Hannah followed close behind him. Brad caught Kenny's eye.

"It looks like Brad needs you," Madison said.

"Yeah, so it seems," Kenny admitted.

"Talk to you later?" Madison asked.

"Absolutely," promised Kenny.

***

The swim party ended early, and everyone left before dark. Brad, Kenny, and Madison stayed to help Trisha and her mom clean up. This gave the nascent couples the opportunity to talk, and saved Trisha's mom from having to spend Saturday morning cleaning everything by herself while her daughter was gone to the revival.

When it was time to go, Kenny offered Madison a ride home.

Madison replied, "Thanks, but my dad's going to pick me up."

"We're going in Brad's car," Kenny pressed. "He has his license."

"I already called him," Madison said. "Besides, he wouldn't be happy with me showing up with some guy he never met before."

Kenny nodded, "Got it. Well, have a good time tomorrow. You can tell me about it when I see you."

"I will," Madison promised.

The guys drove off in Brad's car while the girls remained in front of Trisha's house, waiting for Madison's dad.

As soon as the vehicle was out of sight, Trisha turned to Madison. "What's he like?"

Madison couldn't help but smile. "He's really sweet."

"And cute," Trisha added.

"Yeah. And guess what? He asked for my number."

Trisha did a little dance. "I knew he was into you! Did you give it to him?"

"I did. Do you think that was okay?" Madison asked.

"Totally," Trisha replied.

"I asked him about Brad and Hannah," Madison said.

"You didn't! Do I even want to hear what he said?" Trisha asked.

"He said Brad thinks Hannah is too much drama. Anyway, he's already interested in someone." Madison nudged her friend and raised an eyebrow.

"Well, he did ask me to go to the movies with him on Sunday!" Trisha squealed.

Madison hugged her friend. "That's awesome! Is your mom okay with you going?"

"Probably. I don't see why not. Maybe you and Kenny can go together too, like a double date."

Madison said, "My mom might be okay with it if Kenny asked. But I don't think my dad would let me go."

"You've been to the movies with guys before," Trisha pointed out.

"Yeah, but that's when we went as a group. But a date? With a guy, *alone*?"

"I'll ask your dad when he picks you up," Trisha teased.

"Don't you dare!" Madison was horrified at the thought.

Trisha laughed. "I'm kidding. Honest."

"You're trying to give me a heart attack!" Madison said.

As they spoke, Madison's dad pulled up in front of the house.

"I'll see you in the morning," Madison said.

"Bright and early," Trish answered, waving goodbye.

CHAPTER SIX

Madison Newman was disappointed. She was having a decent time, but after Mr. Slayton's story she had expected...more. She hadn't decided more of what, but she was keeping her eyes open.

The trip had taken a little longer than expected, and there were already a lot of people at the event. Two vans from Madison's church full of young teens, and their chaperones, had arrived before noon.

The three adults knew better than to think they could watch all the young people all the time, so Rule One was never to go anywhere alone; always have a partner. Rule Two was checkpoints every ninety minutes.

Trisha and Madison had paired up, of course, and headed out exploring. A ring of vendors encircled the main tent and the girls stopped at most of them, talking to the people and checking out the merchandise.

"Hey!" Maddie shouted. "You said you were going to share that." She reached out and plucked some pink cotton candy from Trisha's paper cone.

Trisha laughed and tried to pull it away, but she was too slow.

"Check it out, Maddie," Trisha had already moved on to the next table. "Bracelets and charms."

"I wish I had more money," Trisha complained. "I want to buy a ring, but I want to get a taco later."

Madison agreed. "For me it's a necklace or a cheeseburger." The two girls laughed.

They browsed the shiny merchandise, and Trisha finally settled on a bracelet and a ring. Madison purchased a necklace, figuring that her mother would have something for her to eat later when she got home.

They heard a band start to play inside the main tent – a contemporary Christian song. Madison and Trisha made their way closer to the tent, assuming that the main event would be starting soon. Outside the tent stood a table advertising the band's CDs and other merchandise, t-shirts included.

They'd already spent their money for the day, so all they could do was look. That did not dampen their enthusiasm. They were flipping through a rack of t-shirts when the guy working the booth approached them. "Do you see anything you like?"

"We're just looking, thanks," Trisha replied.

The young man was not discouraged. "You're in luck. We're having a half-price special today on 'Just Looking.'"

That earned a chuckle from the girls. He was a good-looking guy, with a friendly, easygoing manner and a nice smile. "I'm Chuck, by the way. If you see anything you like, let me know."

Trisha smiled. "Thanks, Chuck. I'm Trish."

"Nice to meet you, Trish. Who's your friend?"

Madison smiled and felt herself blush, nervously pushing strands of her pale blonde hair out of her face with an index finger. "I'm Madison."

Chuck held out his hand and Madison took it, giving a brief shake. "Glad to meet you," he said. "Are you two from around here?"

Trisha was quick to answer. "No. We came down for the revival. We live up in Monroe County. How about you?"

"I grew up in Florida, but I've been traveling with Pastor Stillman and his show for the past couple of years."

"Are you here for long?" Trisha asked.

"We're never in any one place for long. We got here yesterday," Chuck told Madison. "Tomorrow evening we'll be on our way to Fredericktown, Missouri. We're always on the road."

"Don't you get homesick?" Madison asked.

"Well," the young man gestured around him, "this is my home now. My family wasn't a very…" Chuck paused for a minute as if trying to find the right words, "…welcoming place."

A couple approached, looking at some shirts. "Hang on, I'll be right back," Chuck said, heading off to help the other customers.

They continued to look through the shirts. When Chuck finished ringing up the sale and thanking his customers, he returned to the girls. "Do you see anything you like?"

Madison reiterated, "Seriously, we were just looking. We don't have any money left."

Chuck looked the two of them over and then walked over to his cash register. He reached into a cardboard box underneath the small folding table and pulled out two black t-shirts.

He smiled as he presented them to the two girls. "Behold! The Official Russell Stillman Traveling Revival Road Show T-shirt."

The t-shirts had a graphic on the front depicting an empty two-lane highway stretching to the far horizon with the words, "Road to Redemption." On the back, in the same font as the phrase on the front, it read, "Russell Stillman's Road to Redemption."

Chuck handed the girls their own shirt.

"Oh, no. We can't. We don't have any money!" Madison tried to hand the shirt back.

"It's on the house. Consider it my gift to you for brightening my dreary day."

"Maddie's right," Trisha agreed. "We can't take these for free. You'd get in trouble."

Chuck laughed. "Trouble? Those two shirts didn't even cost five dollars. No one is going to miss them. I promise."

What Chuck didn't tell them was his arrangement with Stillman's people was a set price for the shirts. Anything he gouged from the customers above that was his to keep.

Trisha said, "Thank you. You're really sure it's okay?"

"It's my job. I make the rules."

Trisha dug in her purse, looking for her phone. Chuck took the opportunity to approach Madison. "Hey, thanks for dropping by. I hope you like the shirt."

"Yeah, it's nice, thanks." Madison was uneasy and didn't know what to say.

"I was thinking, maybe you can come back a little later. You know, when the show starts. We can hang out in my camper. Maybe catch a movie?"

"Uh, no. I came to hear Reverend Stillman preach. Besides, I don't even know you."

Trisha grabbed her arm. "Maddie, we have to go. We missed the checkpoint. Mrs. Cady is not going to be happy."

Madison's dismay at being in trouble with Mrs. Cady overshadowed her anger at Chuck, and the two girls ran off to catch up with their group.

When they were clear of the vendor area, Trisha said, "Okay, slow down. I lied. We aren't late. I was just checking the time, but after hearing him come on to you like that, I wanted to get out of there."

"Ewww. That was weird. Thanks, Trisha."

"At least we have t-shirts!"

"Lucky us," Madison deadpanned.

The two walked slowly toward their checkpoint location, silent for the moment.

"So, are you going to start seeing Kenny Warner?" Trisha asked.

"What? No. Well, maybe we could hang out sometimes at school, but as far as going out? My dad wouldn't let me. It's not like that."

Except it *was* like that. At least Madison *hoped* it would be like that. But she knew her parents wouldn't like it, and they probably wouldn't let her go out.

There was just one thing that bothered her about Kenny.

"He made fun of me about being religious," Madison told Trisha.

"What?"

"Yeah. He called me 'church girl.' I asked if he wanted to come to our church and he laughed. He asked, 'Why would I want to do that?' I told him maybe he could take me to his church sometime, but he said his mom and dad don't go to church and he's never really gone."

Trisha shrugged. "Some people don't. A lot of my cousins don't attend church. Did it hurt your feelings when he called you church girl?"

Madison thought for a minute. "No. He wasn't mean about it. He told me he thinks it's cute. Kenny's nice and he makes me laugh. It's just that one thing." Madison sighed. "I'll be patient and pray. Maybe God will open up an opportunity."

***

An hour later, they were in the main tent. The band was playing, and many in the audience were on their feet, praising God. Some had tears in their eyes.

The musicians began to play softer music, and they were singing, "Holy, holy, holy…"

The excitement in the tent was palpable, and Madison felt it along with the others. But she felt something else, too. From deep inside of her, like the bubbling of a well, there was the stirring of something extraordinary. She had no anxiety, but felt an unhurried anticipation, as though she was sent to watch and learn.

The audience was singing along, with hundreds of voices crying out in praise. It was enough to invite the Holy Spirit.

Instead, what they got was the Reverend Russell Stillman. At thirty-four years of age, Russell Stillman cut an imposing figure. Tall and lean, his jet black hair was cut conservatively short, and his impeccably tailored suit hung perfectly.

The band finished with a crescendo, and Stillman whispered into the microphone, "Can I get an amen?"

The audience responded.

"I've been all over this great nation. I've seen the mighty Pacific Ocean beat itself against the rocks of the Oregon coastline. I've seen the silhouette of the Statue of Liberty at dawn against the New York skyline. But my greatest blessing is coming together with God's people and worshipping. Can I get an amen?"

The audience was not stingy.

"I want to thank you all for being here today. Some people say I'm foolish for wanting to preach the gospel. They tell me no one is going to come. They tell me no one wants to listen to what I have to say."

There were some boos from people sprinkled throughout the crowd.

"What do you suppose I tell those naysayers? I tell them they don't know God's people. Whenever I come to Illinois, I have the privilege of meeting some of the strongest and most sincere men and women of God I have ever known. Give yourselves a clap offering!"

The crowd erupted with cheers, clapping, and shouts of, "Amen!"

"Your very presence here is an act of worship. Your decision to spend time gathered together with your brothers and sisters is an act of faith. Rest assured brothers and sisters, God sees your obedience and He will reward you."

Madison looked around. She was excited for the message, and she wanted to focus on his words, but another part felt like there was something else she was waiting for. Something she didn't want to miss.

"Jesus said, 'I have come that they may have life, and that they may have it more abundantly.' More. More time with the family. More time to appreciate each other. More income to afford the good things of life. Who here doesn't wish they could afford the luxury of time off with the ones they love?"

Not a single hand was raised.

"The thing is, we're too busy making a living. After all, we have bills to pay. The kids need braces. The wife's car needs brakes. You just got a call from your doctor. He got your test results, and would you mind coming in as soon as possible?"

By now, Stillman was pacing the stage, waving one arm while holding the mic with the other. He had the audience's full attention.

"I tell you, brothers and sisters, God does not want that kind of life for you. He wants you to live a life of abundance. He wants to give you more of everything so you can stop worrying about the little stuff. God's already taken care of the little stuff if you'd only stop worrying about it and LET IT GO!"

The crowd shouted amen.

"It's a funny thing about God, you know. You can't outgive God. You do understand that He blesses you so that you can bless others, amen? I'm going to tell you how you can help us do that in just a little while, but now I'd like to introduce you to a lady whose voice is nothing short of angelic. She's going to bless us this evening with a song. You can buy her latest CD at the music booth outside."

Madison sighed and looked around her once more. Everyone seemed to be enjoying themselves. Trisha was sitting next to her, watching the singer. They all seemed entertained. Yet unease continued to peck away at Madison. Hoping to understand why she felt as she did, she prayed and asked God to reveal what she needed to know.

Following the music, Stillman began to preach about lack of faith holding people back from claiming the life they deserved to have. Reverend Stillman spent a half hour telling people how to let God bless them richly, so as to be a credit to God's kingdom.

The remaining fifteen minutes he spent on an impassioned appeal to the people for financial assistance to help him spread the word. The band began playing, "In the Presence of the Lord," while a dozen burly ushers/security guards shuffled collection plates back and forth down the rows of bench seats.

The band dropped the volume as Stillman began to speak once more.

"During the service my spirit was heavy, and I didn't understand why. So I asked God to reveal to me why a dark shadow was cast upon my heart. He revealed to me there are people here who are hurting, and I'd like to pray for them. Ushers, if you please, will you escort them up here?"

Madison didn't believe what he was saying. The unease she'd felt had been unlike anything she'd experienced before. Was it the same as the distress felt by Reverend Stillman?

She had her answer soon enough when one of the ushers brought up a middle-aged woman who was using a walker. Her gait was slow and unsteady, and she explained arthritis had all but crippled her.

Madison's heart knew that now was the moment. This is what she was sent to see and understand.

If pressed for an answer, Madison would have been unable to explain how she knew the woman wasn't really suffering, but she knew. She was watching the woman explain her malady to Stillman, but it was as though her eyes had been opened to what was really going on.

Madison gasped. "She's lying!"

"What? Who's lying?" Trisha asked.

Madison blushed. She hadn't intended to speak out loud. Pointing at the stage she said, "The woman who came up with the walker. There's nothing wrong with her."

"How do you know?" Trisha asked.

Madison was tempted to lie. She didn't know if Trisha would accept the truth. Her friend would readily believe her if she said she'd seen the woman earlier and that she had been completely okay. But she was not going to soil the truth that God had allowed her to see by telling a lie.

"I'm going to tell you the truth, okay? The Holy Spirit showed me."

Trisha looked at her doubtfully but nodded.

Madison's attention was drawn back to the stage as Stillman began praying fervently for the woman. With a shout, Stillman proclaimed the woman healed and, as the woman took her first unassisted steps, the crowd went wild with shouts of praise.

The next person ushered to the stage was an older man who walked with a cane. Stillman kneeled in front of the man and gripped the man's hip, rubbing it as he prayed.

"What about him?" Trisha asked.

"It's true. His hip. It hurts him sometimes. Worn cartilage."

Trisha no longer doubted and looked at Madison with her eyes wide. "How do you know?"

"I told you." Madison's eyes pooled with tears. She was unable to explain how she knew. She'd never exposed herself to anyone like this before, not since Frankie so many years before. But they had just been kids. Since then, it had always seemed a necessity to keep it secret, even from her family.

As Stillman prayed, he continued to rub the man's hip. After a couple of minutes, he announced the man was healed.

"Tell me, Sir, how are you feeling now?" Stillman asked the man.

The man flexed his leg and said, "It doesn't hurt as much."

Stillman proclaimed, "That is the healing power of God. The pain in your hip will continue to diminish until it is completely gone. By tomorrow morning, you will never use a cane again."

The audience clapped and cheered.

Madison looked at Trisha and shook her head.

The next person was a man who said he'd been told by his doctor he had cancer. Advanced.

Madison clenched her teeth. By now, she was angry.

"What's wrong, Maddie?" Trisha touched her friend's shoulder gently.

"There's nothing wrong with him either. This isn't what I thought it was going to be. He's lying to all these people."

Mrs. Cady noticed the commotion with the two girls, and she came over and kneeled next to them. She could tell Madison was upset. "Is everything okay?"

Madison didn't know how to answer. She didn't know if Mrs. Cady would understand why she was upset, or if it was even safe to tell her. Madison just nodded her head and said, "I'm a little emotional over all of this. It's a lot to take in."

Mrs. Cady smiled. "It is. Maybe during next week's class we can discuss your experiences."

Madison wished she hadn't come. She didn't really know what to expect. All she had to go on were the stories the adults had told them after VBS a couple of weeks ago, and Mr. Slayton's remarkable account of salvation. She remembered they spoke about it being a very positive spiritual experience. This was more of a carnival.

She understood now what had been bothering her. She'd come with certain expectations. After hearing the story from Mr. Slayton, she expected to come and meet God. Not literally, of course. Madison anticipated this would be more of a holy, reverential experience.

Instead, she was confronted by the world. This was like a county fair with food, merchandise, and games. The preaching and the prayers for healing were nothing more than entertainment to amaze the crowd and had no more to do with God than a carnival sideshow.

A loud commotion shook Madison from her thoughts. Despite the well-ordered and carefully orchestrated parade of people requesting prayer, a woman had managed to approach the stage.

The woman was blind, and she was pushed in a wheelchair by her adult daughter, who had somehow maneuvered past distracted ushers and wheeled her mother to the front where they begged for healing prayer.

Madison watched as two of the ushers tried to block the woman, but the daughter was very vocal. "Please, let the preacher pray for my mama!" She was a small woman, but she was determined, and for her mother's sake refused to be put off.

There was no possibility that Stillman could feign overlooking the duo, Madison realized. Now everyone had seen the two women and waited to see what Reverend Stillman would do.

Madison was captivated by the drama unfolding before her.

Stillman leaned down from the stage to talk to the woman and spoke softly into the microphone, "God bless you, Sister. What can I do for you today?"

"It's my mama, Reverend. She needs prayer real bad. She got cancer in her brain. A brain tumor caused her to go blind and she can't walk. An operation is impossible. The doctor says she won't see year's end."

"That is a lot to deal with, isn't it, Sister?" he said sympathetically.

Then he spoke louder, and with authority. "But your heavenly Father is big enough to take care of anything the old devil can throw at us." He straightened up and addressed the audience.

"Isn't that right?"

The audience shouted their agreement.

Reverend Russell Stillman hopped off the three foot high stage to where the woman and her mother waited. He put the microphone between them and he said, "God wants to do a mighty work in your lives tonight, but it's going to take faith. Do you have sufficient faith to claim the healing He has for you?"

The woman in the wheelchair answered, "I do, Reverend. I surely do."

"Then let us pray together, Sister," Stillman said.

In contrast to those he prayed for previously, this was a very short and simple prayer. He stood in silent meditation for a moment and began his prayer quietly.

"Lord God, hear our prayer. You know the desire of our hearts, Lord. Our desire is that our sister be healed. Begin to remove the tumor from her brain, Lord, and restore her vision. We don't need to shout, Lord. We don't need to fall to our knees as beggars, because you know the prayer in our hearts."

He placed his palm over the woman's eyes and said, "The healing has begun. Can I get an amen?"

The audience gave a loud amen. Amidst the cheering and the shouts of joy, Madison noticed Stillman turning off his microphone and leaning in to talk to the woman and her daughter.

When the women turned to leave, he spoke to the audience again. "Strike me dead if this crowd isn't on fire today! I am privileged to be here with you folks today. We've seen God do some amazing things this afternoon, amen?"

Madison wasn't listening anymore to what Reverend Stillman was saying. She knew what she was being told to do, and she was scared. It had always been private before. Out here, there were people everywhere.

There was no misunderstanding, and Madison began to weep, and pray.

"I will, but please don't leave me," she pleaded.

Trisha looked over with worried expression as she watched her friend crying and whispering.

Madison nodded. Her eyes were closed, and she smiled, "I'd like that."

Trisha laid a hand on her friend's shoulder. "Maddie! What's going on?"

Madison half stood, straining to see where the woman and her daughter had gone. The band started playing, and quite a number of people got up to stretch, or to visit the restroom. There were people standing and milling about, making it difficult to see.

"Hey! Are you okay, Maddie?" Trisha shouted.

There! Madison caught a glimpse of the daughter on the left. She was headed toward the rear of the immense tent.

She sat down and pulled Trisha close. "Listen. I have to go. Don't say anything, okay? I'll be right back."

"Wait, no Maddie, you can't…"

The instructions to always stay with your partner were all but forgotten as she got up and ran toward the back of the tent. There were fewer people, and she hoped to get to the rear exits before the mother and daughter left.

She needn't have worried. Pushing the wheelchair over the uneven terrain of the tent's dirt floor was slow going, and Madison quickly caught up with the pair.

"Excuse me?" Madison said. "May I talk to you for a minute?"

Now that she was close, she could see the woman was in her mid-forties, and her daughter about twenty years younger.

The daughter replied, "I'm sorry, I have to get momma home so she can rest."

The woman said, "It's okay, Gloria. There's no hurry." Then she asked Madison, "What do you want, Miss?"

Madison discovered she didn't have a plan. She just knew she was going to ask the woman questions that her mom would say were being too nosy.

"I'd like to know what the reverend said to you after he prayed."

The woman didn't seem to mind the question and answered, "He said my illness was quite serious and it might take some time before I start to get better. He told me to keep my faith strong and I would see a difference soon."

Even though she suspected that was going to be the answer, Madison was heartbroken. She'd been sent to tell the woman the truth. "I'm so sorry, Ma'am. That's simply not true."

The woman's daughter, Gloria, asked, "What do you mean it's not true?"

"What the reverend said about taking time to heal because her illness is so serious? He's wrong."

Madison addressed the woman now. "It doesn't matter how sick you are, Ma'am. When Jesus heals it's immediate, it's complete, and it's permanent. Jesus raised the dead. It doesn't get more serious than dead."

The woman gave out a weary sigh.

Her daughter began to cry. "Mom, don't listen to her. She's a kid. We'll find someone else. We'll do something."

"No, Gloria," the woman said. "I already knew. As much as I wanted to believe what Stillman told me, I knew it was a lie."

Madison felt urgency now, a need to move forward with...*what?* She didn't know yet. Glancing at the stage, she saw Stillman looking in her direction. She focused back on the woman in the wheelchair and asked her, "May I touch you?"

Without waiting for an answer, she moved forward and placed her palm on the woman's forehead.

The blind woman started in surprise at Madison's touch. "It's okay," Madison reassured her. "It's me."

The Holy Spirit wanted to show her something, and it was breaking Madison's heart. The cancer had started as nothing more than a few cells. In several weeks' time it had grown to the size of a marble. It had stolen her sight and had blocked the nerve impulses to her legs.

As it worked itself through her brain, the woman would lose herself piece by piece until it claimed everything. Eventually, the part of the brain that automatically regulates heartbeat and respiration would begin to fail. It was a death sentence.

Madison gasped and pulled her hand away from the woman. She'd felt her being eaten away by the cancer. It was a lesson for Madison so that she might fully appreciate the healing.

She took the woman's hand in hers and declared, "So that you will know that He is sovereign over all things, and His power is undeniable, it is Christ who heals you."

The effect was immediate and dramatic, and the woman began to shriek, "I can see! I can see!" She leaped from her wheelchair without thinking and grabbed her daughter, "Gloria, I can see!"

The two screamed with excitement as they jumped up and down, overcome with emotion.

The woman was joined by her daughter as she fell to her knees and lifted her arms to cry out, "Thank you, Jesus! I can see, Lord. You healed me. Oh, praise God for His mercy."

Madison had never experienced a reaction like this before. The woman's unashamed joy spilled out like a fountain and caught the attention of most of the people there. The band was still playing, and they were pretty loud, so perhaps the farthest reaches of the tent had no inkling of what had just happened, but those close by saw the whole thing, and they praised God spontaneously and vocally.

***

Reverend Stillman and a couple of his security men headed toward the group, intending to find out exactly what had happened to the woman in the wheelchair.

Stillman was inwardly seething about the security personnel. How could his trained men allow that woman to interrupt his service? They were supposed to stop random people from approaching the stage. She was in a wheelchair, for heaven's sake! Didn't they see that coming?

There weren't ever supposed to be any surprises during the show. It should go just as they'd rehearsed, just as they'd done it in the last dozen towns they'd been in.

***

There were scores of people around, watching and asking questions. All of their attention was on the woman and her daughter and, to her discomfort, on Madison. She never wanted to draw attention to herself in this way.

She had to get back to her people before Mrs. Cady realized she wasn't with them. She saw Stillman. He was still some distance away, but he was approaching the group purposefully.

Her only chance was to move around to the right of the crowd, so she'd be obscured by the knot of people surrounding the woman, and then make her way back to the front of the tent to rejoin her friends. Madison began to rush along the aisle, glancing left and searching for Trisha. They couldn't possibly be this far in the front, could they? Maybe they were further in toward the center of the tent. She couldn't remember.

The milling crowd, the band's loud music, her panic to get back to her group, it all conspired to confuse her. She didn't see anyone she knew and turned to retrace her steps. She didn't watch where she was going and ran straight into Reverend Stillman.

Madison gave a small shriek of surprise, "Oh! Excuse me. I didn't mean to..."

"That's just fine, Miss. No harm done. I was hoping to meet you," Stillman said.

"Me?" Madison asked.

"Yes, you. I'm quite impressed that you prayed for that woman in the wheelchair. All of these people watched her pass by and did nothing, yet you sought her out to pray for her. Why?"

Madison was confused, "She needed prayer."

Stillman persisted. "But why *you*?"

Madison regarded him carefully. What did he want? Should she tell him the truth? Because she didn't want the woman to go away believing God was unwilling to heal her? Or worse yet, too weak?

She reminded herself that Stillman lied to the people that came to hear the truth. He gave them theatrics instead of reality. He flattered them and patted them on the back instead of preaching the Word that would save them.

"Because the Holy Spirit didn't want her to leave without hearing the truth," she said boldly.

Stillman grinned, "Well, whatever your reasons, that's quite a little trick you have there."

"What trick?" Madison asked. "You prayed for her, and now you're surprised she's healed?"

At that moment they were interrupted by Mrs. Cady. Her focus was on Madison. "Madison, where have you been? What's going on here?"

"I'm so sorry, Mrs. Cady. I went to talk to that woman the preacher prayed for."

"You know you're not supposed to go anywhere without your partner. What in the world would you have to say to that woman anyway?"

"Yes," Reverend Stillman agreed. "What indeed?"

Mrs. Cady turned and broke into a smile. "Reverend Stillman!"

She took his offered hand, and they shook.

Stillman said, "I want to thank you personally for coming today, Ms....?"

"Cady. Francine Cady. You're welcome, Reverend."

"And who is this young lady?" Stillman asked.

Madison didn't answer.

Mrs. Cady cut in. "This is Madison. She's part of a youth group from our church that came to hear you today."

Reverend Stillman smiled. "An entire group of young people who are curious about the Lord's work, isn't that something? Ma'am, may God bless the work you do. The youth are the future of the church, and I have to say I am most impressed with young Madison. My heart was heavy for the woman I'd prayed for. I turned to look for her, and there I saw Madison, praying for that woman. You must have a very special church."

"Well, thank you. We certainly like to think so," Francine beamed.

Madison couldn't believe that Mrs. Cady was having a conversation with Reverend Stillman. She didn't want him to ask her any more questions.

"Which church is that, by the way?" he asked.

Madison groaned inwardly.

"We came down from Oracle. We're from Valley Community Church," Mrs. Cady said.

"I am so pleased you did, and I'm pleased to have met you, Francine." He turned to Madison and extended his hand, "I enjoyed meeting you, Madison. Yours is an uncommon faith."

Madison took the man's hand. She shook it, saying, "Thank you, Sir. It was interesting to hear you speak."

At least she didn't lie. It had been an interesting experience.

"May traveling mercies follow you on your journey home." With that, Stillman headed back toward the stage.

"My, he's such a nice man," Mrs. Cady said.

***

When Stillman got back on stage, he went straight to his security detail.

"You see that woman and the girl I was talking to?"

The men nodded.

"Keep an eye on them. Get pictures. The woman is Francine Cady. The girl's name is Madison. Cady says they come from Oracle. Valley Community Church. I want to know who the kid is. I want to know everything."

The head of security nodded. "Yes, Sir. I'll talk to the parking lot attendant and gate security. I'll make sure they get some photos, info about the vehicles, and anything else we can learn."

***

Mrs. Cady and Madison walked back to their seats. Mrs. Cady put her arm around Madison, who hadn't been able to hold back her tears. "Are you okay? Did something happen?"

"I'm fine," Madison answered.

"Why did you pray with the woman in the wheelchair?" she asked.

"I needed to talk to her before she was gone. They were leaving, and...I felt moved to pray for her." Madison was careful to be honest with her answer. The plain truth is, she hadn't simply been moved; she had been commanded. She could no more have disobeyed the order than she could have ignored gravity.

Mrs. Cady sighed. "You scared me to death. I heard commotion going on and the next thing I know, you're missing. Then I saw you talking to some strange man. I didn't realize it was Reverend Stillman. I didn't know what to think."

"I'm really sorry, Mrs. Cady. I couldn't let her leave without talking to her first. It was important. I won't do it again."

"Oh, Madison, I'm not angry with you. I was worried. Reverend Stillman thinks you're pretty special." Then Mrs. Cady smiled and added, "You know what?"

Madison raised her eyebrows. "What?"

"So do I."

***

By dusk, the group from Oracle decided to call it a day. There was another hour of sunlight left in the summer sky. With any luck, they'd be on the Interstate before dark.

On the walk to the parking lot, Trisha and Madison hung back a little. They didn't have the chance to talk earlier because Mrs. Cady had Madison sit with her until the end of the program.

"Are you okay?" Trisha asked her. "I was afraid you were going to get in trouble."

"I'm okay. Mrs. Cady was worried about me, but I'm not in trouble."

"She was pretty upset when she noticed you weren't with me. She asked where you were. I had to tell her. Please don't be mad at me," Trisha said.

Madison put her arm around her friend and gave her a squeeze. "I'm not mad. Besides, Mrs. Cady got to meet Reverend Stillman. I think that helped her not be too angry."

"Is that lady really healed?"

Madison remembered the woman's excitement and smiled. "Yes. She really is."

"What happened today, Maddie?" Trisha asked. "You freaked me out."

Madison was tired. She knew that even a brief answer would lead to more questions, and she wasn't certain she knew the answers. She was pretty sure her friend wasn't ready to hear them.

"I don't think I've processed this day yet," she ventured. "When I figure it out, we can talk. Is that okay? I'm so tired right now."

The group passed through the gate and into the parking lot.

Madison got home very late. Although she was troubled by the things she'd seen, she fell into a deep slumber.

***

With the household retired for the night, there was no one to notice a camper ease down the street, slowing ever so slightly as it passed the Newman residence.

CHAPTER SEVEN

Following the close of the revival service, Russell Stillman sat in his luxury motor home with his key people late into the evening. They debriefed while the worker bees packed everything up for the trip to the next town.

Kevin Wells, Stillman's business manager and publicist, was winding up his report. "We did very well today. After we covered expenses, including our 'gift' to the police department, we ended up doing quite well indeed."

"What about the advance publicity for Missouri?" Stillman asked. "We didn't do well there last time."

Kevin smiled and said, "We've got all the bases covered. I think you're going to like this. A local reporter in town here is going to do a great piece on today's show. I met with him earlier this week and wined and dined him at the best place in town. We have some great shots of your healing prayers and he'll include one with his article."

"How does that help us in Missouri?" Stillman wanted to know.

"He's got a buddy on the paper in Fredericktown. He'll put the story on the AP and his buddy will pick it up. We have flyers out already, along with billboards and – get this – next Thursday morning you'll be interviewed by their local station to promote the event."

"That is sweet, Kevin. Good work. How did you manage to pull that off?"

"It turns out their morning show's host has a daughter on the local soccer team. The very same team that Stillman Ministries, Inc., donated to for their equipment fund."

"God moves in a mysterious way, His wonders to perform," Stillman quoted.

They all burst out laughing. Stillman upended his bottle and drained it. "Grab me another beer, will you?"

Stillman turned to his head of security. "Bill, you're up next."

"It was a good day. We had no fights. One lady sprained her ankle in the tent when she stepped wrong. The doc wrapped it up in a bandage and scolded her for wearing platform shoes. Plus, the lady had been drinking, so there's little chance of liability there. Lastly, we had reports of two lost purses and one lost wallet. Our lost and found reported no items matching their description."

"That is a pretty good day, except I don't care about those things right now, Bill. I think you know what I want to hear. How did two of your guys let some random woman approach the stage? And in a wheelchair! That is *never* supposed to happen."

"I'm sorry, Russ. I had two new guys up front. I already chewed them out."

"You let them keep their jobs?" Stillman asked.

"This one's on me, Russ. I put them in a position they'd never been in before, and I had them working together. They're good, just inexperienced. I don't want to lose them because of my error."

"Rookie move, Bill. We hit Missouri in less than a week. Let's tighten it up. I depend on you guys."

Bill brightened up. "I have a peace offering."

"Yeah? What is it?"

Bill reached into his jacket and pulled out an envelope. He handed it over to Stillman, who leafed through the photos.

"These are the folks from Oracle, eh? It's quite a large crew to make the trip all this way."

"Two vans full. Both of them registered to Valley Community Church. We have Francine Cady's address, and…" Bill paused for dramatic effect, "we know where the girl lives." Bill handed over an index card on which he'd written the addresses.

Russell Stillman smiled.

Bill then handed over his phone. "And a little something extra."

The YouTube app was open on a video. The title read "Stillman Rally Healing." The scene was of the revival meeting earlier in the day, and the camera panned over the crowd. The shot was shaky, and the lighting was off because they were in the tent. There was a babble of voices, and the band played in the background.

Then the screaming began. The camera panned over to the sound, and there stood the woman from the wheelchair. She was shouting and leaping for joy. She hugged her daughter. And there, just behind the woman's wheelchair, was that girl.

Stillman looked at the index card. *Madison Newman.*

Then the woman and her daughter fell to their knees and the mother shouted, "Thank you, Jesus! I can see, Lord, you healed me. Praise God for His mercy."

The video stopped shortly after that.

Bill said, "You can't buy that kind of publicity." He turned to Kevin. "Send that to your reporter friend in Fredericktown. Maybe they'll run it during the interview."

Kevin agreed. "They'll eat this stuff up. Did we post that?"

"No. Apparently it was someone who was here today and caught it on their phone," Bill replied.

"That's even better. No one can claim we were fishing for publicity, or that it was staged," Kevin turned to Stillman. "Great clip, don't you think, Russ?"

Stillman was watching the video again. Watching Madison.

"Boss?" Kevin said.

"Hmm? Oh, yes. Good clip. Definitely send it." Stillman passed the phone back to Bill.

The boss seemed distracted. "Is everything okay, Russ?" Kevin asked.

"Sure. Everything's fine. Listen, Bill, I'd like to know who that woman is. I want to know if she and that girl know each other, or if they're related."

Bill asked, "Do you think they were in it together? Maybe running some sort of con?"

Stillman thought about it for a moment before answering. "I don't think so. But I'd like to eliminate it as a possibility. Ask your guys. Find out if anyone saw them together."

"Will do," Bill acknowledged.

"It was a good show today, guys. Let's see if we can top it in Missouri."

***

After the meeting, Stillman sat in his motor home thinking about this afternoon's show. Every now and then he'd pick up his phone to watch the clip again.

What happened here today?

He didn't believe the woman was faking. Her joy was far too convincing. He'd seen Madison with the woman and watched as she placed her palm on the woman's head. What had she done? He'd prayed for the woman, but he would have laughed at the notion that it was his prayer that had healed her.

Stillman stepped outside in the cool of the night. The wind was a whisper, and here, on the outskirts of town, the night sky was brilliant with stars. He turned his eyes skyward, enjoying relief from the summer heat.

His footsteps crunched on the loose gravel as he made his way through the parking lot. Everything was packed up and ready to roll at first light. Most of his people had turned in for the night, but the one camper he sought still had lights on and he could hear the television as he knocked at the door.

"It's not locked. C'mon in."

Stillman opened the door and climbed up into the camper.

"Well, if it isn't Reverend Stillman. What brings you to my humble door, Rev?"

"I have a job I'd like you to do for me, Chuck," Stillman said.

Chuck Carson was twenty-seven years old, but with his boyish looks and mop of blond hair, he easily passed for a teenager. He was originally from Florida, and he'd been in and out of the system since the age of sixteen. His single mother had done the best she knew how, but she was no match for her delinquent son. He never finished school and made his living with a variety of petty thefts, residential burglaries, and picking pockets.

His numerous arrests finally caught up with him and, for once, he was facing some serious time. He'd done work for Stillman in the past and asked the reverend for a character reference.

Stillman did him one better and showed up at his sentencing. He explained to the judge that Chuck's predilection for trouble was a result of a lack of direction and discipline during his formative years. If the court would permit the accused one last opportunity to turn himself around, Reverend Stillman promised to see that Mister Carson was gainfully employed.

The court agreed to the proposal on condition that Chuck complete the term of his probation with Stillman. Chuck readily accepted the court's decision with the clear understanding that if he ran into any trouble while on probation, he'd be going to prison.

Chuck turned off the TV and hopped down off of his bunk. He and Stillman sat on opposite sides of the tiny dining table. "So, what's up?"

"I need you to leave the show for a while, Chuck. I need you to go up to Oracle and check out a few people." Stillman passed the photographs to Chuck.

He looked them over, and then raised his eyebrows. "Hey. It's Madison and Trish."

"You *know* them?" Stillman asked.

"They came in to check out the merch. We chatted for a bit." Chuck passed the photos back with a smile.

"Why doesn't that surprise me?" Stillman sighed.

Stillman pulled a couple index cards out of his pocket and gave them to Chuck. "Here are addresses, names, everything you need. Most of all, I want to know about the girl." He tapped on the photo of Madison.

Chuck quickly skimmed the cards. "What do you want to know? You know her name and where she lives. What more do you need?"

Stillman passed over an envelope, thick with bills. Chuck fanned through the cash and said, "Dude. This is a *lot* of money. What do you want me…" Chuck went wide-eyed and dropped the envelope. "No way, man. I want no part of–"

Stillman cut him off. "Don't be an imbecile. This is for living expenses. I want you to go up there and settle in. I want you to be part of the landscape. Get a job, go shopping. I want to know what that girl does. I want to know who she sees. Dig deep. Find out if she has problems at home. Does she drink a lot? Does she sleep around?"

"Then what?" Chuck asked.

"I don't know yet. It depends on what you have to tell me," Stillman said.

"Are you looking to blackmail her? What did she do?"

"Blackmail her? No. I want to recruit her."

Chucked laughed. "What's so special about her?"

Stillman stood and headed for the door. "That's what I want you to find out."

CHAPTER EIGHT

It was the last class of the day. Biology. There was a test, but Madison was prepared.

Three questions remained on the exam when she heard the phone buzzing from her backpack on the floor. Her eyes darted to the clock. Two forty-two. Was it Kenny?

Madison looked to the front of the classroom. Mr. Poole was watching the class closely. She wouldn't be sneaking a look at her phone.

When class was over, she grabbed her pack and dug out her phone. The text was from her mom. *Running late. See you in 30. Will text.*

It was cloudy, and it had started sprinkling. Madison put her coat over her head as she ran to the library to wait for her mother. Once she got inside, she texted Kenny. *U still here? In library.* Then she pulled out her sociology textbook, hoping to get a head start on her homework.

It was difficult to concentrate, and she kept glancing at her phone. She didn't want to miss her mom's text. There was no reply from Kenny, which was disappointing, but he was on the track team and was probably practicing.

Madison eventually pushed aside the distractions and was deep into her textbook when someone sat down next to her. She looked over to see Kenny. Her stomach suddenly felt like a flutter of butterflies.

"You're really into that, aren't you? You didn't even see me coming," Kenny teased.

"Not when you're trying to be sneaky!" Madison accused. She smiled and nudged him with her elbow.

Kenny reached down and squeezed Madison's hand. She blushed and looked around, "Kenny, stop. Someone will see," she scolded. Then she added, "Your hands are cold!"

"That's 'cuz it's wet and cold outside. What are you still doing here?" Kenny asked.

"My mom's running late. I was hoping to see you. Did they cancel practice?"

"Yeah, the track's too wet. Our meet is in a couple weeks. This rain just isn't letting up. If we don't get some track time in, we won't stand a chance. Hey, maybe you can, you know…" Kenny put his palms together and looked at Madison, raising his eyebrows in question.

She exhaled in exasperation. "I thought we talked about that. It's like you're making fun of me."

"I know. I'm sorry. I'm just kidding, I promise."

Since meeting at Trisha's party, Madison and Kenny managed to see one another every two or three days at school, depending on their schedules. If you asked either one of them, they'd deny what their friends already took for granted. Madison and Kenny were an item.

"Apology accepted," Madison said. She was avoiding eye contact and absently doodling on her notebook cover. "So…my birthday is coming up in a couple weeks and my parents said I could have some people over. You know. Pizza, cake. Anyway…" She glanced up into his big, blue eyes and said, "Would you like to come?"

Kenny smiled, "You really want me to come to your party?"

Madison blushed and nodded. "Yeah. I do."

"I'd love to," Kenny said.

"Great," was all she managed to say. Madison was thrilled Kenny said he'd come to her birthday, but the silence drew out so long that she felt awkward and didn't know what to say.

"So, like, when is it?" Kenny asked.

"Oh yeah, duh." Madison eye-rolled. *Pull it together.* "I'll text it to you."

Saved by the buzz from her phone, Madison grabbed her backpack. Looking at her phone, Madison said, "My mom's here. I have to go."

"I'll go with you, up to the cafeteria," Kenny offered.

"Yeah, okay," Madison agreed.

When they exited the library, they discovered the light sprinkle of rain had turned into a downpour. Pulling their coats over their heads, the two ran out into the deluge.

"Maybe I should just get going," Kenny said.

Madison shouted in the rain. "No, come with me. My mom can take you home."

"Are you sure?"

"Of course. She'd never let someone walk home in this."

They splashed through the shallow pools of rainwater as they ran across campus. Madison shrieked and laughed. They were soaked through by the time they reached the Camry. The two kids jumped in with Madison taking shotgun, and Kenny climbing into the backseat.

"Hi, Mom," Madison said. She leaned over and kissed her cheek. "Can we take Kenny home? He's on the track team and they canceled practice. He needs a ride. Please?"

Evelyn smiled, "Sure, Sweetie." She looked in the mirror and waved, "Hello, Kenny."

Kenny smiled, "Hi, Mrs. Newman. Thanks for the ride, I really appreciate it. It's not too far."

"Not a problem," Evelyn reassured him. "Where are we headed?" she asked as they pulled out into traffic.

Once her mom knew where to go, Madison announced, "Kenny said he can come to my party. Is that okay?"

"Of course, Maddie. We said you could invite whoever you want."

Madison shot a quick smile to Kenny in the backseat.

"I thought I knew all of Madison's friends. Are you new to the area, Kenny?" Evelyn asked.

"Mom!"

Kenny laughed and said to Madison, "It's okay." Then he replied, "We've been here three years. My dad's job moved him out here from Virginia."

"How do you like it?" Evelyn asked.

"I miss being close to the beach, but it's all right, I guess. I like the woods north of town, but I haven't explored too much."

"Well, I hope you've come to call this place home. We sure like it."

"I do. There's only one thing I haven't done in the three years I've been here," Kenny admitted.

"What's that?" Evelyn asked.

"I haven't been to the county fair."

"You're in luck," Evelyn said as she pulled in front of Kenny's house. "The fair is a few weeks out. You have plenty of time to plan."

"That's great. Then is it okay to ask Madison if she'd go to the fair with me? You know, sort of like an expert guide for a first-timer?"

Evelyn laughed aloud. "Nice try, Kenny. Really, that was smooth. I'll tell you what, when you're at the party, you talk to Maddie's father and ask him. If he says yes, and Maddie wants to go, then you have my permission."

Madison wanted to crawl under her seat, but Kenny said, "Fair enough. Thanks for the ride, Mrs. Newman."

As he left the car, he told Madison, "See you at school tomorrow."

Evelyn drove off accompanied by Madison's silence.

"What are you unhappy about?"

"Does he really have to ask Dad?"

"Of course, Maddie. You remember our deal. We want to meet any of the friends you go out with. I don't think that's unreasonable."

Madison reluctantly agreed. "I guess so."

"If a boy really wants to go out with you, he shouldn't mind meeting your parents and asking them."

Grudgingly, Madison admitted, "You're right."

They drove in silence for a while as Evelyn made her way north up Market Street.

"He seems like a nice boy."

"He really is, Mom."

Madison had told Kenny he'd have to ask her parents if he wanted to take her out, and he readily agreed. She never dreamed he'd do it right in front of her. Still, she reasoned, her mother seemed chill about it, so maybe Kenny talking to her dad wouldn't be as bad as she thought.

Evelyn reached in her purse and glanced at her phone. "Change of plans. Your father is going to be late, so we're on our own."

She dug a twenty and a ten out of her purse and handed it to Madison while pulling into a small shopping center. "I have to pick up a few things at the store. You grab a pizza." She pointed at the local pizzeria near the corner. "Get what you want. I'm good with anything."

***

Madison made the salad while Evelyn put away the groceries. They sat across from each other at the small table, listening to the patter of the rain outside the window as they ate.

"The salad is good," Evelyn complimented.

"Thanks. So's the pizza," said Madison.

"A lot of croutons," Evelyn observed, poking her fork through the greens.

"I like croutons," Madison said, defending her choice.

"I like croutons, too, but a person has to know where to draw the line."

Madison saw her mom was joking, and she smiled.

"You really like Kenny, don't you?" Evelyn asked.

Madison gave a weary sigh, not really wanting to have this conversation, but her mother was silent, waiting.

"Yeah, I do. A lot. The weird thing is how much I want him to like me. It's almost scary."

Evelyn nodded. "Believe it or not, I was in high school. I know how you feel."

"Do you, Mom?" Madison managed to keep the sarcasm out of her voice.

"Do you want to know a secret?"

"Sure."

"You know how you're feeling now? Uncertain and insecure?"

Madison hated to admit it, but maybe her mom really did know how she felt. She hung her head and said, "Yeah?"

"Boys his age feel exactly the same way."

"No way."

"I promise you, Maddie. In high school, *everyone* is trying to figure stuff out. In fact, guys his age are generally less mature than girls the same age."

"But they act all confident and sure of themselves," Madison pointed out.

"Of course they do. That's what they're supposed to do."

"What am *I* supposed to do?" she pleaded. "How do I get Kenny to really like me?"

Evelyn smiled gently. "Just be yourself. That's enough. God has someone waiting just for you. Don't try to force yourself into being someone you're not just to get a person to like you. Respect yourself enough so you don't do something just to keep a boy's attention."

"You really worry about me, don't you, Mom?"

"Yes! Of course I do, silly. You're my baby."

"Why do you worry if you know God is watching out for me?"

Evelyn leaned closer and whispered to her daughter, "Didn't you know? Mothers are God's helpers. Worry is in our job description."

Madison struggled with knowing how much to tell her mother. "Sometimes it feels like my life is going to change forever."

"It is, Sweetie. You're growing up. In a few years your life is going to be much different than it is now. Opportunities will begin to open up for you, and you're going to have decisions to make that will have an impact on your life in ways we can't foresee."

Madison felt her mom watching her closely. "I've never seen you like this, Maddie. Is everything okay?"

"I guess there's just a lot going on."

"Are you sure nothing is wrong?"

Madison smiled. "Positive. I promise I'd tell you. It's just…" Madison turned somber, "… what if I never have anyone?"

"You mean like a boyfriend?"

"Yeah."

Evelyn dismissed her worry. "Madison, that's nonsense. I'm sure God is preparing someone especially for you."

Madison realized she wasn't going to get the answers she needed from her mother unless she told her everything. She wasn't yet prepared to do that, so she changed the subject. "We didn't plan for Kenny to ask you about the fair today. I had no idea he was going to do that in front of me."

Evelyn nodded and laughed. "I could tell by the way you almost died. I thought it was kind of sweet. He really does like you, Maddie."

Madison felt her face grow warm and hoped she wasn't blushing too hard. "Do you think it'll be okay with dad if I go with Kenny?"

"We'll find out when he asks your father."

"Asks me what?" Madison's father came in from the garage carrying his overcoat and briefcase.

"Tom, you're home," Evelyn said. "We saved you some pizza."

"Hi, Dad!" Madison got up and hugged him.

"Hi, Sweetie." He turned to his wife and gave her a kiss on the cheek. "No, I'm okay, Evie. I grabbed some

Panda when I realized I was going to be a while at the office. What are you two conspiring?"

Evelyn answered, "No conspiracy, darling. We were having a theoretical discussion. You know…fate, destiny, that sort of thing."

Tom turned his gaze to Madison as if to ask, *Is this true?*

Madison nodded. "What she said."

"I think I'm outnumbered. Okay, I'm going to go change. You two carry on."

Once Tom was out of earshot, Evelyn said, "I know it seems like the most important thing in the world right now, Maddie, but it will be okay. I promise. And you don't have to do it alone. I'll always be here to listen."

"I know." She hugged her mother. "I'll get the kitchen."

"And stop worrying. I'll talk to your dad and tell him to be nice."

"Thank you!" Madison started clearing away the dishes.

***

Later that evening in bed, Evelyn said to her husband, "Guess who I met today?"

Tom put down his phone and focused on his wife. "How many guesses do I get?"

"I'm feeling generous. I'll give you three."

"Three? You really are feeling generous. Okay, are we related?" Tom asked.

"Nope. One down. Two to go."

"Are they famous?"

Evelyn counted, "Strike two."

"Let's get down to business then," Tom said. "Do they want to give me money?"

"You wish. No. I met Kenny, the boy that Maddie likes."

Tom's expression turned dour. "The boy that Maddie likes?"

"We've talked about this, Hon. You knew it was going to happen sooner or later."

"I was really hoping for later," Tom said. "She's my little girl."

"She's going to be sixteen next weekend. She's not a little girl anymore. Anyway, Kenny asked if he could take Madison to the Harvest Fair."

Tom groaned. "What did you tell him?"

"He's coming to Maddie's party next weekend. I told him he'd have to talk to you."

"Good answer," Tom said.

"I know how you feel about this," Evelyn began. "I feel the same way. But our girl is growing up. She's going to start going out with boys. In fact, that's what's supposed to happen."

"What are you trying to say?"

"I've met him, Tom. He seems like a nice kid. Don't be too hard on him. I'd like us to welcome her relationships so she doesn't feel the need to go behind our backs."

"I promise you I won't bite his head off." Tom smiled and picked up his phone again.

Evelyn groaned good-naturedly. "I guess that'll have to do for now."

***

Chuck Carson sat in his camper finishing the last of his evening meal. He'd rented a space in a small campground outside of town. He was talking into his phone, sending a text message to Russell Stillman.

"Nothing has changed since last week's report. You said not to bother you unless I have something to say, but this girl has no game at all. She goes to school. She goes to church every Sunday, and most Wednesday evenings. Outside of school and church activities she doesn't really do anything. No smoking, drinking, or running around with her friends. Her friends seem to be the same kids she sees at church. The only notable exception is this guy she has lunch with at school, but they don't seem to be dating. She's unremarkable."

Chuck looked it over and tapped 'send.' Not for the first time, Chuck wondered why Stillman was so interested in this kid. It was a game he played with himself. He'd come up with some outlandish plot and then spend the week writing a list of pros and cons. He never came close to the truth.

***

The following Thursday, after dinner, Evelyn told Madison, "C'mon, Sweetie. Get your shoes on. You have to get shopping done for your party Saturday."

Madison was quick to get ready. She brought both of her lists – the Wish list and the Cringe list. Her wish list was lavish, while the cringe list was exactly that – the very bare essentials to the start of a party.

The rain had finally come to an end on Wednesday, and it looked like Madison would enjoy the last of the warm weather for her birthday celebration. Evelyn hung a left on Market Street and headed south.

Madison was convinced her mother had played a trick on her. She didn't say what Madison could buy, and she didn't say what Madison couldn't buy. Instead, she told Madison she would receive a set amount of money and that would be the budget for her party. Drinks, food, decorations, or swag bag, whatever Madison wanted to do was okay with her, as long as she stayed within the budget. Any attempt to pout, plead, beg or renegotiate would result in the reduction of the initial budgeted amount.

Evelyn pulled into Schnuck's Grocery and parked the car. They went in together, but soon parted ways.

"Maddie, you do your shopping. I have some of my own to do. I'll go by the bakery and see about your cake." She pulled an envelope from her purse and said, "Here's your budget money for the party. Spend it wisely."

Madison mentally weighed the envelope. It seemed like there were quite a few bills in it, but what if it was all fives and ones? She didn't want to tear it open in front of her mother, so she waited a decent amount of time after her mother was gone before looking.

She needn't have worried. Her mom and dad had been very generous. A note tucked into the envelope said, "We want you to have a good time. You only turn sixteen once. Dad and I will pay for the drinks. Keep some money to order pizza, but dad said he'd also grill some burgers and hot dogs."

Madison smiled. Her parents were the best.

Her first stop was the snack aisle. Chips, cookies, dip mix, pretzels, crackers...she had a long list of things to pick up, but she'd gone over the items so many times she didn't need to refer to her sheet often.

The chips and dips had been checked off her list and she was ready to move on to the cookies, but a guy was blocking her way. His shopping cart was stopped crossways in the aisle. His back was to her as he kneeled to read a package label on one of the lower shelves.

"Excuse me," she said.

"Oh, pardon me." He stood up and moved his cart. "I didn't mean to be in the way."

Madison smiled, "That's okay. No problem." She paused and did a double take. He looked very familiar.

The young man's face filled with surprise. "Hey, you're Madison!"

"I am," she admitted. "Do I know you?"

"Sort of. We met at Reverend Stillman's revival meeting. I gave you and your friend a shirt. Remember?"

Out of all the remarkable things that had happened that day, Madison did remember meeting Chuck.

"Chuck! What are you doing here?" she asked.

"I left the show," Chuck answered in a dismissive tone. "The season is almost over and Stillman started letting people go. I remembered this place when we passed through, and I really liked it. I'm actually working over at the hardware store."

Chuck seemed genuinely pleased to see her.

"Well, welcome to Oracle," Madison said.

Chuck looked overjoyed. "Running into you like this is an answer to prayer."

"How so?" Madison asked, worried that he'd start hitting on her again.

"Listen, I am so sorry for what I said at the revival. I acted like such a creep. I actually prayed for the chance to apologize to you. And look! God answered my prayer. Will you please accept my apology?"

The last thing Madison had expected was to run into Chuck; it must have been a divine appointment. She was touched by his sincerity and his obvious joy at having his prayer answered.

"Of course I do, Chuck. Thank you for your apology. I accept."

"Aww, thank you. You have no idea what this means to me." He extended his hand and Madison took it by reflex.

Chuck glanced into her basket. "Wow. That's a lot of chips."

Madison said, "We're having some people over on Saturday." Then she teased, "They're not all for me, you know."

He laughed and said, "I swear it never occurred to me they were all for you. Even if it did, I'd never say it out loud."

"Smart man," Madison said.

Chuck said, "I can't believe I ran into you like this. God is amazing, isn't He?"

"He sure is," Madison replied. She was delighted at how Chuck seemed to have changed.

Chuck's job was done. He had wanted to make contact with Madison and put her at ease. If he was going to be in town, he didn't want her to be surprised or suspicious when she saw him around. Now it was time to beat it out of the store. It wouldn't do to linger.

Chuck said, "I better get going and let you get back to shopping. It was great to see you again, God bless!"

"You too!" Madison smiled and waved.

***

On the drive home, Madison reflected on how odd it was to see Chuck again. He must be very brave, she concluded, to leave his home and travel across the country with Reverend Stillman. Then he went off on his own again, and now he's here in her hometown, making his way all by himself.

She'd been so surprised by seeing Chuck again that she hadn't thought to ask him if he knew anybody in town. Maybe he was looking for a church. She should have asked him. Now the chance was lost, and she didn't know if she'd ever see him again.

CHAPTER NINE

Tom and Evelyn discussed how to keep an eye on a house full of teens without looking conspicuous. They didn't want to be an oppressive presence that threw a damper on their daughter's party, but they did want to spot potential problems before they became real problems. That's when Tom suggested he take outside cook duties.

"From my position at the grill, I'll have a view of most of the backyard. Inside, you'll have a view of the patio, and into the great room."

Evelyn snorted, "Would you listen to us? We're planning the job like we're international spies. They're kids, Tom."

"Do you remember when we were their age in high school?"

"You're right," Evelyn admitted. "Let's go over that plan again."

***

Evelyn and Tom were in their bedroom, getting ready for the evening's celebration, and dealing with the uncomfortable combination of trepidation and optimism.

Trepidation, because they were responsible for what happened on the property. This was fine when Madison was seven and the worst that could happen was one of her little friends skinned their knee. But now, at sixteen and seventeen, there was a whole new universe of trouble for kids to get into.

The dread was leavened with optimism because they knew their daughter had a good head on her shoulders. For this, Evelyn was grateful. Her daughter did very well at school. She kept her room picked up, and seldom needed to be prompted to finish her homework. She didn't run around with a bad crowd, and she was always happy to go to church.

Her daughter was exactly the type of girl that Evelyn wouldn't have hung out with when she was in high school. It wasn't that Evelyn was wild, but she didn't always walk the straight and narrow back then. She hadn't always been truthful with her mom and dad about who she was with, or where she was going.

That's why she got on her knees every night and thanked God that Madison was level-headed. She didn't know what she did to deserve such a good kid, but she prayed Madison wouldn't change.

Evelyn finished slipping on her flats and called out, "Tom?"

"Yeah, Evie?" Tom answered.

"Thanks."

"You bet. Anything for you, Babe." Two beats, and then he asked, "For what?"

Tom was barefoot in a pair of charcoal slacks and no shirt. He was standing in front of the bathroom sink, shaving with a blade. He saw Evelyn in the mirror as she came up behind him and wrapped her arms around his torso. Her cool cheek rested against his back, and she answered him.

"For everything."

Her world was as perfect as she could ever hope. Her husband was a hard-working man who was devoted to his family. He was an excellent father to Madison, patient and kind but firm, and he held his daughter to a high standard.

Evelyn continued, "You do a lot for our little family. I appreciate you, Tom Newman."

Evelyn let go of her husband and held a washcloth under the warm water tap. She wrung it out and began wiping away the remains of shaving cream Tom had missed.

"Can you believe our little girl is sixteen years old today?" she asked.

"You're making me feel old, Evie."

Evelyn kissed him – a quick peck – and wiped just under his jaw line. "You missed a spot."

Tom looked in the mirror and grabbed his razor. A couple of strokes and he was done.

Evelyn inspected. "Much better. As I was saying, we are very blessed to have such a great kid."

"I agree," Tom said.

"Mostly that's what the thank you was for. I credit you with how well Madison has turned out. You're a great father. That's important to a girl."

"Thanks, Evie. I don't always get it right, but I want the best for our daughter."

Evelyn kissed him. It was meant to be brief, but Tom held her in place until she'd been kissed proper.

"Easy, Tiger. We're supposed to chaperone this get together, not set a bad example."

"Fair enough. We'll be respectable for now. You can be bad later."

***

Madison and Trisha were downstairs taking care of last-minute preparations in the dining room. Madison ripped open a package of Oreos and laid the cookies out on a serving platter like rows of coins. They reminded her of something she wanted to tell Trisha.

"You'll never guess who I ran into at the store," Madison said.

"Who?" Trisha asked.

"Chuck. That guy who gave us the shirts at the revival."

"Are you serious? What do you mean you ran into him?"

"I was shopping for the party and this guy was blocking the aisle. When he turned around he looked familiar, but I couldn't figure out where I'd seen him. Then he recognized me."

"Weird. What's he doing here?"

Madison shrugged. "He said he'd been through here before and he liked what he saw. He left Stillman and was looking for a place to call home."

"How was he?" Trisha asked, making a cringy face.

"Actually, Chuck was really nice. He said he was sorry for the way he acted that day and felt really bad about it. I wish you could have seen him. He said he'd been praying for a chance to apologize. He was genuinely sorry."

Trisha looked doubtful. "I don't know that I'd trust him, Maddie. The whole thing was weird."

Madison agreed with her friend. "I know, but maybe he was lonely. Think about it, Trish. He's all alone and traveling to a different place every week. He left his family, and he doesn't have a chance to make any friends because he's never in one place long enough. He probably needs a friend."

"Maybe you're right," Trisha conceded. "But what are the odds that he'd come here?"

"I know, right? I worry that maybe he was put in our path for a reason. Like, maybe there was something I should have done."

The girls headed to the patio and began stretching tablecloths over the folding tables.

"So, what exactly happened at the revival?" Trisha asked. "Who were you talking to before you prayed for that lady?"

Madison sighed. She had hoped her friend would have forgotten about that day. She decided to offer at least some information. It wouldn't be right to lie outright, not about a gift that she knew came from God.

"Before we went," she began, "I read a lot about faith healing and watched some clips on YouTube. It turns out a lot of those people are fake. I prayed in faith and asked to know the truth. The Holy Spirit showed me."

"So you really knew? You weren't just fooling around?"

"I really knew," Madison reluctantly admitted.

"Wow! I believed you, but part of me didn't think it could be real," Trisha said.

Much to Madison's relief, her mother stepped outside with a bunch of helium balloons.

"Hi, Trisha. Thanks for coming early to help out."

"Hey, Mrs. Newman. Not a problem."

"You girls got a lot done." She set the balloons down in a corner of the patio where they had set up a backdrop and props for a photo booth.

Addressing Madison, she said, "Your dad's going to bring the coolers out of the garage and wipe them out. Don't put the sodas in until he cleans them, okay?"

"Got it." Madison gave her mom thumbs up.

***

A couple of hours later the party was in full swing. Most everyone she invited had been able to come. Kenny hadn't arrived yet, but he'd texted to say he was on his way.

Trisha was trying to organize some games, but the pizza had arrived, and Madison's dad was serving up meat off the grill. No one was thinking about games at this point, and Trisha gave up for the moment.

Madison looked up and was surprised to see Kenny walking toward her.

"You made it!" Madison said.

"Yeah, sorry I was a little late. I had to wait on Brad," Kenny explained.

"No worries. How are you doing?"

"I'm good," Kenny said. He leaned in a little closer. "To tell you the truth, I'm a little nervous about meeting your dad."

"If it helps, Mom said she'd talk to him. She's kind of prepared the way," Madison said.

"What did she say?" Kenny wanted to know.

Madison shrugged. "I don't know. She didn't tell me."

"Is that him?" Kenny asked, nodding toward the man behind the grill.

"That's the guy. Don't worry. He doesn't bite."

"I'm not worried about being bitten. I want to make a good impression so I can take you to the fair."

"Me too," Madison agreed.

"Wish me luck," Kenny said.

"Wait! You're going now?"

"I want to get this over with." With that, Kenny set off across the lawn.

***

Tom Newman manned the barbeque and watched as his daughter's guests arrived. He was familiar with most of them. It was pretty quiet so far. One of the other moms, whose name he couldn't recall at the moment, had stayed and was inside talking to Evelyn.

He had a pair of tongs in his hand and was turning some franks on the grill when he spied Kenny approaching. Tom had seen him when he first came in and, judging by the way his daughter lit up, he assumed this was the boy Evelyn told him about.

"Pardon me, Mr. Newman?" Kenny ventured.

"What can I do for you, young man?" Tom asked.

"I'm Kenny Warner and I wanted–"

"Kenny!" Tom interrupted. "You're the boy that wants to take Madison to the fair."

Kenny seemed surprised to learn Madison's dad already knew what he was going to ask. "Um, yes sir. I was won–"

Tom wiped his hand on his apron and held it out. As they shook, he said, "I've been looking forward to meeting you, Kenny."

"Thank you, Sir," Kenny said.

Tom stopped short, pretending that he'd had a sudden idea. He pointed at the coolers and asked, "Say, Kenny, can I get you a beer or something?"

"Huh?" replied an obviously shocked Kenny. "No sir. I'm only seventeen. I don't drink."

Tom smiled. "Great answer, Kenny. Perfect answer. I want you to remember that answer if you ever go out with my daughter."

Kenny managed a hesitant half-chuckle. "Yeah, about that, I wanted to ask–"

Tom intentionally interrupted again, "Where are my manners? Do you want a hamburger, or a hot dog?"

"I, uh…"

Tom knew this wasn't going the way Kenny had imagined. He clearly didn't know what to say.

Tom saved him from that challenge. "I'm yanking your chain, Kenny. I know you want to talk to me about Madison but, as you can see, I'm preoccupied at the moment. I'm glad you could come, and I sincerely want you to have a good time. Come and talk to me later, will you, Buddy?"

Kenny smiled broadly. "Yes, Sir. I sure will." He turned to go.

"So, what will it be?" Tom asked.

"What?" Kenny turned back quickly.

"Burger or dog?"

Kenny was quick to reply. "I'll have a burger."

"You bet." Tom gave Kenny a sturdy paper plate with two burgers and a hot dog. "The dog is for Madison. Mayo. Light relish. Plain chips."

Kenny smiled. "Thanks for the tip, Mr. Newman."

Tom wasn't interested in hearing the kid make a pitch to date his daughter. He wanted to watch him at the party and learn what sort of person he really was. Did he enjoy the company of others, or was he a sullen loner? Was he polite and considerate, or was he arrogant and selfish?

He noted with approval that Kenny was carefully preparing Madison's dog and marked a mental tally of one on Kenny's "plus" column.

***

Madison saw Kenny approach with two plates. She was surprised to see he'd prepared the hot dog exactly the way she liked.

"Someone's been talking to my dad," Madison observed.

"Yeah. That was interesting. Your dad is a real character," Kenny said.

Madison tensed up. "What did he say?" She managed to sound casual.

"He cracked a couple jokes and then he said I could come and talk to him later."

"You didn't ask him…?"

Kenny shook his head. "Nah. He was busy with the grill."

"Does that make you more nervous?" Madison wanted to know.

"Your dad was okay. I mean, he told me how to make your hot dog."

Madison laughed. "He must like you already if he's spilling family secrets."

"I guess. We'll see after I talk with him," Kenny said.

"He likes to pretend he's gruff, but he has a good heart," Madison explained. "Just be yourself and God will work out the rest."

"God?" Kenny echoed.

"Yes."

"How exactly does God work out something like that?" Kenny asked.

"Are you going to make fun of me again?" Madison gave him a warning look.

"No. I swear to…I promise I won't," Kenny insisted. "It's just that I've heard people say it before. You know, 'God works everything out for good'. I honestly don't know what that means. How does God do that?"

Madison sighed. She really wanted to help Kenny understand but was afraid she wouldn't be able to explain it correctly. She wasn't a pastor or an elder in the church. "First of all, people who say that are misquoting scripture. They forgot the important part."

"What's the important part?" Kenny asked.

"The verse says, '…all things work together for good to those who love God, to those who are called according to *His* purpose.' Most people completely forget the love God part."

This wasn't the first time Madison and Kenny had talked about God and belief. Madison had quickly learned that Kenny knew very little about the Christian faith. His parents didn't go to church, and they didn't discuss spiritual matters.

Of course, she had asked him to go to her church, but he had declined her invitations, saying he didn't want to meet a lot of strangers and he really didn't know what to do in a church service.

"I admire your faith, even if I don't share your certainty," Kenny admitted. "Maybe that's one of the things that attracted me to you in the first place."

"Oh really?" Madison asked. "In what way?"

Kenny looked uncomfortable. "I think you're really pretty. Whenever I saw you at school, I'd watch you. I figured you had a boyfriend or something, so I never got my hopes up. But I noticed something about you was different. You're always upbeat, like you don't ever have a bad day. It's kind of like you were tuned into a different frequency. I guess I know why."

Madison felt herself blushing, and barely managed to get the words out. "Thanks. That's really sweet."

They were saved from an awkward silence by Trisha, who came running up their table and said, "C'mon. We're going to sing to the birthday girl!"

***

After the cake and ice cream, Trisha finally got everyone together to play some games. A couple of Madison's friends were in the theater arts class, and they did a few improv routines. Madison was thankful that everyone seemed to be having a good time.

After the improv, they broke up into small groups, some to catch up on social media and post some pics from Madison's party, others to take photos in front of the booth with the birthday props.

Pretty soon, someone turned on music and the lights dimmed. Madison's dad was still in the backyard, cleaning the grill, so nothing serious was really going to happen. A few of the guys headed back for seconds of pizza or burgers, now cold, while others returned for more dessert.

Kenny and Madison stood just beyond the glow of the party lights.

"I haven't wished you a happy birthday yet," Kenny confessed.

"No. You haven't," Madison agreed.

"I'll have to get right on that," Kenny said.

"Now seems an ideal opportunity," Madison prompted.

"Yeah, well you see, it's not wishing you happy birthday that's the problem. It's all the other stuff that's so hard to say."

"Like, what other stuff?" Madison felt a little giddy, but also nervous.

Kenny's voice was steady as he said, "Like how I think you're amazing. And smart. And pretty."

Madison could scarcely catch her breath. She wanted to hug him, but even though her dad looked like he was busy, she knew he was still zeroed in on what was going on in his backyard, particularly where it concerned his daughter.

She finally managed to say, "Oh, Kenny. That's sweet. I think you're pretty special, too."

Even in the dark, Madison saw him blush.

"You know, that was supposed to sound smooth and romantic," Kenny said. "Instead, it came out all dorky."

Madison reached out and squeezed his hand. "Believe me, it was perfect."

He pulled a small, carefully wrapped package out of his jacket pocket. "Happy birthday, Madison Newman."

"Kenny! You didn't have to get me anything."

Madison unwrapped the small box and opened it to reveal a small gold heart suspended on a slender golden chain. She pulled it from the box and held it up. "It's beautiful."

"You really like it?"

"Here." Madison handed the necklace to Kenny. "Put it on me."

She turned around and pulled her hair out of the way. Kenny stood behind her as he draped the necklace around her neck. It took him a couple of tries before he managed to secure the clasp.

Madison turned to show Kenny. "Do you like it?"

"You're beautiful," Kenny replied.

"The necklace!"

Kenny smiled. "It suits you perfectly."

"I love it!" Madison said. She pulled her phone out of her back pocket and took a selfie with the focus on the necklace. Handing the phone to Kenny she asked, "Take our picture?"

"Sure!"

Kenny put his arm around her and held the phone at arm's length. "Okay, smile."

When the look was right, he took the shot. Madison admired the photo and gushed, "It's perfect!"

Madison shot a quick glance over to where her father was putting things away. She took advantage while his back was turned and gave Kenny a quick kiss on the cheek.

"Thank you," she whispered.

"You're welcome," he blushed.

Madison was toying with the necklace. "I really do love it."

"I'm glad. I wasn't sure if you'd like it."

She glanced around and saw her dad watching them from where he stood near the grill. "We'd better go mingle. My dad's started to notice us."

***

Eventually, one by one, Madison's friends said goodbye and went home. Trisha and Brad stayed to help pick things up, as did Kenny.

Tom finished cleaning the grill. This was likely the last time he'd use it this year. The weather was turning, and soon it would be too cold to cook outside.

He finished tugging the cover over the barbeque and called out, "Hey, Kenny. Can I get a hand over here?"

Kenny walked over and said, "Sure, Mr. Newman. What do you need?"

"I could use a hand getting this beast over to the shed."

"Sure thing."

Together they wheeled it over to the big aluminum shed in the corner of the yard. As Tom dug in his pocket for the keys to open the shed door, Kenny took the opportunity to broach the subject of taking Madison to the county fair.

"I was wondering if this is a good time to talk to you about Madison," Kenny ventured.

"What's on your mind, Kenny?" Tom figured there was no reason to make it easy for him.

"Well, Sir, the fair is coming up next week and I was wondering if it would be okay if I took Madison."

Tom opened the door to the shed, and together they rolled it in and wrestled it into a corner. When Tom had it where he wanted, he told Kenny, "Thanks for the assist. Why don't we sit down and chat?"

They sat across from each other on an old picnic bench in the backyard.

"You'd like to take Madison to the fair?" Tom asked.

"Yes, I would."

"Here's the deal. I'm going to have to sit down with Madison and her mother so we can discuss her going out with you. If we give her the go ahead, there are a couple of things I absolutely insist on. Make sure she's home on time. Not ten minutes late, not five minutes late. On time. Are we good?"

"Yes, Sir."

Tom was beginning to like this kid more and more. "I'd tell you no drinking, but I think we covered that one already."

Kenny nodded his agreement.

The truth is, Tom had been keeping an eye on Kenny during the party. He'd already decided he was going to let Madison go out with him, but he wanted the pleasure of seeing his daughter's face when he told her she could go.

"One last thing. Respect her, Kenny. If you tell her you're going to pick her up at a certain time, then be there. And another big one; no means no. Do you know what I'm saying?"

"Yes, I do," Kenny answered, nodding to emphasize his sincerity.

"Her mom and I think she's pretty special. The fact that you want to go out with her tells me you must think she's special, too."

Kenny smiled broadly. "I really do, Mr. Newman."

"That's good to hear. I have a few more things to do. Thanks for your help, Kenny. It was good to meet you."

Tom put his hand out and they shook.

"It's good to meet you, too. Thanks."

Kenny rejoined his friends. Madison's face betrayed her eager curiosity regarding Kenny's discussion with her father.

"Well?" Madison finally asked.

"He said he wants to talk to you and your mom."

Madison thought about this for a moment.

Kenny wanted to reassure her, "I think it'll be okay, Mads."

"Really?"

"I'm certain of it."

"Are you ready to go?" Brad asked Kenny. "I've got to get Trish home."

Kenny nodded, and then turned to Madison. "Happy birthday. See you Monday!"

"Thanks," Madison said, fingering her necklace lightly. "This was the best birthday ever!"

***

The party was over, the guests had left, and Madison was alone in the backyard. She'd turned off the lights and it was just her and the twinkling stars.

Tom stepped outside to join his daughter. "How does it feel to be sixteen?"

"I don't think I have the hang of it yet. I haven't had a lot of practice," Madison replied. "It's nice tonight. I thought I'd stay and appreciate it for a while."

Tom turned his eyes to the stars overhead and asked, "Did you make a birthday wish on that big, bright star?"

"Dad, that's Venus."

"Is that a no?" Tom asked.

Madison hugged her dad. "Thanks for letting me have the party. I was out here praying and thinking about all the ways I'm blessed. You and mom top the list."

Praying.

Madison had been doing a lot of that lately. As a little kid, she never needed a reminder to say her prayers. She'd always devoted herself to prayer and reading her Bible, but in the past few months, she'd felt like her relationship with God had surged to a whole new level.

"How does it feel to be the father of a sixteen-year-old girl?" Madison asked, half teasing.

Tom took a deep breath and sat on one side of the picnic bench. "I remember when you were a little girl, and I was teaching you how to ride a bike. You took to it easily. Yet, in spite of your skill, I dreaded the day I'd take off the training wheels. I dreaded it because I knew I'd have to let you go."

Madison clenched her jaw and felt tears welling up as her father spoke.

"I was afraid you'd get hurt," he continued. "Of course, you did. You fell and scraped your knee and cried, as we all do. And you got over it, as we all do. Life is bigger and scarier than a scraped knee, or a bruised elbow. So, I'm still afraid to let you go. But I'm excited, too, because I can't wait to see all the marvelous things you will accomplish in this life."

Madison began crying. "Oh, Daddy! That's beautiful."

Tom stood up and held his daughter closely. "I can't remember the last time you called me daddy," he laughed. His voice sounded gruff, and Madison was pretty sure he was choked up too.

"Transitions aren't always easy, Maddie. Part of that transition is letting you go out with boys. I had a little talk with Kenny. He seems like an okay kid. I hope you two have a good time at the fair."

"Really? I can go? Thank you!" Madison was breathless with excitement, and she couldn't wait to tell Kenny.

"Don't thank me yet," Tom cautioned. "You, and your mother, and I need to sit down and discuss boundaries."

Madison chose to press her advantage. "May I assume the boundaries are adjustable, contingent on a consistent record of reliability?"

Tom grinned. This girl had a future in law. "You may safely assume, subject to review on a case-by-case basis."

"So stipulated," Madison said.

"Don't be in such a hurry," Tom cautioned. "Your mother might have completely different ideas altogether."

Madison nodded. "It's happened before."

They sat in companionable silence on the picnic bench in the backyard. Together, they looked out through the dark silhouette of the trees up into the stars. These fall nights were growing chilly, and the sky was crisp and clear.

"What's been weighing you down lately?" Tom asked.

Madison looked at her dad. "You've been talking to Mom."

"Yes, of course I've been talking to your mother," he answered. "But I noticed on my own, which means there's probably something going on."

"Is it the books I was reading over the summer?"

He smiled. "Your mom did mention the books a while ago, yes."

Madison didn't say anything.

Tom confided, "Listen, I admit they aren't what I imagine an ordinary sixteen-year-old girl reads. That said, I don't have a problem with them except for one thing."

"What's that?" Madison asked.

"You scared your mother."

"What?" Madison protested.

Tom stopped her. "I don't think it's so much the books she cares about, Maddie. I think it's your intensity that worried her. She said you devoured half a dozen books on faith healing in a few days. She was starting to worry you were going to run off and join a cult."

Madison opened her mouth to argue, but her father held up his hand. "Your mom loves you, Maddie. Worrying is her way of working through the anxiety of seeing you grow up and knowing she will eventually need to let you go."

Madison let her dad's comments sink in for a few moments. "Thanks for the perspective, Dad."

"You still haven't answered my question."

"Huh?"

"Why have you been so preoccupied? Mom noticed it even before you brought home all those books. You weren't the same happy, bouncy girl you usually are. Is anyone hurting you, or bullying you?"

"Nothing like that. Honest. I think you raised me to have too much self-respect for that to happen," she replied.

"You're right, but I won't know if I don't ask. I need to be sure you're okay, and I'm concerned."

Madison nodded in the dark. "I'm okay, Dad."

Tom persisted, "Then let me ask again. What's been bothering you?"

It was clear her father wasn't going to be put off. He wasn't demanding, but he was expressing his concern for her out of love. She couldn't tell him *all* of the truth, but would offer as much as she could bring herself to tell.

"I'm starting to understand how serious life is, Dad. It's so much more than honor roll, more than trying out for cheer. It's more than being first, or best, or prettiest."

Once she began to put voice to her fears, they came tumbling out in a rush.

"Will I meet the right guy, get married, and have kids? How will I make a difference in someone's life?"

"All of that sounds like a big weight to carry, Maddie," Tom said.

"There's so much. It's overwhelming!"

"Well of course it's overwhelming when you pile all of those concerns together. You're not being fair to yourself. You turned sixteen today, Madison, yet you're worrying about things that won't happen for another five, ten years. Maybe more."

Then he hit her where she lived.

"What does God's Word say about borrowing trouble?"

She hung her head. "Do not worry about tomorrow, for tomorrow will worry about its own things. Sufficient for the day is its own trouble."

"See?" he challenged her. "You know it better than I do."

"Dad?"

"Yes, Maddie?" Tom replied.

Madison sighed. She tried to put her thoughts together. It was her father who had brought God into the conversation. It was an open door, an invitation to lay bare those concerns she was reluctant to drag out in the open.

Madison took a deep breath. "What if God has a different idea about what He wants me to do?"

"What do you mean?"

"What if it's not about getting good grades, or going to a good university, or landing that sweet job? What if God has a different plan? What if He decides He needs me to do something else?"

Tom was silent for a moment. Then he leaned forward and rested his forearms on the picnic table.

"Madison, I don't think God does that to people."

Madison wouldn't entertain his denial. She knew better. "Oh, but He does, Dad. Look at Jeremiah. He was about my age when God chose him to warn Judah of their coming destruction. That sure didn't win him any friends."

"That's an Old Testament story, Maddie."

She didn't expect her dad to understand. How could he? Still, she decided to try again.

"What about Mary then?" Madison asked. "She was a young girl ready to marry Joseph. They planned a life together. Then the angel Gabriel paid a visit, and everything changed. She had plans. But after the angel visited, her life was never ever the same. What must her family have thought? Or Joseph?"

Tom was out of his depth. He never expected to have this kind of conversation with his daughter. Heck, he never expected to have this kind of conversation with anyone.

He did know one thing, however, and that is his daughter was hurting. To what degree, he couldn't say. She was pretty good at keeping things close and working them out for herself. The fact that she was opening up to him was exactly why he was worried for her now.

What could he tell her that would make a difference? He'd never been to seminary. He didn't have any answers for these big questions. What could possibly have put this burden on her heart that she would worry about God upending her life?

Tom reached out and took his daughter's hands in his. "Madison, I know this is important to you. I don't know that I'm equipped to answer all the questions you've been asking yourself, but I'll tell you the truth as I see it."

Madison nodded. "Okay, I'm ready."

"You trust God, right?"

"Absolutely," she answered.

"What if you got very sick? For example, what if you needed a kidney transplant? Would you stop trusting God?"

"No! I'd need him more than ever," Madison replied.

"Exactly! Let's say I was coming home from work, and someone ran a red light and I died in an accident."

"Dad!" Madison was obviously distressed at the thought of her father dying.

"Hypothetically. Would you stop trusting God?"

"No, and don't use that example again."

Her dad nodded. "Okay. I promise. My point is, people have their lives disrupted all of the time. Illness, auto accidents, job loss, earthquakes, house fires, tornados, airline crashes..."

"I get the idea," Madison cut in. "Despite how circumstances alter our plans, our faith should remain steadfast."

"Smart girl. No wonder you have straight A's. Our conversation brings us full circle to the verse about not worrying about tomorrow. Life has a way of disrupting our plans, and we can't know when or how. Our job is to remain faithful and trust God."

"I guess I knew the answer all along. I just needed reminding," Madison said.

"We all need reminding sometimes. My advice to you is to enjoy the journey you're about to undertake; the journey of growing into an adult. By the time you need to make adult decisions about your career or starting a family, you'll have the experience and wisdom to exercise good judgment."

"Do you really think so?" Madison asked.

"I know so." Tom was still struggling with the earlier part of the conversation, concerned that his daughter was clinging to some terrible idea that God might derail all her work and plans. He believed she worried for nothing, but he couldn't say that to his daughter.

"Listen, Maddie, don't ever let things get so bad that you're ready to do something drastic. You always have one big advantage."

"What's that?"

"You always have me and your mom to talk things out with. You'll never have to do it alone."

"Thanks, Dad."

"You're welcome, Maddie. Happy birthday."

***

When Tom finally came into the bedroom, Evelyn was waiting. "That must have been some conversation."

He sat at the end of the bed and started taking off his shoes. "You have no idea."

Evelyn put her tablet down. "So, tell me."

Tom dropped his socks in the laundry hamper and put his shoes away on the rack in his closet. "She's excited about going to the fair. She tried to be chill about it, but she's very happy."

Evelyn smiled. "I *wish* I could have seen her face! How did your chat with Kenny go?"

"He's a nice kid. I think he'll be okay."

"I think so, too," Evelyn concurred.

"I got Madison to tell me what's been bothering her."

"Do I want to know?" Evelyn asked. "I mean, of course I want to know. What did she say?"

"It's not terrible. She's been stressing over life. Grades, college, and what she's going to do in the future."

Evelyn sighed deeply. "Is that all? I wish that girl would learn to relax a little."

"That's not quite all. She seems very concerned that somehow God is going to disrupt her life."

"What? That doesn't make sense."

Tom agreed, "No, it doesn't, but that's what she's been worried about. It's strange, isn't it? We worry about all the things that our daughter can get into. Running around with the wrong crowd, dropping out of school, drinking or using drugs. Never in my life did I think I'd have to worry about losing my daughter to God."

CHAPTER TEN

The Traveling Revival Road Show was setting up just outside Waterston, Mississippi. Russell Stillman was enjoying the morning's first cup of hot coffee. This mid-October dawn was colder than usual, and he wrapped his hands around the ceramic mug to warm them.

Stillman watched as his crew set up the main tent. They were on a large parcel of land a few miles south of Interstate Fifty-Five, thirty acres of natural meadow among the trees. This weekend was the last show of the season. After this, they'd pack it up for the rest of the year and spend the winter in Florida. When spring rolled around again, they'd start all over, bringing salvation to the lost, and healing to the sick. Or a reasonable facsimile thereof.

He watched as the eastern sky grew brighter. Soon the sun would peek through the line of trees and the day would officially begin. It was his favorite time of day. Brand-new and unspoiled, a new day providing endless opportunities.

Stillman's phone buzzed in his coat pocket. He pulled it out, glanced at the screen, and sighed. Sometimes, along with opportunities, a new day also brings challenges.

"Good morning, Mr. Carson. Quite the early bird, aren't we?"

"The early bird catches the worm, Rev."

"Yes, but the second mouse gets the cheese. What's up? Have there been any developments?"

Chuck got right to the point. "If you wanted to get rid of me, why didn't you just fire me? It's like I'm in exile out here."

"My friend," Stillman soothed, "I need you too much to get rid of you."

"Then why aren't you answering my texts?"

"Send me something interesting and I'll even call you, Chuck. But what do I care if she had a birthday? Was anyone arrested?"

"No," Chuck replied.

"Exactly. Nothing interesting." Stillman recognized the need to keep the machine oiled and running smooth. He took a deep breath and a big swallow of coffee and said, "I'm sorry, Chuck. I don't mean to keep you in the dark. I have a lot going on out here and there's always some problem to take care of."

In fact, Stillman was, at that very moment, watching his next problem do a slow cruise down Peyton Road. The patrolman's brake lights flashed, but he didn't stop, and the car continued its crawl down the rural road.

He'd be back.

Chuck said, "I get it. I'm not on the top of your list, but it's exactly what you said, there's nothing interesting going on. It's been almost two months. What do you say I cut out of here and meet you in Mississippi?"

Stillman drained his cup. Maybe it was time to bring him back. Whatever it was he expected to discover, he was obviously mistaken. Still, he'd seen what he'd seen. He just wasn't certain what that had been.

"Give it another couple of weeks, Chuck. Keep a special eye on her at Halloween. If nothing happens, head out on November first. We'll be at the Florida compound."

"Home sweet home. Will do, Boss. Over and out." Chuck ended the call before Stillman could change his mind.

Stillman pocketed the phone and was not the least bit surprised to see the patrolman pull off the road and head his direction. The heavy cruiser bounced and rocked along the uneven dirt road and came to a stop behind Stillman's motor home.

A young deputy exited the passenger side of the car and waited. The sheriff got out of the driver's side and nodded to his deputy.

Stillman and the older man shared a glance as the young deputy approached.

"Welcome to Tate County, Sir," he said, touching the brim of his hat. "My name is Deputy Harris. This is Sheriff Bradshaw. May I ask your name and the nature of your business?"

"Certainly, Deputy. I am Reverend Stillman, and this is our Road to Redemption Traveling Road Show," Stillman replied.

"Do you have permission to be on this land, Sir?"

Stillman smiled. He'd been around this block before. "Mr. Abraham Crenshaw owns this land, and it was he who provided the permission, Deputy. If you like, I have a signed release in my office." Stillman gestured at his luxury coach.

The deputy was quick to dismiss the necessity of documentation. "That's quite all right, Reverend. I didn't mean to imply that you were being less than honest with me."

"No offense taken. Say, Deputy Harris, why don't you and your wife come out this Saturday? Do you get Saturdays off?"

Stillman charged ahead without waiting for an answer. "Come up to the main box office and give them your name. You will have four front-row seats waiting for you. And thanks for watching out for us." Stillman shook the deputy's hand.

Deputy Harris looked over to his partner for guidance.

Sheriff Bradshaw told the young man, "Harris, why don't you take a look around and make sure everything's on the up and up. We don't want any illegal stills in this county. And check that nobody's running any card games."

"Make sure you stop by the mess tent and grab yourself some breakfast and coffee," Stillman added.

Harris cut another look over to his partner and saw him give a brief nod, then took off in search of the mess tent.

"Dear heaven, they're making them young these days." The sheriff shook his head as he watched his young partner walk away.

"What was that all about?" Stillman asked.

"New recruit. Got him Monday. I'm showing him the ropes."

Stillman laughed aloud. "Geez, Bradshaw, the kid looks barely out of high school. What did you do to pull him as a partner?"

"I wanted him to survive," replied Sheriff Bradshaw. "They were going to cut him loose on his own, right out of the academy with no real experience. The world would eat that boy alive."

The sheriff changed the subject. "How's business, Russ?"

"Not so good these days, I'm afraid," Stillman replied.

"How'd that happen? Are you running out of sinners?" Bradshaw laughed at his own joke.

"It's getting harder to draw a crowd," Stillman explained. "In the wake of 2020, folks were clamoring to hear God's Word. They were crying about their 'rights.' Now that we've had a couple of good years, they've grown complacent. They no longer make time for God in their lives."

The men stopped to watch as workmen began to hoist the main tent.

Bradshaw commented, "I was wondering what happened to you folks. You usually stop by in the early spring and then again before Labor Day. I was beginning to think you'd forgotten all about us."

"I'd never forget my brothers and sisters in Mississippi. We had to adjust our schedule in order to keep the ship afloat. I hope you and the missus can join us Saturday for services," Stillman encouraged.

"We might be able to make it out this weekend. That is, if there's going to be a service."

"What do you mean, Sheriff?" Stillman asked. He was beginning to feel a little tug at his wallet.

"Do you have a current public use permit?" Bradshaw asked.

Russell Stillman nodded his understanding. It was like this in most of the places they stopped. Some officers were more blatant about it. Some were very discreet. Whatever they called it, Public Use Permit, Environmental Recovery Fee, etc., it was understood by both parties to be the cost of doing business.

"You know, Sheriff, I have a number of things demanding my attention this morning, but as soon as I'm done, I'll get right down to the Hall of Records and get that permit," Stillman assured him.

"No need to go to all that trouble, Reverend. I'll be going down to city hall later. My cousin works in licensing. I'll give her the application fee and have her issue the permit."

Stillman's suspicions now confirmed, he asked, "How much is the application fee, Sheriff?"

Bradshaw didn't even blush. "That'll be two hundred dollars, Reverend."

Stillman whistled, but he had his wallet open and was counting out the fee in twenty dollar bills. "This is more than it was last summer, if I remember correctly."

"Darned politicians. They voted for a fee increase across the board." Bradshaw counted the money and said, "Can't trust a one of 'em."

Sheriff Bradshaw tucked the bills into his pants pocket. Their business concluded, Bradshaw said, "You have a great weekend, Russ. Hope you have a good show."

The two men shook hands and Stillman watched as the sheriff made his way to the mess tent to retrieve his deputy and have a little breakfast.

Ordinarily, he might have joined the officers for breakfast. It never hurt to foster a good relationship with the law enforcement wherever you happened to do business, but he had a lot on his mind.

***

By late afternoon, the tents had been erected, the parking areas established, and the vending booths lined up along the approach to the big tent. It was amazing how, at the end of the season, it took half the time to set up as it did at the beginning.

By this time, his crew was experienced. He'd start the next season with a green crew. Sure, some of the men came back from the previous year, and they'd be the ones to train the new guys. It took a new crew a good month or two to learn the ropes. By the time they were done for the season, his men could practically set up camp in their sleep. He strongly suspected some of them did.

Most of his people had gone into town. A couple of them went to post flyers for the weekend show. Some of them wanted to check out the local entertainment. Others wanted to enjoy a meal that wasn't from the mess tent. Whatever their reason, Stillman understood the urge. Sometimes it was therapeutic to do something different.

For Russell Stillman, something different meant getting away and being alone. When he was alone there were no decisions to make, no questions to answer, and no one making demands on his time.

Stillman changed into jeans and hiking boots, and went off to explore the lightly wooded hills to the northwest of the camp. After walking for about a half hour, he chanced upon a narrow dirt road leading up into the hills.

He followed the abandoned road for a while, shedding cares with every step. The only sounds he heard were the chirping of birds, the soft whisper of the breeze through the trees, and the rhythmic crunch of his steps on the dirt. He was only dimly aware of the fact that he'd begun to smile.

Stillman was pulled out of his reverie when he heard the hum of a vehicle approaching from behind. When it rounded the corner, he saw it was one of the electric carts his security team used to patrol the parking lots during their shows. Behind the wheel, he recognized his business manager and friend, Kevin Wells.

"Will wonders never cease?" Wells exclaimed. "Imagine running into you out here."

"Yes," Stillman commented wryly. "It's a remarkable coincidence."

Wells replied, "I thought there were no coincidences in God's kingdom."

"I don't want you to take this the wrong way," Stillman began, "but I was looking forward to spending a little time alone. You know, in quiet reflection."

Wells answered, "Great! Me, too. Get into the cart and we can spend time alone together."

Stillman asked, "Did you listen to what you just said?"

Wells laughed. "C'mon. Jump in. I want to show you something."

Stillman took one last breath of the relative quiet before surrendering, then hopped into the cart.

The narrow dirt road ended at a clearing at the top. It wasn't much of a hill, but it afforded a fine view of the small valley. Below, towards the southeast, lay their camp.

"Isn't this a great view?" Wells enthused. They stood at the edge of an embankment, looking down at the tents and vendor kiosks. "I'll get a guy up here with a camera. We'll get some shots of the crowd, a few at night with the tents lit up from within. Maybe I should get a time-lapse shot of the parking lot filling up."

Stillman nodded absentmindedly. He didn't really need to see all this. He had just wanted a few minutes to himself.

"We have a 'Best Of' Blu Ray in the works from this year's shows, and a live CD from the band," Wells continued. "They'll be available on the website by November with discount offers emailed to members. It's the perfect Christmas gift for that special friend or family member."

"You're always just a couple steps ahead, aren't you?" Stillman asked.

"Oh, yeah. That's why I'm making the big money," Wells snorted.

"Seriously, Kevin. You take excellent care of the business side of things. It isn't a skill you can learn. You have a real talent. Every year, at the end of the season, I worry you're going to tell me you're not coming back."

"Remember that when it's time to renegotiate my contract." Wells grabbed a cooler from the back of the cart and sat at the edge of the embankment to take in the view. Handing Stillman a cold beer, he beckoned Russ to join him. "Really, Russ, where am I going to go? Running around the country with you already cost me a marriage."

Stillman twisted the top off and raised the bottle in salute, "To marriage! A man is incomplete until he's married. Then he's finished."

The both drank until their bottles were empty, and then opened another.

Wells wasted no time in making his pitch. "Listen, Russ, I've got some great ideas for next year's season, and a couple of ways I think we can boost attendance significantly."

Stillman shook his head. "Not now, Kevin. Please. I came up here to forget about the show for a few hours. I'm tired."

"Tired?" Wells asked. "Or distracted?"

"What do you mean?"

"My friend, when it comes to putting on a show and working a crowd, you are second to none. Do you know I've seen over two hundred of your revival meetings? I swear there are times I'm still excited to hear you speak."

"Gee. Thanks, Kevin." Stillman said.

"It wasn't a compliment, Russ. These last few shows weren't up to standard. You didn't generate any excitement. The people who come to your revivals are looking for excitement. Sizzle. Pizzazz! What's happening? It's like you lost interest after we left Illinois."

Stillman was quiet for a long minute. He swallowed the last of his beer. "Got another in there?"

"You sure?" Wells wanted to know.

"I'm not driving," Stillman shrugged.

Wells passed a bottle over to his boss.

"I started thinking about the show," Stillman said. "I mean *seriously* thinking about the show. I've been doing the same thing for years!"

"And it works," Wells reminded him.

"Yes, it works. But…stay with me here. Imagine that you live in the same house for a long time. After a few years the place gets a little shabby. You might need to do some painting. Probably have to get a plumber in there. Maybe you'll put in some carpet, buy a new sofa, or upgrade the appliances in the kitchen. It still works as a house. The roof isn't leaking, it's structurally sound, but it isn't what it *could* be."

"So, the show is a house?" Kevin guessed.

"It feels like I saw the show for what it really is, and...I dunno. It needs an overhaul," Stillman concluded.

Wells eyed his boss thoughtfully. "Of course, this sudden introspection has nothing to do with the girl."

"Huh? Oh, no," Stillman lied. "This has been in the works for a while now. It has nothing to do with her."

"Where's Carson been these last couple of months?" Wells challenged.

Stillman tried to sidestep the question. "Mr. Carson assists me with special projects from time to time. For instance–"

Wells held up his hand, "Don't say another word. I don't want to know what he does for you. You have him up in Illinois following that girl, don't you? Did you ever stop to think about how that might look? How something like that would play out on the evening news?"

Stillman downplayed Kevin's concerns. "No one's going to find out. Besides, I've already told Chuck to abandon the engagement and meet us in Florida. It turned out to be nothing after all."

"What did you think it was going to be, Russ? What surprising revelation did you expect your private investigator was going to uncover about a teenage girl?"

Stillman didn't answer right away. He'd always been able to brush Wells off when he brought up the subject of Madison Newman.

He finished his beer and sat the empty bottle between them. Maybe it was time to shoot straight with

Kevin. "I prayed for that woman in the wheelchair. When I was done, her daughter rolled her out toward the exit. End of story. Then this girl, Madison, runs up and starts talking to them. The next thing I know, she's putting her hand on this woman who starts screaming that she's healed. Don't you think that's a little unusual?"

"Not as unusual as sending a convicted felon to stalk a minor."

Stillman frowned. "Nice. Can we focus here for a minute?"

"Fine. I'll focus," Wells said. "No. I don't think it's at all unusual for a woman to shout about being healed *at a faith healing event*."

Exasperated, Stillman said, "No, Kevin. It's about the girl. She saw me watching and tried to run. She knew I'd seen her do something."

"Do what?" Wells asked.

Stillman shrugged. "I wish I knew. When we locked eyeballs, she looked guilty as sin. So, either she was either running a con, or…"

"Or what?" Wells wanted to know.

"Or she really healed that woman. Either way, I want to know. Is she a con artist, or is she the real deal?"

Wells had no doubt. "Con artist. Kids these days are cold-blooded."

"That's what I would have said. It turns out I'd be wrong. Chuck spent weeks watching her routine, where she goes, who she sees, what she does. It turns out the girl does nothing unless it involves school or church."

"Which leaves the second option of her being the real deal?" Wells asked.

"Yes! But that's absurd," Stillman insisted.

"Is it? If I remember correctly, your job is selling miracles."

"C'mon, Kevin. She's a sixteen-year-old girl. Are you going to be the one to convince me she restored that woman's sight? It's easier to believe she's a criminal mastermind."

Wells clapped Stillman on the back. "I'm glad you realize that, Russ. Who knows what happened that day? It may have seemed odd at the time, but I'm glad to learn it was nothing, and that you called your boy home."

"Yeah." Stillman nodded in the affirmative, but he wasn't at peace.

"What's going on, Russ? Really."

Stillman began tentatively. He'd been holding it inside long enough. He needed to tell someone. "The thing is, I was up on the stage, and I wasn't thinking of that woman at all. Then – and I kid you not – a voice said, *Look*. It was as close to me as you are now. *Look*. I turned to see who had snuck up on stage, but no one was there."

"You never mentioned this before," Wells said.

"No. I haven't."

"Did this voice tell you what to look for?"

Stillman replied, "There was only that one word, but I knew. My eyes were drawn to the girl, and to the woman in the wheelchair."

"God wanted you to see the woman get healed?" Wells asked.

Stillman shook his head. "No. Not her. You know how when you throw a stone into a pond and all the ripples radiate out from the center? The Holy Spirit moved outward from those two like that. As it moved, it touched a woman and she smiled. A young father was touched, and he lifted his hands to praise God. I saw it touch a young man, and when it did, he started crying. Then he dropped to his knees to pray."

"And you saw all of this from the stage?" Wells asked.

"Yes," Stillman admitted. "But that's not all. I *felt* it. As it moved through the crowd, it touched the hearts of saints and sinners alike. It was this that the voice wanted me to see. Then it brushed past me, and I saw the tent, my work, the show, with…" Stillman moved a hand through the air, as if trying to grasp the right word, "…with new eyes, and everything I'd done looked shabby, worn, and worthless."

There was a prolonged silence between the two men. Shadows had grown long, but the cart would get them back to camp quickly.

Wells finally spoke up. "This is the last show of the season. After this, you can take a few months off. As for me, when we pack it in on Monday I'm headed to Charleston. I intend to spend the Thanksgiving holiday with my daughter and her family."

Stillman shot him a look with eyebrow raised.

"Afterwards, I'll head down to Florida."

"You had me a little worried," admitted Stillman.

"You have *me* worried, Russ. What's wrong with you, anyway? You've done a lot of good for a lot of people. Let your detractors say what they will, but you're the one traveling the roads throughout this great land, bringing the message of salvation to town after town."

Wells groaned as he stood up. "I need you to do something for me."

"What's that?" Stillman asked.

"Get yourself down to Florida and go fishing. Relax. Take some time off and clear your head. Can you do that?"

Wells' concern for his friend was obvious, and Stillman was grateful for his advice. "I'll take some time off, I promise."

"That's the spirit! When I get down to Florida, I will blow your mind with some ideas I've got brewing for the road show. You're going to love it."

CHAPTER ELEVEN

The guys showed up at five to pick up Trisha and Madison. It was a perfect night for the fair.

Madison's curfew was eleven o'clock. She thought it was more than generous considering this was the first time she was allowed to go on a date. As they were leaving, her father surprised her by slipping Kenny a couple of twenty-dollar bills.

Trisha grabbed a map as they entered the fairgrounds and headed toward the midway. Trisha and Madison waited while the guys went to get ride bracelets for the four of them.

"I'm starving," Trisha complained. "I've hardly eaten a thing."

"Me neither, but I'm afraid to eat. What if I eat something and then a ride makes me sick? I don't want to throw up in front of Kenny," Madison said.

"Ewww. Bad first date story," Trisha said. "What's the first thing you're going to eat?"

"Corn dog. Definitely," Madison nodded.

"Mmmm. Yeah," Trisha agreed. Vendors were everywhere; they weren't going to go hungry.

Madison looked over Trisha's shoulder as her friend studied the map. There were some local bands playing tonight, and she looked for show times.

Trisha handed the map to Madison and began scanning the crowd. "I bet you we'll see all kinds of people from school. It's Saturday night."

It was already packed. Strolling performers were out in force entertaining the attendees. A unicycle rider juggled. A clown towered above the crowd on stilts. And heading away from them, a one-man band exhibited supernatural coordination.

A lady selling cotton candy was dressed as an old-time chimney sweep, complete with soot on her cheeks. One fellow hawked cups of soda from a tray as he meandered through the crowd.

Trisha nudged Madison. "Does that guy look familiar to you?" She nodded toward a guy selling helium balloons. He was walking around with scores of balloons tethered on long strings which he constantly combed to keep from tangling.

Madison looked up from her map. "What guy?"

"The balloon guy," Trisha answered.

"That's Chuck!" Madison exclaimed.

"The guy from the revival?"

Madison waved her hands back and forth over her head and shouted, "Chuck! Hey!"

He looked genuinely surprised to see them. "Madison. Trisha! Welcome to the fair."

"You're working here?" Madison asked.

Chuck replied, "I am for now. I make a little extra money and get to hang out at the fair."

Trisha asked, "What do you think of our little city?"

"I like it just fine," he answered. "There aren't a lot of jobs though. I'm thinking maybe I'll head for Florida once the fair's over. There's good money to be made in hotel services during the winter. A guy with a little hustle can do okay for himself."

Kenny and Brad returned with the ride bracelets.

"What's going on, Mads?" Kenny asked.

Madison took her bracelet from Kenny and squeezed his hand. "This is Chuck. Trish and I met him when we went to the revival last August."

"Oh, yeah. I remember when you went," Kenny said.

"Chuck's been all over the country with the revival." She turned to Chuck. "This is Kenny, my boyfriend."

Although she'd thought it many times, this was the first time Madison said the word 'boyfriend' out loud. Kenny looked at her and smiled, an eyebrow raised.

Chuck said, "Lucky man. I'm pleased to meet you, Kenny."

"Same here," Kenny said.

Madison finished the introductions, "You've met Trish, and this is Brad."

"Hey, Brad," Chuck said. "Anybody want a balloon? On the house. Guaranteed to contain the finest helium available in North America and inflated personally by yours truly."

Trisha laughed at his spiel. "You really know how to work it, don't you? Thanks for the offer, but I'll have to say no."

"No problemo," Chuck said. "I get it. No one wants to be responsible for hanging onto a balloon all night. Hit me up before you leave. I'm easy to find with all these balloons. Brad, Kenny, nice to meet you guys.

Gotta run. These babies aren't going to sell themselves."

With that, he plunged back into the crowd.

Kenny asked Madison, "How did you meet that guy again?"

Trisha answered, "We went to a revival meeting last August. Down near Chester. Chuck was selling t-shirts and hats and stuff."

"And he remembered you from two months ago?" Brad weighed in.

It was Madison's turn for the perfect comeback. "Are you insinuating that we are so unremarkable as to be easily forgotten?"

Kenny laughed. "Got you, dude." Then he said to Madison, "I don't see how anyone could forget."

"You're sweet," Madison said. She felt herself blushing but maintained eye contact with him.

"Did you mean what you said? About me being your boyfriend?" Kenny asked.

Madison smiled in embarrassment and dropped her eyes, but grew bolder. She lifted her eyes back to his and said, "Yeah. I do mean it. Is that okay?"

"Perfect," he managed to say.

"Hello, let's get the evening started," Brad said, shoving Kenny as if to wake him up. "What do we want to do first?"

The girls answered in unison, "Corn dogs!"

"Corn dogs it is," Brad said.

***

They looked over the map again while devouring their dogs.

"I want to make sure we see the Home Arts Exhibit," Madison said.

Brad said he wanted to see the Photography and Art Pavilion, and everyone agreed that's where they should start.

They were forging through the crowd toward the photography exhibit when they passed the haunted house. On impulse, Trisha grabbed Brad's sleeve and steered him toward the entrance. Kenny and Madison followed.

It wasn't particularly scary, but Madison felt a thrill of excitement with Kenny by her side. It didn't matter what they did, as long as they did it together. She liked the feel of their fingers laced together as they walked the narrow passages.

Her parents had always been fairly strict about where she went, and with whom, so Madison was happy they approved of Kenny. That opened up possibilities for them to do things together in the future.

To ensure that she'd be able to go out again, she wanted to make sure she was home on time. Maybe even a little early. This was one of those "exercise good judgment" moments she and her dad had talked about. She wasn't about to disappoint him.

Their path to the exhibit was not smooth. Following their detour to the haunted house, they stopped to hear a local band. The bass player was a friend of Brad's cousin. They'd played together before, so naturally

Brad wanted to catch up on what he'd been up to. The conversation went longer than expected.

Trisha waited with Brad while Kenny and Madison went on ahead to the art pavilion. They slowly browsed the exhibits, commenting on the ones they particularly liked, and why.

"I can't believe how creative some people are!" Madison said. "Some of these drawings are amazing."

Kenny said, "I think some people are born with talent. Some are adept at art. Some are gifted with the ability to play music."

They began to walk through the photography section.

"What talent do you think you were born with?" Madison asked.

"I don't know that I'd call it a talent, but I do have a good eye for composition, and I know how to take good photographs."

"Really? What kind of pictures?" Madison wanted to know.

"Well, like that one." Kenny pointed to a wall where a large photograph hung.

It was a photograph of the waxing crescent moon. It was big. The moon measured three feet from top to bottom, two feet wide, and revealed clear details on the lunar surface.

"Ooooh, so pretty!" She looked a little closer and saw his name on a small plaque at the side. "You did this? And a first-place ribbon!" Madison exclaimed. "I had no idea I'd be escorted to the fair by a celebrity."

Kenny laughed. "Only the best for my girl. To tell the truth, I'm pretty excited about getting first place."

"I'll bet! Hang on a second," Madison grabbed her phone out of her back pocket. "Stand by the moon."

Kenny stood by his picture, the first-place ribbon just over his shoulder. Madison thought he was looking altogether too serious and started making faces. She snapped the photo just as he started cracking up.

"Congratulations! That's amazing," Madison said.

"You don't think I'm a big nerd now?" Kenny asked.

Brad and Trisha caught up with them in the pavilion in time for Trisha to say, "Your secret's out, Kenny."

Madison said, "Look! Kenny got first place for his photo entry."

Brad said, "Dude. That's so dope. I told you it was a great shot."

"Thanks for making me enter," Kenny replied.

The four of them took off for the midway. They wanted to catch some rides and maybe grab something else to eat before it was time to go.

***

Madison couldn't believe how quickly two hours had passed. Even though they had plenty of time remaining, she wasn't ready for the night to draw to a close. Hooking her arm in Kenny's, she pulled him closer. Madison intended to enjoy every moment they had left.

Walking through the midway, the group caught sight of the Sky Flyer. A shiver of dread washed over

Madison as she watched the carousel of swings, suspended by chains, rise slowly ten feet, then twenty, and continue rising as the mechanism then began to tilt.

She stopped and watched from the ground as riders screamed while they whisked by far above, suspended from a spinning hub. Some riders screamed from excitement, others from terror.

"I *have* to go on this," Kenny declared.

Brad enthusiastically agreed, "I am so with you. C'mon, let's go."

The girls stood still, gazing up at the swings spinning overhead. Madison felt something heavy in her stomach. Was it the corndog?

"Do you want to go?" Brad asked.

Trisha shook her head. "Not me."

Kenny looked at Madison, "How about it, Mads?"

Madison was still looking up at the spinning carousel of swings. Something wasn't sitting right, and she couldn't figure out what it was. "I think maybe not."

"You said you'd take me on the Tilt-A-Whirl," Trisha reminded Brad.

"The swings probably look worse than they really are," Brad suggested.

"The Tilt-A-Whirl doesn't threaten to drop me out of the sky," Trisha countered.

Madison looked at the guys. "She has a point."

"I have an idea," Kenny offered. "Brad, you take Trish to the Tilt-A-Whirl. Mads and I will hit the Ferris wheel. Afterwards, you and I can ride the Sky Flyer while they check out the Home Arts Exhibit. When we're done, we can meet them at the exhibit."

No one objected.

Madison and Kenny waved bye to their friends and found the line for the Ferris wheel. The spinning lights from the ride dazzled, and the music washed over them like a wave, but Madison scarcely noticed as Kenny took her hand.

"I'm not ever going to forget tonight," Kenny said.

"Neither will I," Madison said, shyly.

It was time for them to board the Ferris wheel, and the ride operator held the gondola door open for them. When they were seated, the operator closed the bar in front of them. When he released the gondola, it rocked backwards and Madison shrieked, grabbing reflexively for the bar in front of them.

Kenny laughed at her momentary panic.

"It took me by surprise, that's all," Madison explained.

Kenny gave her a hard time, "Oh, yeah. Sure. I completely understand."

"You're so gonna get it. Just you wait," Madison threatened good-naturedly.

The ride jerked again and moved back one car to let the old passengers off and the new passengers on.

Madison said, "I'm really impressed by your moon picture. How did you take it?"

"I have a telescope, and I mounted a camera where the lens goes. I took hundreds of terrible pictures to get that one good one. Some were out of focus, others were overexposed. I tried several different types of filters. I even…Oh no!"

Alarmed, Madison asked, "What is it?"

"I just exposed my inner geek," Kenny confessed.

Madison reassured him, "Space is legit, so you're covered. No geek points awarded."

The car moved up another space to load new riders.

As the operator cycled through loading the passengers, they eventually found themselves stopped at the top of the Ferris wheel.

Madison looked down to see the fair spread out below them. "Look! You can see everything from up here." She pulled her phone out and took a couple of pictures.

"It's remarkably clear tonight," Kenny said. Although there were no clouds, the lights from the fair washed out all but the brightest stars. Kenny pointed toward the sky in the northwest, "Do you see those two bright stars? The brightest is Vega. The other is Deneb."

"You really know your stuff, don't you?" Madison asked. "You must have spent a lot of time studying the sky."

"I guess I have. It's interesting. There's a lot of mythology in the stars, but no one I knew could tell me about it. I had to learn on my own," Kenny explained.

"The prophet Isaiah wrote, 'Lift up your eyes and look to the heavens. Who created all these? He who brings out the starry host one by one and calls forth each of them by name. Because of His great power and mighty strength, not one of them is missing,'" Madison quoted.

She waited for Kenny to say something, but he remained quiet. "You spent all that time spent learning about the stars. Wouldn't you like to meet the One who created them?" Madison asked.

Kenny didn't know how to respond to Madison's question. He didn't want to offend his new girlfriend, much less hurt her feelings, but he simply didn't believe.

To him, the universe was a magnificent, but random, series of events. There was no grand design. There was no designer.

He reasoned that even if there was a God, and this God actually did speak the universe into being, what possible notice would such a God pay to an insignificant hunk of rock orbiting an obscure star out in the galaxy's backwater?

Kenny replied honestly, "I can't imagine what that meeting would be like."

"You never know when you might get the chance," Madison said.

Their ride began in earnest, and the two settled back into their seats. Kenny reached his arm around Madison as they rode up, up, up, and over the top, and then down again. The downward side gave Kenny the feeling of falling.

Madison gripped Kenny's arm and he leaned closer to her. "Don't worry. I got you."

They'd begun another upward spin when he caught sight of Trisha and Brad on the ground and pointed them out to Madison. "They look so small from here," she said.

When they neared the top of the spin, Madison scooted to the edge of the seat, away from Kenny, and grabbed the bar that secured them in their seats.

"What's wrong?" he asked.

She glanced over at him. "Nothing. I just want to be prepared for the descent."

Kenny laughed as Madison leaned over to look down on the people below.

"Trish!" she screamed. Kenny leaned forward and saw Trisha and Brad peering up at them. "Wait for us!" Madison called out.

As she leaned, the car tipped forward, catching Kenny unaware. He gasped and tightened his grip on the handrail, crying out, "Whoa!"

Madison looked over at him and laughed, "Now who's scared?" She shifted her weight a couple of times and the car tilted back and forth.

The ride operator shouted over the loudspeaker, "Stop rocking the cars!"

Madison leaned back. "That's embarrassing."

Kenny leaned in and teased her, "I can't believe your dad was worried that I'd be the bad influence. Does he have any idea what a troublemaker you are?"

"That's not true," Madison said nudging him gently. "I'm exuberant."

"Does that mean troublemaker?" Kenny asked.

"No. It means I'm glad you asked me to come to the fair and I'm having a wonderful time," Madison said.

"Me too," Kenny agreed. He felt a little giddy as they stepped off the ride, happy that their first date was going so well.

Madison and Trisha headed off to see the Home Arts exhibits, and Brad and Kenny went to ride the Sky Flyer.

While standing in line, Kenny noticed they were behind Jeremy Zellers. Jeremy was a tall, wiry redhead on the track team with Kenny.

"Jeremy, my man!" Kenny said.

"Hey, what's up?" Jeremy high-fived them.

"Hey, Jeremy," Brad said.

Kenny told Brad, "We had a track meet last week and Jeremy totally smoked them on the relay. Without him we would have ended up in third place. We finished first by the end of the day."

Brad raised an eyebrow. "Congrats, Jeremy."

"All in a day's work," Jeremy said. "I only hope I don't betray my secret identity as The Flash."

Kenny wanted to give him his due. Jeremy was fast, and a real asset to the team, but he was also something of a jerk. He loved playing practical jokes on people, and he always took it a little too far to where, instead of laughing along with him, you wanted to punch him. He was a real nice guy when he wasn't being a pain.

After a moderate wait, they got on the ride. Kenny grabbed a swing on the outside of the circle. Brad was one swing ahead of him while Jeremy was one swing to the inside on his right. The operator made the usual rounds, checking each rider to ensure the lap restraint was in place. When everyone had been checked, the operator cranked the tunes and started the ride.

It was slow at first, but the ride steadily built up speed until the centrifugal force started to pull the swings out of plumb.

The operator yelled into the microphone, "Does anyone want to go faster?"

The answer was a unanimous, "Yes!"

He pushed the lever forward and the swings accelerated in their circle. Air whooshed past the riders, and everyone clung a little more tightly to the chains holding them. A few cries of fright sounded as the hydraulics lifted the central pillar, hauling the swings skyward.

Kenny was surrounded by the sounds of hysterical laughter, screams of fear, and the rush of the wind. The chains, which seemed perfectly capable of supporting a rider's weight while the ride was at rest, now seemed inadequate to the task.

Kenny looked over to see Jeremy with a big grin plastered on his face.

"Watch this!" Jeremy yelled. He began to pull on the chains, as one might pull the lines on a parasail, and began rocking side to side.

Kenny called out, "Jeremy, that's not a good idea. You could get hurt."

That's all Jeremy needed to hear. He began pulling harder on the chains, working up a good rhythm. Soon he swayed back and forth like a pendulum gone mad.

The ride operator pulled another lever and the hub tilted, and the passengers shouted with delight and alarm as their tight orbit took them up into the sky, then angled back down. Jeremy's sideways sway became unstable and, as he pulled harder on the chain, his seat collided with Kenny's.

"Dude!" Kenny yelled. "Stop it! What's wrong with you?"

Brad thought he heard people shouting. He could barely hear above the music and the rushing wind, but something was going on behind him. He turned in time to see Jeremy crash into Kenny.

It was a hard impact, and it started Kenny's swing rocking from side to side. Brad heard Kenny yelling something, but he couldn't quite make out what he was saying. He wasn't able to turn completely around to see what was happening. Brad heard other riders screaming at Jeremy, yelling at him to stop.

Jeremy's swing took him far in toward the hub, and then back out toward Kenny. Kenny saw him coming but had no chance of avoiding the collision. He wrapped his arms around the chains and held on tight. The impact tangled them together as they spun around each other.

Jeremy grabbed one of the chains on Kenny's swing and pulled hard to free it from his own, but as they spun, the stress on the chains proved to be too much, and one side of Kenny's swing broke free.

The crowd below gasped as Kenny's swing flipped him headfirst toward the pavement. The ride continued spinning as Kenny slipped through his seat. His fall was stopped abruptly as his leg caught in the security strap that had been across his waist. He felt something crack in his leg and dimly, through the pain, realized it was his femur.

"Help! Help me!" Kenny screamed, flailing helplessly as the ride continued to spin him in circles.

Brad was panic stricken to see his friend slipping from the seat. "Kenny! Hang on," Brad shouted. "We're going to get you down. Hang on."

***

People on the ground looked skyward to see what was going on above them. It looked as though the two passengers were fighting.

Spectators screamed as they watched Kenny hang from his leg as the ride continued to spin. A few were on their phones to 911, and several ran off in search of security personnel. Some people were recording the incident on their phones, and live streaming. Some began to pray.

The local stations first noticed mention of the accident on Twitter, then on Facebook. They sent everyone they had to cover the story.

The ride operator had stepped away for a smoke. What could possibly go wrong in the space of a few minutes? From his position along the back fence, he had no inkling of any problems with his ride. It was against the rules, but everyone did it.

No one knew how to stop the ride. A couple of guys from security who heard the commotion on the midway ran over to see what was going on, but they didn't know the first thing about running the ride. None of the switches or levers made any sense to them. What if they threw a switch and it brought the ride abruptly to the ground? What would happen to the boy hanging from the ride?

The more experienced security guard had his walkie-talkie out. He needed backup. He needed an ambulance. He needed police. And he needed them NOW.

***

Kenny had never known such agony as he hung from his broken leg.

Despite the pain, despite his terror, the thought crossed his mind that this would likely be the end of his track career. He made one last, futile attempt to grab the chain and pull himself up when his leg finally slipped through his seat.

Like a stone from a sling, he was flung some eighty feet away into the metal barrier surrounding a ride called The Scrambler.

***

Stephan Torres had been an EMT for a little over a year. He had seen a few things in that time, but he felt completely unprepared for the chaos that greeted him as he reached the midway. There had obviously been a major accident. The entire area was thick with civilians, sightseers who wanted a firsthand look at whatever had happened.

Security personnel were joined by city police as they held the crowd back for the ambulance. Stephan witnessed the police handcuffing an older guy wearing a sweatshirt and jeans as they prepared to plant him in the back of a police cruiser.

Officers were helping people off one of the rides, and a couple civilians crouched over what appeared to be a young male who lay motionless on the ground. There was a lot of blood. Stephan swallowed hard.

Making a quick exit from the ambulance, he and the lead technician, Victor Morelli, ran over to the patient.

"What do we have here?" Victor asked, announcing his presence.

A woman who looked to be in her mid-thirties introduced herself. "Heather, trauma nurse at County Hospital." She nodded toward the body. "Young male, teens. Multiple major injuries, heavy loss of blood, major head trauma, broken ribs, broken leg. Patient is unresponsive, breathing is irregular and shallow."

Stephan listened carefully as she spoke through tears. She'd been here first and, although she had no equipment, she'd managed to tell them everything they needed to know.

"I need blood, stat!" Victor snapped. Stephan immediately got to work. If they didn't do something immediately, they were going to lose this guy.

He slid a needle into Kenny's arm. "How many units?"

"All of them," Victor replied, his voice calm but serious.

Stephan worked quickly as Victor attempted to stabilize the young man's vitals. "I gotta stop this bleeding," Victor muttered.

Stephan clenched his jaw as he took in the sight. Blood was running from the kid's head like a faucet. He looked into Heather's eyes, and she shook her head.

"Inform County of our pending arrival. Major trauma," Victor instructed. "And grab the gurney. We have to get him in quick."

A police officer approached. "How's it look?"

"He has serious injuries," Victor answered abruptly.

"We were hoping to ask him a few questions," the officer said.

Stephan cut in. "That's not possible. Look at him. He's not even aware *we're* here."

"All right. If you don't mind, I'm going to need a statement and contact info before you leave."

Stephan glanced at Victor, who rolled his eyes. "We're EMTs. We're just here to handle the emergency."

"I can help," Heather offered.

The officer turned to her. "Did you see what happened, Ma'am?"

"I did," she answered.

"What happened?" Stephan couldn't help but ask. He wanted to know how this boy could have gotten this badly hurt.

She pointed not far down the midway at a ride that had been stopped. A neon sign announced that it was called the Sky Flyer.

"He was thrown from that ride."

Victor shook his head slowly as Stephan exhaled. There was no way this boy would be walking away from such a horrific accident.

The officer turned to go when the teen's body convulsed beneath the EMT's careful work. His back arched off of the pavement as his eyes opened wide, unseeing, rolling in their sockets. Then a last breath left his body, and he was at rest.

Victor felt for Kenny's carotid artery while Heather took a wrist.

"I detect no pulse," the EMT said.

"I concur," Heather answered.

Stephan kneeled in silence. He looked over at Victor who had been in the business twelve long years. Sometimes, during slow shifts, he would talk about some of the emergencies he'd attended. The man had seen a lot of nasty accidents, and now Stephan understood the horror firsthand. This was the worst thing he'd ever seen.

"Do we try to resuscitate?" Stephan asked.

Victor shook his head. "Not with injuries this extensive. There's no way."

"Call it," Heather said gently. "It's the right thing to do."

"Time of death, 9:23 p.m.," the EMT said.

***

When the police arrived following Kenny's fatal accident, they'd arrested the ride's operator. They'd heard enough from the witnesses on the ground to know his negligence was partially responsible for the tragedy.

The police made him bring the ride to a stop, whereupon they released the ride's passengers one by one to get contact information and a brief statement.

Through witness statements, it was readily apparent that Jeremy was the direct cause of the accident. They held him until his parents could be notified prior to questioning.

As the officer was walking Jeremy off the ride's platform, another officer was releasing Brad from his seat. As soon as he was free, Brad bolted from the ride and tackled Jeremy from behind.

Jeremy went down immediately, and Brad got in a couple of punches before Jeremy scrambled away and got back on his feet.

"You son of a bitch! You killed Kenny," Brad screamed.

Jeremy returned a punch and caught Brad with a glancing blow to the cheek. Brad shook it off easily.

Jeremy was taller, and had a longer reach, but Brad was solid muscle and could take a punch. His fury rendered him unstoppable.

Brad landed a two-punch combo to the face, and Jeremy spit out a tooth. Jeremy lunged for Brad, and they went down, rolling on the ground. Brad ended up on top and threw a volley of punches. The only time Brad smiled was when he felt Jeremy's nose crunch under his fist.

The cops were on the two boys an instant later, pulling Brad off of Jeremy. They placed Brad under arrest for assault and handcuffed him. An officer was taking him to his cruiser when Brad heard someone call his name.

He looked around. It was Hannah.

"Brad! What happened?"

The officer didn't stop. Brad had only one chance. "Hannah. Go to the Home Arts building. Tell Madison. Kenny had an accident. Home Arts. Trisha and Madison are there."

Brad dragged his feet to slow the officer down, but he pulled Brad all the harder. Brad wasn't sure Hannah had understood his message, or if she'd deliver it even if she did understand.

In the end, it was out of his hands. He wondered how much trouble he was going to be in for beating the crap out of Jeremy in front of the police. He didn't really care. Brad thought about his friend Kenny and cried, and when his tears dried, he began to pray.

CHAPTER TWELVE

Chuck sat in one of the stalls in the men's room at the fair. The bathroom was crowded, noisy, and no matter how diligently the janitorial staff cleaned, it possessed an unpleasant aroma.

He reached into his pants for a wallet and removed the cash. He ignored the credit cards, the debit cards, and the driver's license. Those are the things that slow you down. Those are the things that will get you locked up quicker than you can say, "Miranda Rights."

Chuck tucked the wallet into the front of his pants, flushed, and walked out of the stall up to the row of sinks near the exit. There he washed his hands, yanked a couple of paper towels out of the dispenser, and proceeded to dry his hands.

With an uncanny skill that made him such a success in his chosen profession, he managed to remove the wallet from his pants, wrap it in the paper towels, and casually toss the wad of towels into the trash. No one noticed. No one would ever know.

Chuck Carson was a man who'd made up his mind. It didn't matter how long he remained in this suffocating little town. He had no idea why Stillman wanted him to keep an eye on the girl, but he was done.

Maybe he'd make his way over to the east coast, and then grab Highway I95 south. If he took his time and enjoyed the sights, he might stretch it out to three weeks. Then he could report to Stillman's camp.

Although this was only the second night of the fair, he was itching to get back on the road. He'd miss the money, of course. He was doing very well. Not from selling balloons, but from the many opportunities to lift the wallet of a completely unsuspecting bystander.

It was like taking candy from a baby, really. People were so enthralled by the enormous bouquet of helium balloons that everything else ceased to exist for them. It was the next best thing to an invisibility shield.

He'd cleared thirty-five hundred dollars in a few hours. This was the fair, after all. People were throwing cash around for snacks, for drinks, for rides, t-shirts, and beer. This was probably the one place where cash was more convenient than inserting your chip, and a whole lot more secure.

Whenever possible, Chuck went where the cash was. Fairs, carnivals, anywhere things were wildly overpriced and it was easier and safer to pay with cash. People carried wads of it. With what he'd made in the last couple of days, he could go just about anywhere he wanted.

As Chuck emerged from the restroom, he watched three girls running out of the Home Arts building. They were in a big hurry. The blonde was crying as they ran toward the midway. Something bad must have happened.

Then he recognized the brunette. It was Trisha. And the blonde. Was that Madison? Something serious must have happened, and Chuck took off after them.

***

Madison and Trisha had been wandering the Home Arts exhibit, admiring the hand-crafted quilts hanging on the walls. A couple of girls from their class had entered the event, and they wanted to see how well they'd done. One didn't win an award, but the other got a second-place ribbon.

They were headed toward the sewing and design exhibit when Madison spied Hannah hurrying toward them.

"I wonder what's up," Madison said.

"We'll know in a second," Trisha replied.

Hannah had run the entire way and was breathing hard. She leaned over with her hands on her knees and gulped air. "Trisha! Brad…" She took a deep breath. "The police took Brad. They arrested him. He was–"

Trisha interrupted, "Arrested? Who told you that?"

"I saw it, Trisha. I swear. Brad was handcuffed and the police took him."

Madison asked, "Where? What about Kenny?"

Hannah caught her breath and said, "The midway. The news trucks are there, and the police, and an ambulance. I asked this girl what happened, and she said there was an accident. Maddie, Brad sent me to tell you. Kenny had an accident."

"An accident? What kind of accident? What happened?" Madison was frantic. She held her phone in a shaking hand and called Kenny. No answer. Tears spilled onto her cheeks.

"What about Brad?" Trisha asked.

"I don't know. I didn't see where they took him," Hannah answered.

Trisha had her phone out and was trying to call Brad as the three girls ran toward the midway. Foot traffic was moderate, and they had no problem making it to the other side of the fairgrounds. The crowd grew heavier as they drew close to the midway.

They asked a few people if they knew what was going on, but no one knew anything for sure. They'd heard someone had been hurt on a ride. Someone else heard a lady had a heart attack.

Madison prayed that Kenny was safe, and she prayed for peace in her soul so that she might discern the leading of the Holy Spirit. She pushed herself to the front of the crowd, close to the police line.

The crowd of onlookers was spellbound with what felt to Madison like a horrible fascination. Parked near The Scrambler were two police cars and an ambulance. She saw news vans from local stations and network affiliates parked along the fence, as reporters talked to police and witnesses. The air was full of serious conversations from squawking police radios, and the entire scene was awash in flashing red and blue lights.

Madison saw a reporter standing in front of The Scrambler giving a live report about the accident that had taken place. Madison couldn't make out what the woman was saying. The reporter gestured to the two EMTs in the background. At their feet was a body covered with a blanket.

Madison's blood ran cold. It was Kenny. There was no doubt.

She ran toward the body, dimly aware that she was screaming.

Madison jumped over the low fence surrounding the ride, and two police officers intercepted her before she got to the body.

"Let me go!" she shrieked. Madison beat and kicked and clawed at them with a fury she'd never felt. "I have to see him! Please!" she cried, as she twisted and fought. "He's my boyfriend. Please, let me see him!" Madison broke down crying. "Please."

Try as she might, she could not break free. "Please," she begged, exhausted.

As soon as she crossed the police line, the news cameras began tracking her. This was wholly unexpected, and no news crew worth their paycheck was going to miss capitalizing on this dramatic turn of events.

The two officers exchanged a look and slowly eased their grip on her. They weren't without sympathy. Both men had lost someone close and couldn't imagine being kept from seeing them one last time.

The girl was harmless. A kid, really. As for her boyfriend? There was a very solid consensus about what had happened. It was an accident. A foolish prank turned deadly. It wasn't like she was going to contaminate a crime scene or compromise a murder investigation.

The officers looked at Madison and their hearts knew compassion. One of the officers spoke softly and said, "We can only give you a few minutes."

Madison nodded and whispered, "Thank you."

She staggered those final few steps and fell to her knees next to Kenny. Then she bowed her head and began to pray.

The crowd grew silent as they watched Madison pour out her grief.

The news cameras were focused on her, as were many smart phones. Some were live streaming the scene to their social media accounts.

Chuck had followed the girls, and he was dumbstruck when Madison ran past the police line. *Was that her guy?* he wondered. *What happened here?* He had no answers for his many questions. Like the others, he sensed something remarkable was about to happen, and he couldn't tear his eyes away.

He drew closer, watching intently. Madison lifted her head and, reaching out to Kenny, she pulled away the blanket.

There were murmurs in the crowd. People cried. Many turned their eyes away from the horrible sight. Someone right in front of Chuck fainted. It gave him the opportunity to get even closer.

"Oh, Kenny," Madison said, resting a hand gently on his cheek. "Why did you leave me before we even had a chance?"

Of course, there was no answer.

Madison seemed unaware of anything else around her as she said softly. "Please don't take him. He wasn't ready. He didn't know."

Chuck furrowed his brow. He knew she was praying, but she seemed so casual, like she was talking to a close friend. She turned her tear-streaked face to the stars, as if searching for an answer.

"I'm not being selfish," she said loudly. "Examine my heart, Lord. You know I'm not asking for myself. You have searched me, Lord, and you know me. You know when I sit and when I rise; you perceive my thoughts from afar. You discern my going out and my lying down; you are familiar with all my ways."

Chuck noticed Trisha and the other girl holding hands. Both of them were crying.

A woman next to them asked, "Who's she talking to?"

"God," Trisha answered. "She's talking to God."

The crowd watched spellbound as Madison seemingly held a one-sided conversation. Chuck saw some of them whispering under their breath, possibly praying as well. Most seemed very upset and frightened by the scene playing out before them now.

"That's not the reason!" Madison said, as if she were arguing with someone. "I ask because he died without asking Jesus to be in his life." Madison looked down again. She closed her eyes. "Without Him, Kenny will be lost forever. Please give him that chance."

Madison understood the price she was being asked to pay for her prayer to be answered. Kenny was already lost to her in death, but at least this way he'd have another opportunity to make his peace with God through His son, Jesus. She was ready to pay that price.

She felt strength rising in her spirit as she spoke clearly. "You are worthy, Lord God, to receive glory and honor and power, for You created all things, and by Your will they were created and have their being. Kenny, so that you will know salvation comes through Jesus Christ alone, be whole by His grace."

Although she had no doubt her prayer would be answered, she was still startled when Kenny sat up like a man who had been dragged out of a deep slumber. He appeared disoriented, looking every which way in an attempt to make sense of his surroundings.

She heard the people around her issue a collective gasp. Many retreated several paces. Some began to cry. Some raised their hands and shouted spontaneously, "Hallelujah! Glory to God!"

Madison closed her eyes and thanked Jesus. Then she held out her hand to Kenny. "Can I help you up?"

Kenny shook his head and tears filled his eyes. "Stay away from me," he pleaded. He scrambled away from her, backwards, crablike, until he backed up against the iron barrier.

Madison bowed her head and tried to keep her own tears from spilling over once more. She'd understood, when she prayed, that things would never be the same between them. She readily agreed so that Kenny might live. Even if she had known how profound their estrangement would be, she would have agreed. Nevertheless, it hurt, and she felt the loss deeply within her heart.

***

Stephan Torres, the rookie EMT, felt the hairs on the back of his neck rising at the sight of the boy sitting up, alive. He had seen the kid die. He'd confirmed it with his own fingers on the boy's nonexistent pulse.

He wasn't surprised to see police officers rushing forward. Their job was to keep the peace, and whatever had happened here tonight was far from a peaceful event. He felt bad for the boy, who he knew had been dead only moments before. He felt even worse for the girl, who had seemed so broken up, but he knew the officers couldn't let the two kids walk away after such a disaster.

The officers handcuffed the two young people to the accompaniment of boos and insults shouted from those still watching. Then they were placed in the back of separate police cars, most likely to prevent them from coordinating a cover story. Someone was definitely going to want to sit down and have a lengthy chat with them.

One of the police officers waved Stephan over and told him to take a look at the kid, who had identified himself as Kenny.

Stephan checked Kenny's vitals. The boy was still bloodied, and his clothes were a ruin, but physically he was uninjured. It made no sense. He shook his head in wonder.

"Didn't you declare him dead a few minutes ago?" the officer questioned.

"You saw him," Stephan replied. "He was as dead as dead gets. There's no walking away from that."

"Yet, there he sits," the officer said, gesturing to his car. "As a medical professional, what do *you* think happened here?"

The EMT shook his head again. "It's a miracle."

CHAPTER THIRTEEN

Evelyn slipped off her husband and fell back on the bed. "Whew!"

"See?" asked Tom. "There are benefits to having our daughter out of the house for a few hours."

"If you promise to keep doing what you just did, then she can go out every weekend as far as I'm concerned," Evelyn sighed contentedly.

Tom rolled over, wrapped his wife up in his arms, and began kissing her. Small pecks. Her chin, her cheeks, her eyelids. "You'll wear me out, woman. I'll die of exhaustion."

"Maybe," Evelyn conceded. "At least you'll die with a smile on your face."

"That I would," Tom agreed.

Evelyn turned on her side to face her husband. "Did you see how excited our daughter was to be going out with her fella?"

"Yes. She was excited, and I was feeling old. Our little girl is grown up and dating, Evie. How did we get here so quickly?"

"It only seems quick."

Tom glanced over her shoulder to read the clock on the end table. It was 10:25.

Evelyn misread Tom's motive and said, "Don't worry. She'll be on time."

"Are you kidding? She'll be at least ten minutes early." Tom explained, "I was looking to see if we had time for another...you know."

"No, we don't. And if you're entertaining thoughts about taking advantage of me again, then you need to quit complaining about feeling old," Evelyn scolded. "I'm going to take a quick shower and change. I can't wait to ask Maddie how it went."

Evelyn's phone rang and her heart skipped. Her first thought was Madison.

She reached over and grabbed her phone from the nightstand.

"It's Lillian," Evelyn said.

"Trisha's mom?"

"You talk to her, I'm going to get in the shower," Evelyn said, tossing Tom her phone and jumping out of bed.

Tom answered, "Hey, Lillian. What's up?"

Tom had been relaxed and at ease, but Evelyn saw the change register on his face, and in his body language.

"An accident? Where?" he asked.

Evelyn's knees nearly buckled.

"I'm going to put you on speaker," he told Lillian.

"I'm so sorry to be the one to tell you this," Lillian said. "Trisha called a few minutes ago. She was talking so fast I'm not even sure I understood her."

Evelyn's hand trembled as she covered her mouth.

Tom asked, "You're sorry to tell us what, Lil?"

Lillian's voice broke as she began to cry. "She said Kenny died. Madison's date? He had an accident."

Tom's face went white. "What about Madison? Is she okay?"

"She was arrested."

"What?!" Tom bellowed. "For what? What happened?"

"I don't know, Tom. Trisha is on her way home with a friend. The boy that Trisha went to the fair with? Brad? He was arrested, too."

Tom was frantic for details about his daughter, but Lillian was too upset, and she didn't know much more than what she already told.

"Thanks for calling, Lillian," Tom said. "Are you going to be okay over there?"

"I'll be okay," Lillian answered. "But I'm worried about you guys. Let me know if you need anything. Give Evelyn a hug for me."

"Will do. Thanks again."

"TOM!" Evelyn screamed as soon as Tom cut the call. "My baby!"

"Hang on, Evie. We don't know anything yet. Maddie's safe. She wasn't hurt."

"She was arrested, Tom!" Evelyn felt her breath coming in short gasps, and she was afraid she was going to pass out.

Tom embraced his wife and gently led her to sit down on the bed. He grabbed her robe from where it had been draped over a chair and spread it over her shoulders.

"Evie. Listen to me, Sweetie. I know this is scary, but we know she's not hurt. Whatever else is going on we can handle together. You and me."

Tom put his arm around Evelyn. "Okay?" he asked.

"Okay," Evelyn answered. Then a horrific thought came to her, and she felt her body tense up. "Do you think she saw Kenny's accident?

"Everything I know is what you heard on the phone, Baby."

"Oh, Tom. What if she saw him die? His poor parents." Evelyn felt her voice crack as she began to cry.

"If it was an accident at the fair–" Tom grabbed the TV remote and hit the power button.

The television came on in the middle of a report. "...a tragic fatality on this second night of the annual Harvest Festival."

Evelyn's breath caught at the image on the screen. An exterior shot of a ride titled Sky Flyer in bright neon, empty of passengers. The next shot was a tight focus of a swing dangling empty and broken from one set of chains.

The voiceover intoned, "Early reports stated that this is the ride that sent an area teen plunging to his death less than an hour ago. As new details emerge, investigators continue their probe into the incident."

The image quickly cut to another reporter on the scene interviewing witnesses. Against the dark of night, the camera's lights did no favors to one woman they interviewed. Her naturally pale skin was washed out in the harsh lights and stood in stark contrast to the dark mascara streaked on her face from crying.

"I've never seen anything like it," the woman said. "The ride kept spinning and he was hanging from the little chair, and he was screaming. When he fell, we all screamed, but there was nothing we could do."

The woman pulled a wadded tissue from her purse and patted away her tears. "Then this girl ran up to the body and started praying for him. I thought she was crazy, but whatever she did freakin' worked. When that dead boy sat up, I'm sorry, I had to get out of there. I swear to God I'm going to have nightmares for a week."

The reporter turned to face the camera. "There you have it. An eyewitness to what must be the most bizarre story I've ever covered. But you don't have to take my word for it, right Liz?"

Elizabeth Ashford was the anchor for the local late-night news. "That's right, Rob. Tonight's tragedy took an unexpected and dramatic turn, as you will see in this exclusive video from tonight's Harvest Fair. Sensitive viewers are warned this disturbing footage contains some graphic scenes."

The station rolled the tape. A female reporter was giving a rundown of what had transpired when a girl came into the frame, running toward the body. Two police grabbed her, and she began to fight.

Evelyn gasped. "Tom, that's Maddie!" She gripped her husband's hand.

They watched as she fought the police until, surprisingly, they relented and allowed her to approach the body. Evelyn cried as she watched her daughter praying over Kenny's body, but nothing could have prepared her for what happened next.

The camera operator abandoned the reporter and moved in closer to Madison. He was only a few yards away. The camera and microphone missed nothing. Not the gruesome, lethal injuries that were revealed as she pulled the blanket from his body, not Madison's conversation with, and subsequent praise of God, not her declaration of Jesus, and especially not when life surged back into Kenny's body.

The footage then showed their only daughter getting handcuffed and being placed in the back of a police cruiser.

Tom switched off the television and sat, staring at the black screen. Evelyn saw tears welling up in her husband's eyes. "What are we going to do, Tom?" she whispered.

He wiped his tears away with the back of his hand. "We're going to pray, Evie. Then I'm going to call Morris. If anyone can untangle whatever legal knot she's tied up in, Morris can."

***

Sleep did not come quick for Tom, and it was not a restful night.

His repeated calls to the juvenile detention facility proved fruitless. Madison had not yet been processed, and she was not allowed incoming or outgoing calls until she'd been booked into the system.

He tossed and turned and had begun to give up on the idea of sleep when the phone rang. It was their friend, Morris Abbott, the attorney Tom had called earlier. Morris was at the juvenile hall, making sure

Madison was being treated properly. He even arranged for her to be housed away from the general population of detainees.

"Don't worry about her, Tom," Morris said. "Your girl has a strong character. She seems to be taking all of this in stride."

"Thanks, Morris. I really appreciate it. Is there any chance she can come home tonight?" Tom asked.

"I wish I could say yes, but the earliest she'll be released is Monday. She has to appear before a judge. Before that happens, I'll talk to the district attorney and get a feel for what he wants to do about the case," Morris explained.

"What case?" Tom asked. "What charge are they holding her on?"

"Conspiracy to commit fraud," Morris answered.

"Wha–"

"I know, I know. It's BS. Believe me, friend, I'll have her home for dinner on Monday. How's Evie taking this?"

"She's a wreck, Morris. This has hit us hard. It's…It's like…" Tom ran his hand over his face. He couldn't go on.

"I know, Tom. Believe me, with three daughters of my own, I have an idea of what you might be going through. You guys need to get some rest. Oh, and no talking to the press. You got that?"

"Yeah. No problem," Tom acknowledged. "Thanks, Morris. We really appreciate everything you've done."

"I'm just getting warmed up. You take care of Evie and get some rest. I'll call you if anything changes." Morris hung up.

With only a thin strand of hope to hang on to, Tom finally slept.

***

Back at his camper, Chuck sat outside by a small campfire, laughing. So, *this* was what Stillman had been obsessing about. Somehow, he must have got an inkling of what Madison could do and sent him to keep an eye on her to verify if his suspicion was correct.

There was no point in texting Stillman at this hour. The man was probably asleep. No doubt he'd find out just as soon as he turned on a TV or radio. When he did, he'd be certain to call.

Chuck stirred the hot coals with a stick and put another log on the fire. He turned his busy mind to how he could turn this situation to his advantage.

***

Morning arrived all too soon. Wanting nothing more than to turn over and go back to sleep, Tom realized it was unhealthy to allow fear and uncertainty to control their lives. He carefully got out of bed, not wanting to wake his wife.

He remembered talking to Madison about the fair the previous afternoon. He had asked her if she was still scared to get on some of the rides now that she was sixteen.

She had answered, "God has not given us a spirit of fear; but yeah, you bet I am."

That kid, he thought, and a wave of despair washed over him.

Tom filled the Mr. Coffee and fired it up. He hoped things would begin to look better after some caffeine and a little breakfast.

He walked across the living room and pulled back the drapes to let the sunshine in, only to be greeted by the sight of a street full of news trucks and about fifty sightseers milling out in front of his house. Tom sighed and closed the curtains. *So, this is how the day is shaping up.*

***

The story was picked up by news agencies all over the country, and quickly gained traction in the international markets as well. Sunday morning television and radio news programs featured the unbelievable story of a young high school track star whose life had come to a horrific and tragic end on what should have been a joyous occasion.

But the story didn't end there!

His date, disregarding a police barricade, uncovered the body and prayed for him. Miraculously, the boy was resuscitated, with every moment captured on camera in front of hundreds of witnesses.

If it hadn't been such a grisly sequence of events, the news team would have broken out the champagne and celebrated their good fortune.

But the Internet was where the story really went viral. There were thousands of people that night at the fair, and many of them had active social media accounts. There were scores of clips from every possible angle of Kenny hanging from the spinning ride, and of his tragic, fatal fall.

Madison's struggle with the police was documented and posted, as were clips of her praying for Kenny, and his miraculous return to life. These clips had been viewed and shared thousands of times before the first news team even arrived at the scene. The story rocketed up the trending lists and, just as swiftly, people began to take sides.

Some believed Madison to be a manifestation of New Age enlightenment, the quintessential "woke" soul, in tune with the positive vibration of the universe. To them, she was a brilliant beacon of hope for these dark times. They posted messages of encouragement and declared they were sending positive thoughts and energy.

Some believed she was evil. A wolf in sheep's clothing sent to prey on the weak minded. Many of the devout feared Madison was sent to lure the unsuspecting from their faith in Jesus, thereby condemning them to an eternity of suffering in the lake of fire. In spite of Madison's declaration of Jesus, they denounced her as a servant of Satan.

Some called her a fraud. There were a growing number of people vocal about their belief that this was an elaborate hoax perpetrated by a young teenage couple. Bitter and cynical from years of being lied to by elected officials and mainstream media, they saw her as another false hope, and another empty promise. She was the embodiment of all that was destructive, corrupt, and malevolent in this calamitous decade.

***

The phone jarred Chuck out of a deep sleep. He hadn't gotten to bed until well after midnight. There was too much on his mind, and too many questions to answer. The second ring forced him to open one eye to check the time.

Six-thirty. Who in their right mind gets up at this hour of the morning?

"Hello, Rev," Chuck answered the phone groggily.

"Did you see it?" Stillman demanded.

"I was right there, Russ. I saw everything. It was absolutely incredible."

"Some people say it's a hoax."

"No one who saw it live would ever believe that. I saw it, Russ. There's no way it was a hoax," Chuck reassured him.

"I knew I was right! I knew she did something to that woman. Why didn't you call me last night?" Stillman asked. "Where is the girl now?"

"She's probably in jail. The last I saw of her she was in the back of a police car," Chuck said.

"Do not lose track of that girl, Chuck."

"What do you want me to do, just follow her around?"

"I don't know yet. Ideally, I'd like her to come to Florida," Stillman said.

"Outside of me kidnapping her, I don't see how that's going to happen. God knows I'm no Boy Scout, but I'm not going to go that far."

"No. Sure. I mean, I wouldn't want you to. Who knows? If you tried, she might strike you dead," Stillman pointed out.

"What? Is that even possible?" Chuck never considered a sixteen-year-old girl might be a lethal threat.

"You saw what happened last night. She brought a dead person back to life. She could probably stop your heart without breaking a sweat."

Chuck admitted, "I never thought about that."

"A little patience paid off, didn't it? And you wanted to leave. This is incredible," Stillman marveled.

"So, what do you want to do now?" Chuck asked.

"I don't know. I never expected her to do something so spectacular, or so public. This is beyond anything I imagined. Hang out there for a few more weeks as we originally planned, and I'll let you know what I decide," Stillman concluded.

"Okay, Russ. If I'm going to be out here any longer, I'm going to need some cash. Expenses, fuel, food, etc. You can PayPal me," Chuck said.

He knew that Stillman was probably thinking about the envelope full of cash he'd given him. True, it should have lasted longer. But Chuck also knew that Stillman was in no place to argue. Chuck was flush with cash from his haul at the fair, but with this latest development, he was confident Stillman would pay whatever was needed to keep him there and keep his eyes open.

"Sure thing, Chuck," Stillman said. "You'll have it in the next few minutes. Stay in touch!"

"Ten-four, Boss. Talk to you soon." Chuck clicked off.

***

When Tom caught sight of the news vans outside his house, his first thought was to shelter Evelyn.

It was only a matter of time before someone came to the door for a few words. Maybe they'd even try to call him on his phone.

The phone! Tom dashed upstairs and grabbed Evelyn's phone and turned it off. He took it downstairs with him and placed it on the kitchen counter. He used his own phone to take a photo of the chaos outside and sent it, along with a text, to Morris Abbott.

Under siege. Please advise.

Tom started slicing mushrooms for omelets. There was a bell pepper in the fridge, and some cheese. He'd been thinking ham but decided instead to fry up a few slices of thick-cut bacon. He had a feeling they'd need their strength to get through the day.

He laid out silverware, napkins, and a plate. At Evelyn's place on the table, he set a cup of coffee and a flute of chardonnay. When everything was in place, he went upstairs.

Evelyn was already up. She must have been up for a while considering the small mountain of soggy and crumpled tissues next to her on the bed.

"Hey, Sunshine. How did you sleep?"

Evelyn blew her nose. "Don't look at me."

"Grab your robe and come downstairs," encouraged Tom.

"I can't find my phone," Evelyn complained.

"It's downstairs." Tom took the robe off the end of the bed and held it for her. "I've made some coffee and we can have some breakfast."

"I don't feel like getting up," Evelyn said.

He gave her a look that said Please work with me here, I'm at the end of my rope.

Evelyn felt a stab of guilt. Yes, she was devastated by what she'd seen last night, and by her daughter's arrest, but she also had a responsibility to her husband. She wasn't meant to be a weight to carry. As God designed it, she was supposed to be a helpmeet, a partner, a co-owner of their precious marriage relationship.

"On second thought, kind sir, I've heard the dining in this establishment is second to none, and I will be happy to accept your gracious invitation." Evelyn smiled and batted her eyelashes.

Tom felt the weight on his chest ease a little. "Right this way, Madam," he said, crooking his elbow for her to take.

Breakfast wasn't strained, but a shadow hung over them, dampening the spirits. Tom re-filled her coffee, and her chardonnay. By time they finished breakfast, they were almost back to normal.

Almost.

"So, why did you take my phone?" Evelyn asked.

"I didn't know if anyone was going to call you. You know, like the press calling for a statement or something? I didn't want anyone disturbing your rest or saying something to upset you."

"What makes you think that would happen?" Evelyn asked.

Tom nodded toward the front window.

Evelyn glanced outside and her stomach lurched. "My goodness! When did they get here?"

"I don't know," Tom replied. "I was up at six, but I didn't notice them until later."

"What are we going to do about *them*?" Evelyn asked.

Tom's phone announced an incoming text message. He smiled. "We're going to have a press conference."

***

Morris Abbott sat in one of the interview rooms at the county jail. "Thanks for meeting with me on a Sunday, Rick. I know you have better things to do."

"I got your text as I was leaving church. We were heading over for lunch at my mother-in-law's house." He groaned. "They'll get along fine without me for a couple of hours."

Rick Bennett was the Monroe County District Attorney. He and Morris Abbott had been on opposite sides of the table on many occasions.

"As you can probably guess, I'm here about the Madison Newman incident. I'd like to take her home to her folks, Rick. They're worried sick."

"I wish I could help them out, Morris. We'll have to wait until Monday to see what the judge has to say."

Morris gave a broad smile and asked, "Does that mean you intend to pursue a conviction on the charge of conspiracy to commit fraud?"

"Does that amuse you?" Bennett asked.

"Where's the fraud?" Morris pressed. "What did they gain from staging this theoretically fraudulent accident?"

"I don't have to prove they gained anything from their actions, I only have to prove they acted, in concert, to deliberately deceive. Maybe they wanted to sue the fair association for an accident. Maybe they wanted to cash in with a big GoFundMe windfall. For all I know they wanted TikTok views or Twitter likes. Who knows why kids do some of the things they do?"

"This stinks, Rick. You're going to go after a seventeen-year-old boy and a sixteen-year-old girl on a weak conspiracy charge? Madison has been sixteen a little more than a week. She's taking honors classes in high school."

"Those are all very good points to bring up in her defense," Bennett conceded. "Listen, people are angry about this. They're no longer willing to put up with anything that smacks of lawlessness. After a few years of violence in the streets, riots, and looting, I can't say that I blame them."

"What are you going to base your case on? You have the sworn testimony of two EMTs. You have two policemen who were also witnesses. That kid wasn't just dead, Rick, he was destroyed. Are you saying

Kenneth Warner got up and walked away from those kinds of injuries?" Morris asked.

"To be honest, I find that a lot easier to swallow than thinking the girl healed his injuries through the power of prayer," Bennett said.

Morris was not about to let that go. "Is the office of the Monroe County District Attorney willing to go on record that God is not able to heal?"

"C'mon, Morris, do you actually believe that boy was magically healed?"

"Not magically. He was prayerfully and divinely healed. What I believe is immaterial. It's what you can prove in court that matters. I only need to provide reasonable doubt."

Bennett mulled over his options. It was true, the case was weak, and the optics were truly bad. His initial reservations about pursuing a conviction had been overridden by the mayor.

It didn't matter how high profile the case was, or how many people in the community called for prosecution. The truth is he had very little on which to build a case. If evidence should turn up later proving otherwise, he could always formally charge them at a later time.

Bennett sighed, "What do you want?"

"I want Madison Newman released. No charges. As it stands, you can't possibly prove conspiracy. My client wishes to spare his daughter the additional trauma of a court appearance. She's already been through the wringer."

"You realize by dropping this, the press is going to accuse me of being indecisive and soft on crime. Not good during an election year," Bennett observed.

"Nonsense. I'd like to think they'd see you as a man of compassion, one who knows how to administer the rule of law without losing that touch of humanity," Morris said. "In fact, I'll tell them as much during the inevitable press conference."

CHAPTER FOURTEEN

The press conference took place at 2:00 p.m. that very Sunday at the residence of Thomas and Evelyn Newman. Keeping the press abreast of current developments was not, however, the purpose of the conference.

Morris had arranged for a small and informal conference. Apparently, word had spread within the news community because there were considerably more in attendance than he anticipated. At precisely 2:00, Morris appeared with Tom and Evelyn on the front porch of the Newman home.

The cameras were on, and Morris began with the introductions. "Members of the press, thank you for coming. I know some of you have been waiting for an opportunity since early this morning. My name is Morris Abbott. I am an attorney. The couple you see here are Thomas and Evelyn Newman, the parents of Madison Newman."

Immediately, a reporter's hand lifted to ask a question.

Morris held his hand up, "If you'll bear with me for another minute, I promise you'll have an opportunity to ask some questions."

Morris surveyed the group in front of him. They seemed willing to let him finish.

"Very well then. By now you're all aware of the terrible accident at the fair last night. We've all seen that shocking footage from the news broadcast last night. Am I right?"

Most of the reporters nodded in agreement.

Morris continued, "The coverage was very dramatic and emotional. I want to provide some context for what happened last night. This wasn't reported by the press, but Kenny Warner and Madison Newman went on their first official date last night."

A small rumble rose from the small crowd.

"There have been some comments that what occurred last night was a deliberate fraud. Nothing could be further from the truth. While they do attend the same school, last night they went to the fair on their very first date. If that isn't a scene right out of Rockwell's America, I don't know what is."

Behind him, Evelyn began to weep.

"The Newman family is now prepared to answer your questions. As you can imagine, this has been very difficult for them," Morris concluded.

A hand went up and the reporter asked, "Did you see the news coverage last night, and if so, what was your reaction?"

"Yes, we did see the news coverage," Tom answered. "My wife and I were wholly unprepared for what we witnessed."

Morris approved. He'd spent the last hour coaching them.

Answer questions briefly and directly. Do not volunteer information. If you're unsure if you should answer, look for my guidance. It is perfectly acceptable, and often preferable, to answer, "I don't know."

Another reporter shouted, "Where is your daughter now?"

Morris was quick to step in. "As you probably saw last night, she was taken into custody. She was subsequently booked into the juvenile detention facility."

Not quite a direct answer, but it would have to do. Hoping to avoid a follow-up question, he was quick to grab the next reporter's question.

"Mrs. Newman, what went through your mind when you saw your daughter kneeling by the boy's body?"

It was plain that she was still shaken, but Evelyn answered thoughtfully. "If you're asking if I was surprised that she would pray for someone, the answer is no. That is very much in character for Madison."

"If I may," the reporter quickly interjected, "do you believe your daughter brought Kenny Warner back from the dead?"

Morris Abbott, a believer, closed his eyes and silently thanked God. The reporter brought up the question up. Morris didn't. This introduced the idea that bringing someone back from the dead was a possibility worth considering.

Tom spoke up. "I don't know. I mean, we've talked about it," he said.

He looked at Evelyn with a question in his eyes. She returned the look and nodded. "Yes, we've talked about it, of course, but we haven't arrived at any conclusions.

Our focus has been on getting our daughter home and assessing how she's been affected emotionally."

Some fellow in the back had his hand up for a while now. Morris pointed at him.

"Police Chief Darryl Hunt said earlier today that the investigation is ongoing, but there are discrepancies that need to be reconciled. Do you have any idea what these discrepancies are? And how does that impact your client?" he asked.

Morris knew this is where he could tip the court of public opinion in his favor.

"I understand why they might have questions about what exactly happened. I imagine many of you are having the same struggle. On one hand, we have the expert medical testimony of two paramedics who say that, despite their skill and experience, the patient's injuries were so severe as to be fatal. Then we have a girl who fervently prays for the deceased, and by some miracle he's brought back from the dead to life again."

Morris continued, "How does this happen? How is this possible? The law doesn't make provisions for praying people back to life. The law recognizes only two possibilities. Either everyone was wrong, including trained medical professionals, and Kenny Warner never died, or these two teens, on their very first date, conspired to deceive everyone."

A hand went up in the crowd and Morris called on the reporter.

"Are you saying that the girl actually brought that dead boy back to life?" she asked.

"That's the big question, isn't it?" Morris answered. "There is a lot to look at in the way of evidence before I'd be willing to say for certain. But one thing I do know, there is absolutely no evidence at all to support the idea that last night's accident at the fair was a hoax."

Several hands went up for the next question, but Morris wasn't done yet. "I know our district attorney well enough to say that he won't pursue a conviction if the evidence doesn't support one. Rick Bennett is a brilliant prosecutor, and he is not one to apply the rule of law haphazardly."

"I'm very sorry," Morris said quickly before any more questions could be asked. "I'm afraid we're out of time. I promised my clients they'd be done here quickly. They have a previous commitment."

He leaned into the microphone. "Thank you for your time."

With that, Tom and Evelyn got into Evelyn's car and drove away.

***

Morris had told Tom to make a quick exit and drive straight to the Fashion Center Mall.

The trip took seventeen minutes. Per instructions, he parked by the entrance to Macy's. He and Evelyn got out of the car and entered the mall.

They made their way to the bridal registry. There, just as they were told, stood a young brunette with a red blazer. She had a Macy's employee name tag. Jennifer.

Evelyn said, "Uncle Morris sent me."

Jennifer smiled. "He's my favorite uncle."

She handed Evelyn a set of car keys. Evelyn handed over the keys to her Camry.

"Exit on the east side of the mall," Jennifer said. "You're looking for a red Altima. Good luck."

"Thanks so much." Evelyn turned to Tom. "Let's go."

***

Jennifer wasn't Morris Abbott's niece. In addition to her job at Macy's, she did the occasional odd job for him to help pay for college. She was working on a degree in Criminal Justice. Morris tried to convince her to study law, but Jennifer liked to get her hands dirty. The dream was far off, but she hoped one day to work for the FBI.

Her shift was over, and Jennifer clocked out. There was no problem finding Mrs. Newman's car. She took off her blazer and laid it on the back seat. Thumbing an icon on her phone, she scanned the Camry with an app. It registered positive.

Unless Mr. Newman was keeping track of Mrs. Newman on the sly, one of the reporters had placed a GPS tracker on the car. She switched functions and tried to ping the tracker.

Jennifer started by the driver's door, and then moved toward the front of the car. As she advanced, the signal became fainter. She stopped, and then backtracked. Once Jennifer neared the back of the car, the signal became stronger.

Kneeling by the rear fender, she bent over to examine the underside of the car. There, just as her app told her, was the GPS tracker, magnetically attached to the frame. She had to crouch low to reach it, but she eventually pulled it from underneath the car.

She was crouched by the rear of the Camry when a car rolled by slowly.

"Well, if you aren't the prettiest thing I've seen today," the driver said.

Clutching the tracker in her right hand, Jennifer stood slowly. She kept herself from making a snide remark to the sleazy driver. He was exactly what she needed at the moment.

Jennifer smiled and said, "And that's the nicest thing I've heard today. Isn't that a coincidence?"

"Maybe it's fate," he said in an oily voice. "Perhaps we should discuss this over drinks?"

Jennifer leaned slightly into the driver's window, letting him get a good whiff of her perfume. She dropped the tracker on the floor behind the driver's seat as she whispered into his ear, "A man wearing a wedding ring shouldn't be out looking for trouble."

The would-be Lothario momentarily looked embarrassed, and then lashed out. "You're nothing but a tease!" He sped off, tires squealing in protest.

Jennifer sighed, "Good luck explaining to your wife why the news truck is following you all over town."

She got into the Camry and drove away.

***

Tom and Evelyn located the Altima. Tom popped the trunk, and there was the suitcase they'd thrown together earlier at Morris' request. They got in the car, buckled up, and headed north on State Route Three. Their destination was over the river and across the state line into Saint Louis.

An envelope in the glove compartment gave them the name of the hotel where they'd be staying, a room key, and a few simple instructions: *Lay low for the next couple of days and maybe this will blow over. Don't talk to reporters.*

The drive took less than an hour. They dropped the car off with the valet, grabbed the suitcase out of the back, and went up to their room.

As the elevator doors closed, Tom said, "Morris thought of everything. I don't think I could live at home with all those reporters parked outside."

"That was unnerving," Evelyn agreed. "I wonder what they thought was going to happen?"

The elevator stopped at the seventh floor, and they exited into the hall. Tom had the luggage, Evelyn had the room's pass card, and he followed her down the hallway to their room.

"They were probably waiting for a chance to talk to Maddie," Tom guessed.

Evelyn slipped the pass card into the slot on the door. "Now we're farther from her than ever. What if the police release her tomorrow? What if she needs us?"

The door made a soft click and the tiny light flashed green. Evelyn pulled the door open and stepped inside. Her breath caught at the sight.

There, by the window that overlooked the city, stood her daughter, Madison.

"Mom!" Madison shouted. She ran to her mother, throwing her arms around her, holding her tight.

Evelyn held her daughter and cried. She was so grateful to see her daughter safe. Even Tom was taken completely by surprise by his daughter's presence, and wept tears of gratitude.

When the tears were over and they'd settled into their suite, Madison said, "I'm so sorry for what happened. You're probably never going to trust me again."

Tom answered, "Maddie, we were worried sick for you. What happened wasn't your fault. I'm so happy you're safe."

They looked their daughter over. It had been barely twenty-four hours earlier that they'd sent her off on a date to the fair. She'd been a carefree teenage girl, bubbling over with excitement about going out with Kenny. Now she looked as though she'd lost weight and hadn't slept a wink.

"How did they treat you, Maddie?" Evelyn was holding her hand and she gave it a squeeze.

"Mom, I was so upset with everything that happened, but it was okay. I mean, I didn't want to be there. I was worried about you guys." She shot a look at her dad. "I didn't want you to worry. I didn't want…" Madison sighed and shrugged.

"How's Kenny?" Tom asked.

Tears filled her eyes. "He was okay the last time I saw him." She cast a hopeful look to her mom. "Has he tried to get hold of me?"

"Not that I know of, Maddie. We pretty much had to turn our phones off. They started ringing non-stop. Reporters called wanting interviews. The talk shows want you; the late-night shows want you. It's completely nuts. People were calling to ask you to pray for them. Some of them offered thousands of dollars if you would pray for them."

"Then there's the other ones," Tom muttered.

Evelyn gave him a warning look.

"What?" Madison asked.

"She deserves to know, Evie. She's not a child anymore. She needs to know so she can protect herself."

Evelyn didn't say anything, but nodded her agreement.

"Some people have called saying you serve the devil. Some claim you're a false prophet. And sometimes those are the nicer things people say," Tom said. He swallowed. "I'm not trying to hurt your feelings, Maddie."

Madison nodded as she dabbed away her tears with a tissue. "I know, Dad."

"Whatever happened last night triggered something deep in a lot of people," Tom said. "It's created a real divide at a time when we already have enough division between people. It's all over the Internet. Everyone has an opinion and a blog to post it on."

There was a knock at the door. Tom got up and walked over to peek out the peephole.

"Well, if this isn't a surprise!" Tom opened the door and grabbed one of the brown shopping bags that Morris was holding. "Come in, come in!"

Morris was elated. "I see you discovered my little surprise."

Evelyn was out of her chair and hugged Morris, kissing him on the cheek. "Thank you so much, Morrie. I don't know how we can ever possibly thank you."

"Don't you worry about it, Evie. I'm charging your husband plenty!"

Tom laughed but added, "He's not kidding."

Evelyn asked, "What's in the bags?"

"Dinner! Chef Ma's. You can spend more, but you'll rarely find better. I ordered something for everyone and a lot more just in case. You'll have enough for breakfast tomorrow."

"It smells yummy," Madison said.

Morris had brought plates and remembered flatware for the cowards who didn't want to use chopsticks. The Newman's suite had rooms for three, a living room, and a dining area overlooking the city from the seventh floor.

The view was spectacular. The food was even better.

After they'd served themselves and begun eating, Morris said, "I thought it was best if you got out of town for a few days. You need the time alone, especially since you're going to be with your daughter."

"How did you pull that off?" Tom asked. "I thought you said it was impossible."

"In the courtroom, our district attorney is a single-minded warrior for justice. Get him outside of a courtroom for a simple conversation, and the man is a pussycat with a soft heart. He won't pursue charges against our girl here, or against Mr. Warner."

Madison jumped up and hugged Morris. "Thank you, Mr. Abbott!"

"I did very little except to speak the truth. If you want to thank someone, thank God. It is written, 'The king's heart is in the hand of the Lord, Like the rivers of water; He turns it wherever He wishes,'" Morris quoted.

"Lawyer and theologian," admired Tom.

"Hey, you don't go to a Jesuit college for six years without learning something," Morris said with a chuckle.

"Where do we go from here?" Evelyn asked.

"Bringing you to Saint Louis was meant to give you a little break from the crazy," Morris answered. "I suggest you talk among yourselves about how you want to deal with the press and the fanatics. Also, you might want to consider letting Madison do an interview or two when you get back. Or not. I'm not sure it would help at this point. You'll probably need to change your phone numbers if you ever want a moment's peace."

"Surely you're exaggerating," Tom said. "I mean, if the DA isn't going to press charges, and nobody really got hurt, aren't we pretty much done?"

"I'll let you decide." Morris grabbed the TV remote and clicked it on. He only had to change the station twice before hitting a news broadcast.

"...the highest single night attendance in the history of the fair. Fair officials are citing last night's sensational accident, where a young man was initially believed to have been killed when thrown from the Sky Flyer ride."

The station showed the clip from the previous night, with the seat dangling from a single pair of chains. "Fair officials report that a small shrine was erected where the boy was believed to have died. They removed the shrine, only to have a different group erect a second shrine where people have gathered to pray.

"Oracle police say they have not yet closed the investigation, but all indications are there was no foul play in the incident."

Morris changed the station.

"...is how horrified fairgoers described the carnage at an Illinois fair last night as a high school senior was ejected from the..."

Madison got up from the table, sobbing, and ran to the bathroom.

Evelyn quickly stood and went after Madison.

"Geez, Morris," Tom said.

"I'm sorry, Tom. I wasn't thinking. But now you see what you're going to go back home to. I don't think this is going to disappear any time soon. This story has everything, including a mystery. What exactly happened last night? People are going to want to know. If you stonewall them, they're going to get angry."

"Or they'll completely forget once the next calamity hits the evening news," Tom countered.

Morris nodded his agreement. "Could be."

Evelyn and Madison returned to the table. Madison looked embarrassed. "Sorry. It got to me for a second. I'll be okay."

Morris was quick to apologize. "No. Please accept my apologies. That was insensitive, and entirely too soon."

"Is everyone finished eating?" Evelyn asked a little too airily. "If so, I'll clean this up."

"I'm stuffed, thanks," Tom said.

"Me too," groaned Madison.

"No more for me," Morris answered. "Hey. We haven't had our fortune cookies!"

Morris upended a small bag and half dozen fortune cookies spilled out on the table. Evelyn took one, as did Madison. Tom took some time making his selection while an impatient Morris snatched one off the table. This narrowed the selection to three, and Tom selected the farthest from him.

Evelyn tore open the plastic wrapper and broke open her cookie. Reading the slender slip of paper, she said, "You will find that which you seek."

"Commendably vague," Morris said, ever the lawyer.

Morris cracked open his cookie and read the fortune. "He who divines truth is wise." Morris held his fortune up for all to see. "What a wonderfully prophetic cookie!"

They all had a good laugh at that, but the laughter stopped when Tom read his fortune. "No man can tame the tongue; it is a restless evil."

"That's pretty grim," Tom observed.

Madison already had hers out and was reading it. "That's just great," she deadpanned.

"What does yours say, Maddie?" her mom asked.

Madison passed the fortune over to her mother who read it aloud. "Your path is paved with woe, but you do not travel alone."

They all looked at Madison, who sat in her chair looking small and very alone indeed.

CHAPTER FIFTEEN

Monday brought another press conference. District Attorney Rick Bennett thanked Police Chief Darryl Hunt, and his department, for their swift and thorough investigation of the accident on Saturday night. He was pleased to inform members of the press that his department would not file charges against the two teenagers in question. There was simply no evidence to support the charge.

A religious rights group protested the sudden outbreaks of prayer occurring throughout the city. They alleged that the enthusiasm displayed while praising the Christian God infringed upon the rights of other, non-Christian faiths. They vowed to push for a bill outlawing public prayer or vocal worship outside of a recognized house of worship or private home.

An outraged citizens group asked for an independent review of the two officers who allowed Madison to disturb the boy's body. When it was pointed out that there was no body, their reply was, "No, but there could have been if not for that girl's interference."

Bishop Marcus Wright was decidedly not of the Catholic Church. This self-styled bishop was an author of many books on Christian faith and prosperity. He was an enthusiastic proponent of the "Name It and Claim It" gospel. Bishop Wright was heavily involved in television ministries, radio programs, and big-event evangelical revivals. He'd used his Sunday podcast to strongly condemn Madison Newman.

Monday morning, he was a guest on one of the network talk fests. The network wanted to capitalize on the buzz this story was receiving across all demographics. They figured correctly that America's most flamboyantly vocal preacher might have some interesting observations.

"Bishop Wright, thank you for joining us on such short notice," the host began. "I understand you've seen footage of the accident at the fair in Oracle, Illinois last Saturday night."

Wright nodded and adopted his serious and thoughtful face. "I've seen it."

The station ran the now-famous clip of Madison as she pulled the blanket off Kenny and prayed. They stopped and held on the image of Kenny as he sat up and exchanged a look with Madison.

The interviewer asked, "Do you see events such as we saw this past Saturday as evidence that there's a new spiritual awakening in our country?"

"Quite the opposite," Bishop Wright proclaimed. "What happened in Illinois this past weekend is a shameful indictment on how we've allowed ourselves to be spiritually blinded. This girl is a fraud."

The interviewer countered, "There are some who see this girl, Madison, as a shining light that the world needs in these dark times. I take it you don't share that view."

Marcus Wright replied, "I certainly do not share that view. Pay close attention to what people are saying about this girl. Some say she's a shining light. But that claim was rightfully made by someone else over two thousand years ago. Jesus told the Pharisees, 'I am the light of the world.'"

"Do you worry she has a hidden agenda?"

"I worry that people won't recognize lies because they aren't familiar with the truth. We live in an age when the spiritual health of the world is at an all-time low. We can't afford to cast our gaze to a hope that's counterfeit."

Bishop Wright took off his glasses and cleaned them with a microfiber cloth as he expounded,

"This is not at all unexpected. In fact, Jesus said that he was warning us in advance about this very thing. He said, 'For false messiahs and false prophets will appear and perform great signs and wonders to deceive.' If Jesus felt it was important to warn us, I think we should pay attention."

***

Tom was a habitual early riser. Monday was no exception. He walked into the suite's living area and spent some time figuring out how to use the hotel coffee maker. Once he cleared that hurdle, he checked the hallway. As he'd hoped, the hotel left a copy of *USA Today* at the door.

The plan was to drink some coffee and read the paper, but Tom soon soured on the idea when he saw the accident at the fair was still headlining. Witnesses provided graphic descriptions of Kenny's injuries. Additionally, an investigation had uncovered that the operator of the ride was in the country illegally on an expired visa and repeated requests for interviews had been met with silence.

Tom tucked the paper into the bottom of the trash.

After having changed their numbers, Tom was no longer reluctant to use his phone. He quickly learned that reading the news online was no better. As bad as the stories were, it was reader comments to the online articles that really got to him.

Some people were truly nice, but the majority who commented said terrible things. One person wrote that Madison was a witch, and that when Kenny came back, it was a demon that animated the body.

Tom heard Evelyn moving around in the bedroom. He fixed her a cup of coffee and took it to her. On the way, he glanced at Madison's door. It was shut. He didn't know if she was still asleep, or if she just didn't want to face the world.

I wouldn't blame her at all.

When everyone was awake, and with no one objecting, they had leftover Chinese food for breakfast as they admired sunrise over the Mississippi River.

"We should go do something today. It's going to be too nice to stay cooped up in a hotel room," Tom said.

"Morris said we should be inconspicuous," Evelyn reminded her husband. "It's still all over the news and they have Madison's picture everywhere. I don't think it's safe, Tom."

Madison frowned at the way this conversation was going. Was she going to have to hide for the rest of her life? She hadn't done anything wrong.

"Maybe if this was Oracle, Mom. No one knows me in Saint Louis. I'll wear sunglasses, or a hat. Maybe I'll buy a hoodie at the shop downstairs and look like a tourist."

"Great idea, Maddie," Tom said. "The Wax Museum is less than a mile away. We can walk there and enjoy the day. What do you say, Evie?"

Evelyn wasn't feeling it, but Tom was intent on doing something. He didn't stop to ask what her reservations were. She wasn't even sure she would have been able to articulate what she was feeling.

She compromised and said, "Let's get ready. If I haven't warmed to the idea when you're ready to go, you two can go ahead without me and I'll find something else to do. I'll be okay."

They tried to cajole her into joining them, but her heart was not at peace. She encouraged them to go and explained she needed some alone time for a few hours.

In the end, Tom and Madison went together and left her at the hotel. She envied their easy relationship, and she was glad Tom was so engaged as a father. Evelyn appreciated how Tom wanted things to get back to normal for Madison, and he tried to keep her mind busy on other things.

Evelyn recalled the call from Lillian. Things had gone from good to horrible in the space of a few heartbeats. When she'd heard Madison had been arrested, she had seriously begun to lose it, but Tom had been right there for her.

He was amazing. He encouraged her and let her know that together the two of them could face anything. Just the two of them.

She loved him for that. Just the two of them. But…where was God in this? If it was the two of them, then where was God's place in their lives? Where was God's place in their hope of getting through these events that had only just begun?

When Tom had lost his job early in their marriage, she'd worried about a dozen different things. He said, "This is God's way of giving me the kick in the pants I need to open my own firm." He realized the dream of opening his own business, and Tom never forgot to give God credit for the increase.

When God had blessed them with Madison, Evelyn had wondered how they would manage the expense of a child when they were barely getting by. It was Tom who had pointed out, "God wouldn't bless us with a child and fail to provide for her."

Evelyn missed the man that Tom had been. That man had been missing for a couple of years. The blame wasn't all his. She shared in it also. She'd grown lax in praying and reading her Bible. They still attended church regularly, but she was quickly realizing that kind of passive faith was not enough.

Their current situation involved heavenly realms. What had happened with Madison directly involved God. Tom wanted it to be the two of them, but that wasn't even enough to handle earthly problems. They needed to be firmly in the spirit if they hoped to understand what was happening to their daughter.

Evelyn began to pray. She prayed long and hard, and when her resolve began to flag, the Holy Spirit buoyed her, encouraged her, and revealed spiritual truths. She prayed for strength to face the challenges that lay ahead, and for discernment to know God's will.

Finally, she prayed that God would use her husband to help Madison realize God's will, and help Madison choose her path.

Her final prayer would soon be answered, but not in the way she expected.

***

The camper cruised carefully down the residential street, cautious of pets, children, and the speed limit. No reason to call attention to oneself. Not when you're already at a distinct disadvantage by virtue of driving a massive pickup truck with a camper shell on it. It was a sweet rig, but it was one people would notice and remember. This was Chuck's second trip today.

There was still no sign of the Newman family, and no sign of the news people. Yet at the end of the street, in that two-year-old Prius, sat that same guy he'd seen since Sunday. Cop, or network news snitch? He couldn't make himself believe a cop was sitting in that Prius. His vote was newsperson.

Chuck would have to give Stillman an update later. He'd gone ballistic when Chuck had given him word that Madison and her family were missing. It had taken a while to calm him down.

"They went somewhere, Russ. It's that simple," Chuck explained. "With everything going on, why wouldn't they want to get away by themselves for a couple of days?"

"Didn't they let anyone know where they were going?" Stillman asked.

"They're free people, Russ. Like you and me. They're under no obligation to let anyone know when they go anywhere. There's no need to worry. They have roots here. They're entrenched. They have a house, and a business. They're not going anywhere. Relax."

Stillman sighed. "You're right. I'm supposed to be relaxing out here. I promised Kevin. All right, I'll let you take care of it. Keep me in the loop…"

"...if anything happens." Chuck completed the sentence.

***

The Newman family returned from their brief exile late Tuesday afternoon. They stopped on the way to pick up a bucket of chicken. No one felt like cooking. They didn't know quite what to expect when they turned the corner to their house.

The news aggregators on their phones still carried articles related to the accident. They included accident statistics by state for amusement parks as a whole, and articles on the most infamous ride fatalities. Tom had a feeling any future lists would include the accident his daughter had been involved in.

The radio reported fallout from the accident. The latest news was that the city council wanted an audit of their emergency medical contracts. It was an understandable request in light of Saturday's accident.

Two EMTs had declared a patient dead, yet the boy was clearly unharmed. How is it possible that a qualified EMT could make such a mistake? The city council intended to find out.

Until it was straightened out, Victor Morelli and Stephan Torres, the EMTs at the accident, were suspended without pay pending the results of the investigation.

While it was a relief to turn the corner and not see any news vans parked in front of the house, Tom knew they'd probably be back. No need to plant the entire crew outside when they just needed one person to blow the whistle when the subjects returned.

Tom backed the car into the garage. They didn't have a lot of luggage, and they got everything into the house in one trip.

Madison made a beeline to the kitchen. Morris said he left her phone on the counter after he'd picked up her property from the jail. Even though she hadn't used it, the battery had run out. She went upstairs to her room and let the phone charge while she showered and changed.

Evelyn and Tom agreed they'd have to tackle a job they'd put off while they were in Saint Louis. Now that Madison was upstairs, it seemed the perfect time. They got out their phones and started calling to thank their friends and neighbors, the ones who supported them with prayers and good wishes, and who said they'd watch the house while they were away.

Madison was on her bed, scrolling through her phone. She had a lot of messages from Trisha. Most of them were from Saturday night and Sunday. There were a few from other friends. She frowned – none from Kenny.

Her social media were flooded with messages and posts with clips from the accident. Some were messages of encouragement. Others made horrible accusations. Some called her foul and evil names, and some were simply disgusting.

If the extent of the situation hadn't been clear to her before, she was now inundated with thousands of messages from people she'd never known. Complete strangers cursed her with hate and venom spilling out on her screen.

Dear God, she thought, *the whole world knows.*

She tapped Trisha's number. The phone rang, but there was no answer.

She figured she'd try later, after dinner. Madison was about to go downstairs when her phone rang. It was Trisha.

"Hey, Trish."

"Maddie, where have you been?"

"They released me from custody on Sunday, and I've been in Saint Louis. Our lawyer said I had to lay low. Did I miss anything?"

"Are you freaking kidding me?" Trisha shouted into the phone. "Everyone wants to know where you are. They want to know where Kenny is."

Madison sat up on the bed. "Kenny hasn't been to school?"

"No one's seen him. He's not answering calls or texts. A lot of people believe he's still dead. Some people are saying you two ran off to California to start a life together."

Madison wiped tears with her sleeve. "Yeah, that's not going to happen."

"You've talked to Kenny?" Trisha wanted to know.

"No. I haven't talked to him. But I know, Trish. That's done."

"Did he break up with you?" Trisha asked.

"I *know*, Trish."

"Oh," Trisha said, finally understanding. "Are you okay? How do you feel?"

"I don't know, Trish," Madison said. "I feel so many ways right now it's hard to sort them all out. I feel scared because I'm not sure what's supposed to happen next. I feel grateful, because Kenny is alive and has an opportunity to accept Christ."

"That sounds like a lot to deal with," Trisha sympathized.

"It is a lot," Madison replied.

Trisha said, "My mom's pretty freaked out by the whole thing."

"So's mine."

"Yeah," Trisha began, "but the thing is, my mom says she doesn't want me hanging out with you anymore."

"What? Trish, she knows me. I thought she liked me."

"She does like you, but what you did scared her. I mean, she knows we hang out at church and go to Bible study, but you went next-level on this one. I have to be honest with you, what happened at the fair freaked me out, too."

"Trish," Madison pleaded, "please don't tell me you're going to bail on me."

"You're my friend, Maddie. More than that, you are my sister in Christ. I'm not going anywhere."

Madison began crying. She'd always valued Trisha's friendship. It meant a lot to know the feeling was reciprocated.

"Thanks, Trish," was all she could manage.

"Mom will come around eventually," Trisha reassured her friend. "Don't worry."

Madison's phone buzzed and she looked at the message. "Mom's calling me to dinner. Talk to you tomorrow?"

"You bet. Later."

***

Madison sat at the dinner table and her father said grace. She didn't have much of an appetite, but she knew if she didn't eat, her parents would worry. She didn't think she could take their scrutiny along with everything else, so she filled her plate as she ordinarily would. That did not, however, shield her from comments.

"You've been crying," her mom observed.

"Yeah. I was talking to Trish. Talking about school, people that miss me, gossip. All that kind of stuff."

"Did she have any news about Kenny?"

Madison focused on her plate. She didn't want to look up. *I am NOT going to cry.*

"Maddie?" her mom prompted.

She shook her head and looked up, eyes bright, but no tears. "No one's seen him or talked to him."

"Have you thought of when you're going back to school?" Her father asked. "The school gave a week off, but you'll have to go back sometime."

Madison was eager to change the subject. "I can go tomorrow if you want. I don't think anything's going to change by staying out. It'll be harder to catch up the longer I wait."

Tom seemed grateful for her daughter's sensible and mature outlook regarding her return to school.

Evelyn, on the other hand, voiced a concern that Madison was rushing things. In her natural desire to return to a normal routine, Maddie might be refusing to deal with emotional issues that needed to be resolved.

"I think tomorrow is entirely too early," Evelyn said, fighting back tears of her own. "I can give you half a dozen good reasons why you shouldn't be so eager to rush back to school, but the truth is *I'm* not ready. I don't want to be selfish, or hold you back, but I'm not ready to hand you back to the world just yet. Monday will be soon enough."

Tom and Madison shared a look of agreement and Madison said, "Monday it is."

Tom suggested, "My understanding is there are distance learning options avail–"

Madison interrupted, "Oh no, no, no. Please no." She clasped her hands together, "I'm begging you, never again, please no."

Tom acceded, "Monday it is."

As they ate dessert, Tom spoke up again. "Your mom and I have been talking about this, and there's no casual way to bring it up so I'll just ask you. What really happened at the fair last Saturday night?"

Madison knew the question was coming. Maybe not now, but she knew she'd eventually have to tell her parents. How they were going to respond was anybody's guess, but she was determined to tell them the truth. Silently, she said a quick prayer to ask God to be with her.

"Brad and Kenny wanted to go on that stupid ride. Trish and I said no way. So, they went on the ride by themselves. Trish and I went to look at the Home Arts exhibit. Then this girl we know, Hannah, ran up to us and said Kenny had an accident."

Madison wiped her tears with a napkin.

"Mom, Dad, there's no doubt at all. Kenny was dead. I didn't see him fall, but I saw the result. I prayed. I begged God to heal him. God answered my prayer."

Tom and Evelyn exchanged a look. Tom asked, "Are you sure, Maddie?"

"I'm absolutely certain," Madison replied. Unintentionally or not, they gave her an out. She could say she wasn't certain, or that she was so emotional it was difficult to really know for sure. Madison knew if she exhibited any uncertainty, they would hold onto it. They would use that as an excuse to deny that God was involved.

Evelyn asked, "Was that the first time that…you know?"

Madison knew it was time to tell the whole truth. "Remember that summer we spent a week on Lake Michigan with Uncle Donnie and Grandma?"

"Yes. That was a lot of fun," Evelyn reminisced. "You were ten that summer."

"Do you remember the lady on the beach?" Madison asked.

"I do! She was frantic," Evelyn recalled. "Her little granddaughter wandered away and got lost. You found her Maddie. She'd lost her way in the brush and had fallen in a stream. You brought her back to her grandma."

Madison shook her head, "She didn't simply fall in, Mom. She drowned."

"Madison, I hope you're not making this up," Tom cautioned. He didn't raise his voice, but there was an edge to it.

Madison insisted, "I'm not making it up. That little girl wandered away, fell into a shallow stream, and drowned. I felt bad for the woman, and I wanted to do something for her. God told me the girl had died, but I could take her back alive to her grandma if I wanted. I remembered the Lord's Prayer. You know, the part where it says, 'Thy will be done'? I prayed and told God I wanted Him to save the girl. Then I said exactly what Jesus said. Not my will, but yours. And God let me take the girl back to her family."

"That's an extraordinary story, Maddie," her father said. "Why do you suppose God wants you to do this?"

"I've wondered about that for a long time," Madison replied. "I think He was building my confidence. He's prepared me for something."

Evelyn visibly flinched. "Prepared you for what, Maddie?"

Madison finished her last bite of pie and wiped her mouth. "He hasn't told me yet."

***

They'd only been gone for a couple of days, but Tom and Evelyn were grateful to be back in their own house, and back in their own bed. It gave them the sense of stability they sorely needed.

"What do you think, Tom?" Evelyn asked.

"I think I'd like to go down to the church and find out what in hell they're telling these kids."

"What do you mean?"

"Where do you think she got these crazy ideas?" Tom asked. "She heard them at church! Then she ran down to the library and grabbed a load of books on faith healing. You were worried, remember? I should have listened to you, Evie. I apologize."

"Do you think Maddie made that story up? About that girl drowning?"

"Of course," Tom replied. "What else? She took a dramatic story that we all remember and added an eerie twist. You don't think she actually found that kid dead and brought her back to life, do you?"

"Well…"

"Evie, c'mon. Look me in the eye and tell me you believe without a shadow of doubt that Kenny was dead, and Madison healed him."

Evelyn closed her eyes and took a deep breath. "I can't. Not one hundred percent."

"Exactly right," Tom affirmed.

"Then why is she claiming that she did? Why make up an elaborate lie about the girl drowning?" Evelyn countered.

Tom shook his head and one tear rolled down his cheek. "I don't know, Evie, but we're going to find out. I think we did a good job of raising our girl. What I mean is, I don't think she's deliberately lying."

Evelyn said, "I don't think so, either. What do you think is going on?"

Another tear that Tom brushed away. "I think we need to have her talk to someone, maybe a psychological professional. I want to know that she's mentally stable. If she's cleared, then we have her checked out medically. No brain cancer or tumor or something blocking blood to the brain…"

"Our daughter isn't crazy," Evelyn argued.

They went back and forth for hours and reached no conclusions. They fought and yelled, then cried and comforted one another. They tried in vain to believe that Madison was guided by divine influences, but they found it impossible to take that crucial, final leap of faith.

Instead, they considered the fearsome possibility that some organic disease might be gnawing away at their daughter's ability to discern reality from imagination, or that she might be caught in the grip of some madness.

Evelyn finally agreed that Madison should see medical professionals as soon as possible. Beyond that, they were at odds.

Evelyn wanted to believe what Madison told them. She didn't believe her daughter was lying. Her daughter behaved as she always had in all other respects, so she didn't believe Madison was suffering from some psychiatric affliction.

By contrast, Tom was almost hoping for some chemical imbalance in her brain, or some psychological malady. These were things that had a physical reality and could be managed through medicine or therapy.

He wanted to eliminate other possibilities before he'd allow himself to entertain the notion that Madison's prayers could raise the dead.

***

Madison heard them arguing. They'd get loud, then things would quiet down for a little while, then they'd get loud again. She couldn't quite hear what they were saying, but she knew what they were talking about.

She blamed herself for bringing such turmoil into the home. This was exactly why Madison had never spoken about the things God asked her to do. She never wanted to call attention to herself. When people suspected, they regarded her with suspicion and fear.

As Madison picked up belongings in her room and unpacked from the long weekend, she poured her heart out to God.

What she had told her parents was true. God hadn't told her what was next, but it was also true that He didn't have to. Madison clearly saw the direction the Lord was leading, and now the moment was upon her. Its arrival was swift and unexpected.

She knew she was being called to leave home. Where and how, she didn't know. Exactly when, she didn't know, much less how she would explain it to her mom and dad.

As she lay down to sleep, a thousand questions ran through her mind. How was she going to finish school? How could she broach the subject with her parents?

Madison didn't know how to bring herself to say the words, "I need to leave home," but she understood she couldn't keep delaying God's will indefinitely.

***

After Tom had gone to sleep, Evelyn found she was unable to rest. She went downstairs to pray, seeking God with her heart and her spirit. Praying for wisdom and understanding, she asked that God would always be there for her daughter even when she failed as a mother.

It was a mother's cry on behalf of her only child. Evelyn acknowledged that she wasn't equipped to help guide her daughter through what she was experiencing. How could she hope to counsel her daughter when Madison received direction from God himself?

At first, she was angry with God for usurping her role as a mother. She soon realized that it wasn't about her feelings, but about Madison and what was best for her.

Evelyn ceased praying. Her mind was unquiet, and her heart was not at rest. She examined herself to understand why.

"Lord, give me wisdom," she whispered, and wisdom came. Evelyn understood her prayers had been full of cries for God to meet her needs. Instead, her prayers should have asked God what He required of her.

She was reminded of what Madison had said at the dinner table. She described how she told God it was His will she wished to do, not hers. Evelyn began to pray again, and this time she sought God's will.

Evelyn didn't remember how long she stayed downstairs, but she woke in her own bed straight out of a vivid dream. In that dream she was having a conversation with someone about Madison. Evelyn never saw the person she was talking to, but she was reassured that Madison would be watched most carefully. As she woke, Evelyn remembered only three words.

Trust your daughter.

CHAPTER SIXTEEN

Madison rose later than usual, shrugged on a robe, and went downstairs to the kitchen. Her mom was awake and watched the news on a small portable television. Bacon was popping in a pan, and Evelyn was mixing up batter in a bowl.

"Good morning, Maddie. How are you doing?"

Madison poured herself a cup of coffee and added generous amounts of cream and sugar.

"Good morning, Mom. I'm good." Madison gasped, "Are those pancakes?"

"As a matter of fact, they are," her mom answered. "How many?"

"Three," Madison responded.

"Three pancakes coming up. Do you want a couple of eggs, too?"

"Absolutely! What's the occasion?"

"No occasion. Well, maybe nostalgia. Your dad left for work, and I started thinking of when you were in elementary school. I'd cook breakfast for you and dad. You and he would talk while I made your toast and eggs. You'd tell him everything you planned to do that day. Then you two would kiss me goodbye and he'd take you to school on his way to the office. Those are good memories."

After several minutes, Evelyn put a plate in front of her daughter.

"Thanks, Mom," Madison said.

Evelyn bent over to kiss the top of her head, "You're very welcome, Sweetie."

Evelyn joined her for breakfast at the table.

Madison crumbled a slice of bacon over her pancakes and dug in.

"This is so good. Thanks."

"It's good to see you have an appetite," Evelyn said.

"Have you ever known me to turn down a pancake?" Madison asked.

"True. I'll take this as a good sign," Evelyn responded.

The television demanded their attention as the news anchor said, "The attorney for the family of Kenny Warner issued a terse statement to the press this morning, saying, 'While the family understands the interest in their son's accident, they ask the public to respect their privacy at this time.' Viewers will remember Saturday's dramatic fair accident where it was originally believed the boy died of his injuries."

The station played the now famous clip of Madison kneeling next to the body. Evelyn snatched anxious glances of Madison as they watched the coverage.

The anchor narrated over the clip, "Controversy still rages over whether Kenny Warner actually died that night, or if he'd been knocked unconscious, only to later be revived. Meanwhile, other than a brief press conference this past Sunday, no information has come from the family of the girl said to have prayed him back from the dead."

The co-anchor said, "That's quite a story, Craig. I still get the willies every time I see that video."

"It is quite a story indeed. It almost makes a believer out of me. Next up, an–"

Evelyn clicked the TV off, "I'm sorry you had to see that, Maddie."

Madison said, "It's okay, Mom. I promise. I've made my peace with it."

"Have you heard from Kenny?" her mom asked.

"No, I haven't. Trish said no one's heard from him," Madison replied.

Evelyn nearly cursed when her phone rang. She and Maddie were talking and, for once, her daughter didn't seem reluctant to open up. Evelyn hoped she would be willing to talk frankly about what happened at the fair. She no longer felt resistant to hearing what her daughter had to say.

Evelyn's phone rang a second time, and she answered before it stopped. "Hey, Tom."

"Evie, I have only a few minutes. Morris is going to be there around eleven. He said he has a deal from one of the networks for an exclusive interview with Madison. Listen to what he has to say, and if it doesn't sound like a good idea to you, then tell him no. Madison is our first priority."

"Okay. If Madison doesn't want to do it, I won't try to talk her into it," Evelyn explained.

"Right there with you, Evie. I totally agree," Tom said.

"Good. About last night…sorry I got a little intense."

"Don't think twice about it. I'm sorry for being pigheaded," Tom apologized.

"Oh, Honey, I always forgive you for that," Evelyn laughed.

"Ouch," Tom said, but he laughed, too.

"I better go if Morris is going to be here at eleven. Maddie and I lingered over breakfast chatting."

"Nice. I hope I didn't interrupt you two," Tom said.

"You did. I haven't decided yet if I'll forgive you. Gotta run." Evelyn clicked off.

Madison immediately asked, "If Madison doesn't want to do what?"

"I don't know anything except Morris has something going on with a network television interview. He'll be here in an hour, and you can ask him all the questions you want."

***

Morris Abbott sat with Evelyn and Madison in the Newman's living room. He jumped right in. "I was contacted directly by Sharon Sterling."

Evelyn raised her eyebrows. "Sharon Sterling from *Morning Review*?"

"The one and only. The anchor of America's number one weekday morning show." Morris turned to Madison. "She is very eager to interview you."

"Sharon Sterling wants to interview *me*?" Madison watched her show every morning while she was getting ready for school. She'd never known a host other than Sterling.

"Madison, everybody wants to interview you. From 60 Minutes, to Kelly Ripa, to the guy running the classic rock station on the outskirts of town. People are fascinated by your story. Doing an interview would give you the opportunity to tell what really happened."

"Do you think they'll be fair?" Madison asked.

"I think so, but I can't promise," Morris replied. "I do know one thing. Right now, everybody else is talking about you, and they don't know anything except for what they see on the news and on the Internet. This will be your chance to change the narrative and give people an opportunity to hear what happened from your own lips."

"What exactly do they want?" Evelyn asked.

"Sharon Sterling doesn't want to do the interview live. If you agree, the network will send a jet Friday morning and take the three of you to New York. There you'll get a suite at a five-star hotel for the weekend. When you're settled in, a limo will take you to the station and they'll start the interview. Ms. Sterling said the process will take about a day."

"What? Why so long?" Evelyn asked.

Morris explained, "The final interview won't be that long. They'll edit the tapes down to an hour and air it a week from Friday as a Special Report."

"Do you hear that, Mom? I get my own TV special! Red Carpet, here I come."

Evelyn laughed, "Don't rehearse your Emmy speech just yet. Let's get past the interview first."

"Of course, that's *if* you decide to do the interview," Morris reminded.

"Are there any reasons we wouldn't want to?" Evelyn asked.

Morris shrugged, "I'm no media expert. I'm just a humble lawyer."

"You're a miracle worker to us," Evelyn said.

"Thanks, Evie." Morris pointed to Madison. "There's the real miracle worker. In fact, the Internet is hotly debating that issue even as we speak. An interview may stir the pot and generate even more acrimony between the various groups."

"Why is that? Wouldn't my statement clear things up for them?" Madison asked.

"You'd think so, but it won't," Morris answered. "The reasons are rather complex and worthy of a paper examining the sociological reasons behind *why* it won't. Keep that in mind when you attend college.

"While the majority of American families identify as Christian, very few practice their faith or even attend church regularly. In fact, many of them can't tell you the basic tenets of their religion. Yet, if you do something to offend their sense of religious propriety, it sparks moral outrage. You can see this now from personal experience. They turn on you, vilify you, and denounce you in the harshest terms possible, even when such behavior is proscribed by the very Bible they claim to believe."

"Are you saying it would be better if Madison didn't do the interview?" Evelyn asked.

"Not at all. I'm merely pointing out that an interview probably won't make the controversy disappear."

Evelyn turned toward her daughter. "It looks like there's no easy answer here. What do you think?"

"I think I've let people talk about me long enough. Now it's my turn to talk. With Ms. Sterling doing the interview, maybe more people will be willing to listen," Madison said.

"Maybe so," Morris said. "I don't want you to be disappointed if it doesn't work out the way you want."

"It'll be fine," Madison assured him.

"How can you be so sure?" Morris asked.

"Because it will work out the way God wants," she replied.

"You can't argue with that," Evelyn said with a smile.

"With that, ladies, I'll run back to my office and make the final arrangements." He cast a quick glance at Maddie and asked, "You're sure?"

Madison looked at her mom.

"It's your decision, Maddie."

Maddie nodded decisively. "Let's do this."

"Great. I'll be in touch with Ms. Sterling and touch bases if there are any surprises."

Morris draped his coat over his arm and grabbed his briefcase. "Evie, is it okay if I have a few words with Maddie in private?"

"Sure," Evelyn replied.

They stopped by his car, and he placed his coat and briefcase on the backseat. The wind had picked up from the northeast, and clouds, dark and thick, had begun to sail in on the breeze.

"Let's take a walk," Morris suggested.

They walked in silence. When they reached the end of the block, Madison said, "Mr. Abbott! That guy took our picture." She pointed to a silver Honda at the corner.

Morris nodded to the guy in the driver's seat and got a nod in reply.

"Do you know him?" Madison asked.

"I don't know him personally, but I know of him. He takes photos or videos of news events and shops them around to the stations or to the local paper. In a little while, someone's going to call my office saying I was seen with Madison Newman, and they'll want to know if your family is planning a legal action, or if there's been a development of some sort. They're looking for a story, and right now you're the biggest story around."

"But he took our picture. Is that legal? Didn't he violate our privacy?" Madison was indignant.

Morris chuckled and shook his head. "Privacy? We're outside, walking down a public street. A court would rule that, here and now, we have no reasonable expectation of privacy. The same is true if we were eating at McDonald's or walking through a mall."

"I didn't know that." Madison felt her jaw clenching.

"That's one of the reasons I wanted you to come with me. I wanted you to see. There's probably someone else at the other end of the street for all I know." Morris explained, "I want you to be prepared for the public's intense interest in you."

"What do I need to be prepared for?" Madison asked.

"Keep your eyes open. If you don't want to answer questions, tell them no. You don't have to go out of your way to be nice, but don't be rude. It's not a good idea to make an enemy of the press. During Friday's interview, or any interview for that matter, don't let them browbeat you or get you to backtrack. They'll come up with hypothetical questions designed to trip you up. Stick to God's truth and you won't go wrong," Morris replied.

"I promise, Mr. Abbott. Why are you telling me this?"

"You won't always be with your parents. You might be out with friends, or out shopping. I don't want you to be caught unaware. If you're unsure what to do, ask God for wisdom. God is an ever-present help in trouble."

"I appreciate your advice, Mr. Abbott," Madison said. "Were you worried about scaring Mom? Is that why you wanted to tell me in private?"

"What? No, nothing like that. Your mom is one tough cookie," Morris said. "No, I wanted to ask you to go easy on your mom and dad."

"What do you mean?" Madison asked.

"It's going to take them a while to adjust to this. Please be patient with them. I'm pretty sure your mom is close to believing, but I think it's going to take longer for your dad," Morris said. "He absolutely adores you, and I think this has been hardest for him."

"Wait a minute." Madison stopped and looked up at the man. "You actually believe me, don't you?"

"Absolutely." Morris did not hesitate. "From the moment I saw the news broadcast, I knew it was true. I saw you pray, and I saw the mercy of Jesus Christ. Nothing I've seen since then makes me want to change my mind."

"I think you're the one person who hasn't asked me what really happened. Why is that?" Madison asked.

"You know," Morris replied, "I think the Apostle Paul is my favorite of the apostles. In one letter he wrote, '...my speech and my preaching were not with persuasive words of human wisdom, but in demonstration of the Spirit and of power, that your faith should not be in the wisdom of men but in the power of God.'"

Morris continued to walk, and Madison kept up with him. "I don't have to ask you what happened. You have already demonstrated it in the Spirit. I saw the power of the almighty God. If I asked you questions, it would be only my flesh trying to understand it intellectually. The things of God can only be understood if you are in the spirit of God."

Madison smiled, relieved. "You really do understand and believe."

"Yes," Morris replied. "One last warning since we're talking about things of the spirit. You've invited a powerful enemy by publicly proclaiming Jesus Christ. Satan will use everything he has to attack you. He'll even use the things you least expect. He'll make you doubt your faith to turn you away from God."

The two completed circling the block. It started to sprinkle, and the clouds now nearly obscured the afternoon sky. Morris opened his car door.

"Be careful, Madison. Say good-bye to your mom for me."

"Will do, Mr. Abbott." She didn't wait to watch him drive away. Madison had taken their conversation seriously and didn't want to expose herself unnecessarily. Suddenly self-conscious, she went inside the house.

Madison was immediately met by her mom. "Can you believe it? You're going to New York to be interviewed by Sharon Sterling!"

"Is dad okay with it?" Madison asked.

"He said if it looked like a good idea, then go for it."

"Then I guess we're going to New York!" Madison hugged her mother.

***

Madison planned to spend the dreary afternoon in her room. She certainly didn't feel like going out. Trisha was still at school. As tempting as it was to text Kenny, she knew better than to pick at that scab not yet healed.

After a while, her mom knocked and opened her door. She seemed very happy. "Maddie? You have a visitor."

"What? Who is it?" she asked. She couldn't imagine who'd come to the house to visit unless it was Trish.

Her mom called downstairs, "Come on up!"

Now Madison was very curious. Who would her mom invite up to her room?

She heard the footsteps climbing the stairs and a friendly face appeared at her door.

"Frankie!" Madison shrieked. She jumped off her bed and threw her arms around him.

Frankie was a little embarrassed to be hugging her in front of her mom.

"It's good to see you Frankie," Evelyn said. As she backed out of the room she said, "You kids have a good visit."

"I can't believe you're here!" Madison said.

"Yeah. Me neither," Frankie said. "Sorry it's been so long."

Madison drank in the sight of her friend, the one she once thought of as a brother. It *had* been a long time. Over two years. Sure, she saw him at school, but they'd stopped hanging out as they used to long ago.

Frankie had brought his backpack, and he reached into it now and gave Madison a card. "Happy birthday," he said. "Sorry I didn't make it to your party."

"Thank you, Frankie," Madison said, taking the card. "You didn't have to get me anything. I'm just happy to see you."

"It's good to see you too, Maddie."

"What made you decide to come and see me?" she asked.

"I was home from school, and I saw you walking outside with that man. I figured if you were out walking around then it was probably okay to come and see you. I've wanted to come for a while."

"Why didn't you? We used to hang out all the time, Frankie. Then after a while you stopped." Madison began to tear up. "I used to call you. Remember? I asked if you wanted to do something, and you never had the time. Why did you stop wanting to see me?"

"You were my best friend, Maddie. We did everything together. Then you brought Buddy back to life. I am so grateful to you for that, but it was like there was a whole hidden part of your life I never knew about. It was scary, Maddie."

"I did tell you," Madison insisted. "You're the only person I ever told. I never even told my parents. Not even Trish knows everything. I never intended to tell anyone."

"Now everyone knows," Frankie said. "It's everywhere on the Internet and on TV."

"Yeah," Madison agreed, nodding.

"That's why I came," Frankie said. "Everybody's talking about you. They post ugly things online, and the news talks smack about you. I'm sorry that I wasted so much time feeling scared just because there was something peculiar about you."

Frankie was crying now, and it was breaking Madison's heart.

"If I'd been a real friend," Frankie continued, "I would have thought about how you might need someone who had your back. That person should have been me, and I failed you."

Madison went to her friend now and held him. As Frankie cried, his big frame shook as he clung to her.

"I'm sorry, Maddie. Can you forgive me?"

"Of course, I forgive you," Madison whispered. "Stop crying, Frankie. Don't blame yourself for something that's not your fault."

Madison grabbed some tissues and patted away his tears, ignoring her own in order to comfort her friend.

After a few moments they composed themselves. Madison was thrilled to see her friend again, and desperately wanted to lighten the mood.

"Hey, do you want to go down and get some ice cream?" Madison asked.

"No, I have to get back home. I'm sick. At least, that's what I told mom so I could stay home. She was glad I wanted to see you, so she let me come, but she said not to stay long."

"You're not going to leave already, are you?" asked a dismayed Madison.

"Not yet," Frankie said. He turned to look out the open door into the hallway. "Have you talked to Kenny?"

Madison was unprepared for the question. She saw from Frankie's face that it hurt him to ask. "I haven't spoken to him at all since…"

Frankie nodded his understanding.

"Kenny called me last night," he said.

"What?!" Madison leaned forward and grabbed Frankie's arm. "Why? What did he say?"

"He asked if I was still friends with you. He wanted me to tell you something."

Madison could barely breathe. "What?"

"He said now he understands what you tried to tell him about Jesus. He said thank you. He'll never forget you and prays for you every day."

Madison was bawling now, and it was Frankie's turn to get her a tissue. "I'm sorry, Maddie. I didn't mean to make you sad. I thought you'd want to know."

She smiled through her tears. "I'm not sad. Really, that's perfect. Did he say anything else?"

"I didn't really understand the rest of it. He said Jesus showed him the lives you'd touch, and he couldn't be a part of that. I didn't understand what he meant. I was going to ask, but his dad came in and started yelling at him for being on the phone. Then he disconnected."

Madison sighed and wiped her tears. "Thanks, Frankie."

"I didn't get to talk to him a lot, Maddie. I can tell you this, he was really into you. I don't think he wanted to hurt your feelings. It sounded like he was afraid of something."

There was no point in asking any more questions. Madison knew everything she needed to know. Kenny knew Jesus.

It was an absolutely amazing day! She was reunited with her friend, and she learned that Kenny was now a saved Christian.

"Hey," Madison teased. "Are you sure you want to pass on that ice cream?"

***

When her dad came home, she and her mother overwhelmed him with the news that they were going to New York, but Tom had the last laugh. He'd stopped by Morris' office on the way home and picked up a folder with all the information they needed. He had their itinerary, hotel reservations, and even where to go at the airport to board the network's private jet.

They discussed everything they'd like to do while in New York, but soon realized they'd have to stay a few extra days to get it all in. Madison didn't want to miss anything during her trip, but she also intended to be back to school on Monday. She'd already been gone too long.

After dinner, when she'd finished the dishes, Madison went up to her room and laid out some clothes, trying to figure out what to pack. She wasn't going to be gone for long, but she wanted some choices.

Madison checked her phone for the time. It wasn't yet ten. She called Trisha and shared everything she knew about going to New York. Trisha was excited to hear about her friend's trip, especially when she learned that Madison was going to be interviewed by Sharon Sterling.

There was a knock at Madison's bedroom door. Soft. Tentative. Then the door opened. Madison looked at her mother and saw she was upset about something.

"Mom, what's up? Is everything okay?"

"Maddie, can you come downstairs?"

"Okay."

Evelyn turned and headed for the stairs. Madison rushed to follow.

Her dad was sitting on the couch and was watching the evening news. The station ran a story on Madison, and he wanted his daughter's reaction. Tom paused the newscast and backed it up to the beginning of the story.

"Dad? Is everything all right?" She could plainly see he was displeased. His posture was rigid, and he clenched his jaw. Madison was shocked to see her father had been crying.

"Maddie. Come and sit down."

Her dad pressed play.

The anchor in the newsroom smiled into the camera and said, "The world has been following the remarkable story of the accident that occurred last Saturday night in Oracle, Illinois, where a local high school track star was believed to have died following an accident on a ride at their annual Harvest Fair."

Again, the station played the instantly recognizable clip of Madison praying for Kenny.

"Controversy centers around this young woman," they showed a tight close-up of Madison's face from when the police walked her to their car, "who prayed for, and apparently completely healed, the accident victim. Many people who witnessed the Harvest Fair Miracle, as it's being called, agree the victim died at the scene, and was subsequently brought back to life by this girl, Madison Newman. Others, most notably Bishop Marcus Wright, denounced Saturday's 'Faith Healing' as, at best, a cruel hoax."

Madison looked at her mom, then her dad. They had heard all this before, but they were still watching. She turned her attention to the screen once more.

"It now seems last Saturday's spectacular healing wasn't the first time that Madison Newman used the power of prayer to save a life."

They cut away from the reporter and showed a video of a black woman in her late sixties playing with her grandchildren, a teenage boy and a younger girl, in the backyard of a private residence. She appeared fit and active, sporting sweatpants and an official Detroit Tigers sweatshirt.

A male reporter did the voiceover while the camera remained on the woman and the kids. "Two years ago, Andrea Parker lay in a hospital bed at the Auburn Hill Convalescent Care Center in Grand Rapids, Michigan. After suffering a broken hip from a fall, and having to undergo dialysis three times a week, she was, in her own words…"

The scene switched to a living room with Andrea Parker sitting on a sofa. She said, "I was waiting to die."

Another quick cut to a physician's office, with a reporter introducing Mrs. Parker's doctor. "This is Doctor Calvin Isaacs, Andrea Parker's former Nephrologist. Doctor Isaacs, how long was Mrs. Parker your patient?"

"Mrs. Parker was under my care for approximately two and a half years. She was referred to me by her primary care physician after receiving laboratory results that indicated serious problems with Mrs. Parker's kidney function."

"Dr. Isaacs, what happened then?"

"Mrs. Parker's kidney function rapidly deteriorated to the point where it was necessary to begin hemodialysis. Shortly thereafter, she experienced renal failure and was completely dependent on dialysis. Due to mobility issues and other health concerns, she was admitted to the care facility in Auburn Hill."

The scene cut back to the living room, where a reporter was talking to Andrea.

Madison was happy to see Mrs. Parker in what must be her son's living room. Andrea looked healthy and beautiful. Madison said a quiet prayer of thanks.

"What was the turning point for you, Mrs. Parker?" the reporter asked.

"I was lying in the dark. I'd just finished my treatment and was trying to not feel so sick and exhausted. Then this little blonde girl came into my room and struck up a conversation. I asked her name, and she told me she was Madison Newman. Sweet little thing. She had a lot of questions."

The reporter asked, "Can you tell our audience what she told you?"

"She came over to the side of the bed and she took my hand. She told me about Jesus Christ. She said that my time on earth was not yet over, and that I needed to be a holy influence in my grandchildren's lives. I still remember the words she used. She said, 'By the grace of our Lord Jesus, you are healed.'"

"Did you feel any different?" the reporter asked.

Andrea said, "I didn't feel as tired. In fact, I was feeling pretty good. The nurse on duty even commented that I was looking perky. The next day they took my blood for lab work, and there was all sorts of commotion when they got the results. Doctor Isaacs couldn't believe it. He said he'd never seen anything like it, but my kidneys were fully functional, and I no longer needed dialysis."

The reporter prompted Mrs. Parker with the question, "But that wasn't the end of it, was it?"

"Praise God, no," Mrs. Parker said. "I discovered my hip was completely healed. They did an x-ray and compared it to the one they took when I broke my hip. They couldn't even find where the fracture had been on the new x-ray. Our God is a mighty God indeed. They rolled me into that place in a wheelchair, and I walked out on my own two feet."

They cut back to the office of Doctor Isaacs where he said, "We conducted a battery of tests and they all pointed to the same conclusion. Mrs. Parker's kidneys were completely healthy and functional. This was something wholly beyond my experience."

"How do you account for the spontaneous return of Mrs. Parker's kidney function?" the reporter asked.

"There's really only one word for it," Doctor Isaacs said. "It's a miracle."

Back at Mrs. Parker's son's house, the reporter asked, "Can you tell us why you contacted the station, Mrs. Parker?"

"I was watching the news last Sunday after church, and I saw what happened to that poor boy at the fair.

Then I saw Madison go and pray for him. I shouted to my son, Bradley, and he came into the living room to see what I wanted. I pointed. 'There,' I said. 'That's the girl who prayed for me.' She's older now, but there's no doubt about it."

Then Andrea looked into the camera and said, "Thank you, Madison Newman. I pray for you every night. May God bless you for what you did for me and my family."

They cut back to the newsroom where the anchor said, "There you have it; corroborating testimony from another individual who was apparently healed by the power of prayer. It's a surprising addition to an already astounding story. For me, this unexpected new revelation tips the scales in favor of Miracle Madison being the real deal. What do you think? You can take our Instapoll online, or on our 800 number, both of which are on the bottom of your screen."

Tom turned the television off and turned toward his daughter. "Can you tell me what happened here?"

Evelyn watched from the kitchen entrance, praying.

Madison wasn't sure what her dad was asking. "That was when we went to visit grandma. Before..." Madison caught herself too late. She felt bad mentioning her grandma's death in the light of this miraculous healing.

Tom finished the sentence for her, "Before she died. Right? Isn't that what you were going to say?"

Evelyn said, "Tom, why–"

"Not now, Evelyn," Tom snapped.

Madison was scared. Why was her father acting like this?

Tom turned back to Madison and demanded, "Before she died. Right?"

Madison's eyes pooled with tears. She looked down and nodded.

"I didn't want to believe it was true, that you healed Kenny. Because if *that* was true, then that means you could have saved your grandmother. You certainly wouldn't have walked away and let her die. *Would you*, Madison?" Tom barked out the last three words as an accusation.

His words were like a blow. "Dad, please understand, it's–"

Tom's blast of anger drowned out her explanation as he shouted, "Imagine how I felt when I learned that my daughter healed a total stranger and let my mother die!"

"Tom! Stop it," Evelyn screamed.

Tom wouldn't stop it. Where this anger came from, he didn't know. But it felt good. All his shame for his imagined failures as a son, all his self-recrimination, all his guilt for not doing more for his mother was being burned away in the crucible of his rage, and he poured it all out on the daughter he mistakenly believed should have saved her.

Satan delighted in it.

Madison stood up quickly. "Dad, I don't choose! It's not up to me. I prayed and I cried when Grandma died. I pleaded, but it wasn't God's will to keep her on this earth. He brought her to glory. It wasn't a punishment. It was a blessing!"

"No excuses!" Tom snarled, backhanding her. Madison fell backwards over the coffee table, shouting in pain and fear.

Evelyn screamed and ran to her husband, pulling on him, hoping to stop him. He tried wrestling her off, but she wouldn't be stopped. Screaming, she pounded on him with her fists, distracting him as Madison scrambled away and ran upstairs.

***

With the broadcast of the story of Andrea Parker's healing, several different news vans had already showed up at the Newman home. They parked on the street, waiting for an interesting scoop following the revelation that Saturday's Harvest Fair Miracle wasn't the first time Madison had healed someone.

They heard the fight going on inside the Newman house but were content to let things ride until they heard crashing glass and screaming. That's when they decided to call the police.

The police were minutes away. When the officer heard the address, he groaned, knowing he'd be on camera while dealing with a domestic disturbance call. This was going to require a large measure of diplomacy.

***

Madison stood in her bathroom tasting blood. The blow her father delivered had split her lip, and her right cheek was red. By the look of it in the mirror, it would turn into a bruise. She touched her lip gingerly with a trembling hand and winced.

She washed her face, careful to avoid her lip. Madison knew her father loved her. She remembered Morris Abbott's warning, that Satan would be fighting, and fighting hard.

Tears welled up in Madison's eyes as she realized she had to leave. The Holy Spirit had been leading her in that direction, but she hadn't wanted to believe it would be so soon.

She emptied her school backpack and filled it with clothes, shoes, makeup, and personal care accessories. She sent a text to Trisha.

Not going to ny after all. pray 4 me. ttyl

While packing her charging cord, she realized she couldn't take her phone. Her phone would give her away. She could be tracked everywhere she went.

Madison texted Trisha one last time, sending the selfie Kenny had taken of them on her birthday. She included a quick message: *keep this for me.*

She factory wiped her phone and then finished packing.

Madison moved carefully down the stairs with her backpack. She saw flashing lights through the rain speckled windows and through the kaleidoscope of her tears. Her parents were in the kitchen talking to someone. The voice was unfamiliar.

She was confused for a minute but then realized it was the police. They must have been called because of the disturbance when her father had been shouting and hit her. She was grateful for the distraction. At least her mom and dad were occupied and wouldn't immediately become aware of her absence.

Madison slipped around the corner and tiptoed down the hall toward the backdoor. Peering out the window into the darkness, she looked for signs of movement. She'd seen enough cop shows to know the police always stake out the backyard just in case the perp wants to take it on the lam.

Apparently, this group missed the memo. The backyard was clear.

Madison carefully eased the door open and stepped out into the darkness. She stood on the back porch waiting for her eyes to adjust to the dark, but she was eager to leave, afraid to linger in case her parents discovered she wasn't in the house.

Scanning the sky, she was grateful there were no lights from news drones. All the action was happening in the front of the house, so that's where their attention was.

Police drones? That was another story. They ran in stealth mode. They also had night vision capabilities and infrared. If they sent a police drone to look for her, there would be no escaping detection. She needed to get some distance from the house before someone noticed her absence.

Madison whispered softly, "It is God who arms me with strength and keeps my way secure. He makes my feet like the feet of a deer; he causes me to stand on the heights."

Running across the yard, she easily pulled herself over the low fence into the neighbor's backyard. Madison ran across their yard and along the side of the house until she came out to their front yard and into the street.

The rain was now just a sprinkle, but she was glad she'd put on a sweatshirt and a jacket. It wasn't too cold now, but it soon would be. She pulled a knit beanie over her head and jogged north through the neighborhood. Even though it was late, she kept her eyes open for anyone who might see her.

Where she traveled, she did not know…but she did not travel alone.

CHAPTER SEVENTEEN

Madison stopped her headlong flight to catch her breath. She stopped to rest under the shelter of a tree, where she was less likely to be seen in the shadows. Under the boughs she was sheltered from the drizzle. It was half past eleven, and most of the houses were dark, their occupants having turned in for the night.

She walked north to the next street and then turned east. Her neighborhood had no sidewalks, and in the dark it was easier to walk in the road. It was safer, too, but it left her visible to anyone who happened to turn down the street. Madison wanted to pass unnoticed.

Three more blocks to the east and then she turned north. Another half mile north would bring her to the woods. Five more minutes and then she'd be safe. She'd be able to slow down and think.

As kids, she and Frankie had spent countless hours exploring that small patch of wilderness. It wasn't more than three miles wide and two deep, neither was it densely wooded. She knew every square yard of path and hiding place. No one would find her.

Her plan was to work her way to the northern edge of the woods. There, across a small road, was a failed industrial park. These abandoned warehouses and manufacturing facilities would shield her from being seen. They also had the advantage of being close to State Route Three, where she hoped to catch a ride out of town.

Madison soon reached the northernmost edge of her neighborhood. There were no more homes past this last, seldom-used road. Her attention was drawn to the sound of an engine. Glancing to the far end of the road, a truck rounded a corner and headed her way. Madison ran into the trees and ducked behind a large shrub as the truck eased down the street, headlights shining on the wet pavement.

The camper passed without slowing, and Madison said a prayer of thanks.

Where she once felt safe, she now felt exposed. She couldn't explain the sense of urgency she felt; she only knew she needed to move. Madison headed north, and she picked her way through the dark.

***

Chuck Carson had been half listening to the police scanner when a call came in for a domestic disturbance. He almost didn't hear the call on the scanner until they mentioned the address. It was Madison's house.

Ordinarily he'd drive into her neighborhood from the main road, but tonight there would be police. Maybe they'd send a couple of cars in case backup was needed. You never knew how those domestic quarrels were going to go. Chuck could personally testify to how quickly a small disagreement could blow up in your face.

This meant it would be unwise to drive straight into the neighborhood and drive past the house. It was likely there'd be a news team or two hoping for a story. A big camper squeezing past the news vans and police cars would surely draw attention, and a set of Florida plates in Illinois would raise eyebrows.

Chuck drove up the main street toward the northern end of town. There was a road near the woods that would take him into her neighborhood. He pulled onto the old road and turned right.

For the briefest moment he thought he saw someone crossing the road into the woods. It was hard to tell. It was dark, and his windshield was speckled with raindrops. He flipped his wipers on, but when the window cleared, he saw nothing.

Three blocks from Madison's house, Chuck parked and walked the rest of the way.

He was glad he had thought it through. There were news vans on the side of the street and a police car in the driveway. He had reservations about walking up to where the action was taking place, but curiosity won out. Chuck figured he might learn something useful.

Chuck approached a neighbor standing in the street across from Madison's house.

"That's a real shame," Chuck observed.

The neighbor agreed, "Yep."

Chuck simply acted like he was from the neighborhood as he nodded and observed, "Haven't those poor people been through enough already?"

The man shook his head. "Everyone has arguments, but I've never heard anything like that before. I thought someone was going to get killed."

Chuck said, "My wife and I try not to fight in front of the kids. There's no reason to make them suffer for our problems."

"True," the neighbor agreed. "In this case, though, I think he was yelling at Madison. Then Evelyn started screaming at Tom. They're a great family. It's hard to see them go through this."

Chuck pulled his collar up around his neck against the drizzle, which was starting to fall heavier. "I'll remember to keep them in prayer." He looked skyward. "I hoped this rain was over for the night. I'd better get home before I get soaked."

"Yeah, I should get in, too," the man said. "Have a good night."

"You too," Chuck said as he waved good-bye. He hunched over, stuck his hands in his pockets as though preparing to leave. He'd learned far more than he hoped.

Chuck had seen enough in the last couple of months to know that Madison's home life was perfect compared to his when he'd been her age.

Apparently, things had blown up big time at the Newman household. It was considerably worse when he was a kid. His stepfather didn't hesitate to use his fists, and his temper was easily triggered when he'd been drinking.

A small seed of an idea took root in Chuck's mind. When things blow up at home, your first instinct is to get out.

Madison had run.

Chuck laughed aloud. What a crazy idea! Yet somehow it wouldn't let him go.

That caused Chuck to start thinking. What would it take for Madison to want to leave home? By any standard, she lived a privileged life. She had two parents who had a solid marriage. If not wealthy, they were at least well-off and wanted for nothing. What would make her want to walk away from that?

Maybe she and her boyfriend were plotting to run away together, and somehow her parents found out. Then there was a fight, and someone called the police. It was probably the news people. They'd do anything for a story.

Chuck took a good look at Madison's house. The lights were on in the living room. No doubt mom and pop were talking to the police right this very minute. It looked like the kitchen lights were on, but at this angle it was hard to be sure.

Then Chuck looked at the windows on the second floor. The lights in Madison's room were off. From his many weeks of monitoring her movements, he knew her lights were almost *never* off. She only turned off the lights when she was gone. It was a feeble theory, but Chuck couldn't shake the idea that he was right, and that Madison had run away.

Maybe he hadn't been seeing things after all. Could that have been Madison he'd seen disappearing into the night?

Chuck hurried back to his truck, his mind already assessing the possibilities.

***

Madison admitted to herself she'd made a mistake. The woods might be fun at dusk, but it was an entirely different experience in the dark of night, when the black clouds overhead prevented even the moon from shining a little light. She was on one of the main paths through the trees. Even so, she could hardly see her hand in front of her face, and the going was slow.

As she walked, she prayed, and God spoke to her about her father. Madison was hurt, yet she could find no anger in her heart against her dad. It wasn't about him. Her father had been a weapon used against her.

"Lord, You are my rock and my fortress. For the sake of Your name, lead and guide me," Madison prayed.

It began to sprinkle again, and Madison pulled the collar of her jacket close. She stumbled and startled something in the dark. Something big.

Madison screamed and took a step backwards, tripping on an exposed root that sent her sprawling on her back into the damp grass. Her fall was broken by her backpack, but the impact knocked the wind out of her.

She lay where she fell, crying. Her lip and the side of her face ached where her father had struck her. God wanted her in the world to do His work, but she didn't know where she was supposed to go, or how she was supposed to get there.

She was just a sixteen-year-old girl, cold and afraid. Her tears mixed with rain as she longed to be home with her parents, but she was resolute as she said a last good-bye to the life she knew.

"Help me, Lord," Madison prayed. "What You want I can't do by myself. I need You."

It reminded her of a worship song, and Madison began to sing aloud. With praise for Jesus on her lips, she felt renewed. In the dark, and in the rain, Madison stood up and brushed herself off, physically as well as spiritually. She adjusted her backpack and resumed her northward march.

"Thank you, Lord," she prayed. "Thank You for Your encouragement. You are a mighty God, and You are with me. If I fall, You will catch me. If I am beset by my enemy, Your angels will defend me."

Madison walked through the darkness with confidence, never faltering. She was keenly aware of the Holy Spirit with her. When she came to the deeper portion of the woods, her confidence didn't wane. As she walked, she listened and learned.

***

After Tom had struck Madison and she'd run up the stairs to her room, Evelyn kept holding on to him from behind, hitting him with her fists. He turned on her with a vicious snarl, but Evelyn stood her ground.

Then Tom stopped, and his countenance changed from anger to bewilderment. When he realized where he'd allowed his anger to take him, he cried out, "Dear heaven, Evie. What have I done?"

Tom fell to his knees and covered his face with his hands. "Lord God," he implored, "forgive me."

Evelyn was torn. She wanted to hate him. At this moment she could walk out the door and never see him again. But she saw the look on his face and knew he was horrified at what he'd done. Evelyn knew well the husband and father he truly was, and it wasn't the man she witnessed a few minutes ago.

"Thomas Newman, what in the world is wrong with you?" Evelyn demanded. "How dare you hit our daughter!"

She wanted to slap him. She wanted him to hurt as much as she was hurting.

The doorbell rang, distracting her momentarily.

"Who could that be?" Tom asked.

His answer came immediately when the doorbell rang a second time, and a man announced, "Police."

The officer rapped on the glass panel in the door. "Mr. and Mrs. Newman? I'm Officer Driscoll. I'd like a word."

"I'd better answer the door," Tom said, standing up.

"No," Evelyn insisted. "Go clean yourself up. I'll answer the door," she said, pushing him toward the guest bathroom. "Wash your face. Tuck in your shirt."

Tom left for the bathroom. After a moment, Evelyn opened the front door.

"Good evening, Officer."

"Good evening, Ma'am. Are you Evelyn Newman?" the officer asked.

"I am. May I ask what this is about?" Evelyn asked.

"Yes, Mrs. Newman. Our dispatcher received a domestic disturbance call for this address. May I come in and ask you a few questions?"

"It's awfully late, Officer. As you probably know, my family has had a rough week. My husband and I are still trying to sort things out, and sometimes things get pretty heated."

"Yes, Ma'am. Still, I do need to speak to you and Mr. Newman so that my report is complete. I'd appreciate your cooperation."

Evelyn wasn't sure what she should do, but Tom came up behind her and said, "Good evening, Officer Driscoll. Listen, I'm sorry about the disturbance. This is so embarrassing. Why don't you come in and we'll answer your questions."

Tom took his lead from Evelyn. She hadn't answered the door to turn him over to the police. She admitted the argument readily and wanted to put the whole ugly thing behind her. He took great comfort in the idea that she didn't seem ready to give up on him just yet.

He ushered them into the kitchen, and they sat around the table.

"Can I get you anything, Officer? Coffee maybe?" Evelyn offered.

"No, thank you. You are Thomas and Evelyn Newman, and you reside at this address?"

Evelyn nodded while Tom said, "Yes."

"Does anyone else live here with you?" Driscoll asked.

"Our daughter, Madison," Tom replied.

"Where is she now?" the officer asked.

"She's upstairs. In her room," Tom answered.

Evelyn added, "She's probably asleep. We got back home only yesterday. This whole thing has really turned our lives upside down."

Officer Driscoll sympathized. "I imagine it would, Ma'am. Look you guys, I'm here to make sure you're okay. It seems one of the reporters out there called when they heard you two fighting. I'm married. I get it. Do you want to tell me what happened?"

Evelyn decided to go all in. "We were about to go to bed and he, my husband that is, announced that we are going to New York so that Madison can be interviewed on national television. He didn't even ask me."

She asked Officer Driscoll, "Me. Her own mother. I should have a say in where she goes and who she talks to, shouldn't I?"

This was only one of the reasons Driscoll hated domestic disturbance calls. One spouse always wanted to recruit him to advocate for their side.

"That's not for me to say, Ma'am. I'm here to keep the peace. We all have disagreements with our spouse. All I'm asking is to not disturb your neighbors with the arguments, and not to put hands on one another. Can I get an agreement on that?" Driscoll asked.

"Absolutely," Tom replied. "We're sorry for the disturbance."

"He's right, Officer. I'm mortified," Evelyn said.

It was the performance of a lifetime. Tom was forced to play the friendly dad, calmly cooperating with the officer's investigation.

Inside, he was in agony. He desperately needed to talk to Evelyn about what had happened. He had no idea how things had escalated to the point that he yelled at Madison and struck her. He prayed he'd have the opportunity to make it up to both of them, and he would need God to help him on the way.

Evelyn believed she might break any minute. Serious violence had been done in her house, and here she was, deliberately lying to the officer investigating the domestic disturbance call. If Officer Driscoll asked to talk to Madison, they could both go to jail.

As furious as she was with Tom, she didn't want her husband arrested. That man who'd acted out simply hadn't been Tom. Tom wasn't an abusive person. In fact, he rarely even got angry. It was completely unlike his ordinary behavior.

The thought chilled her. She looked over to her husband as he talked to Officer Driscoll. It *was* her husband. What had happened when he'd ordered her to bring Madison downstairs? What was going on when he lashed out at her? Had that truly been Tom then?

He hadn't acted like the Tom she knew.

Evelyn had been praying for her husband, and for her daughter. Now she prayed for understanding. She prayed she wouldn't let emotion get in the way of seeing the truth. Through her anger, and through her love, she saw that the man who lashed out at Madison had been her husband, but it hadn't been her husband alone.

He'd been pushed and tripped up by spirits of darkness who knew where he was weak. They used his hurt at losing his mother. They amplified the shame he had felt because his brother had been the one to care for their mother in her final months on earth. They fed his self-loathing because he never had the chance to tell his mother how sorry he was that he hadn't been there for her.

They managed to do substantial damage in a few brief moments.

She turned her attention back to Officer Driscoll who was saying, "I can't imagine what you're going through."

"My first priority is keeping my daughter safe," Evelyn asserted.

"As a parent, I understand completely. I know the public scrutiny of your daughter has been pretty severe at times, and I'm sure that's difficult to deal with," Driscoll sympathized.

"Thank you for understanding, Officer. We worry how it's going to affect her," Tom said.

When Officer Driscoll first knocked on their door, he seemed stern, and very much there in his official capacity. As they talked, he gradually softened and became more relatable. He began talking to them, if not as a friend, but as a close acquaintance.

"Are you sure I can't get you something? Coffee would be good on this wet and chilly night," Evelyn asked.

"It would, but I'd hate for you to go to the bother. There's a fresh pot waiting for me when I get back to the station and file my report," Driscoll said.

"Is there anything else you need, Officer?" Tom asked.

"No. I guess my business here is done as long as you two aren't going to go at each other when I leave. I'd hate to have to come out a second time tonight." He paused, letting the unspoken message sink in.

"There is one more thing, but this is more personal in nature," Driscoll said. "I have a buddy on the force who was at the fair last Saturday. He was one of the officers there when your daughter prayed for that boy. He said he felt the presence of God that night. Anyway, my sister, she lives in Chicago. She's pregnant and is having a rough go of it. The doctor told her she could lose the baby. I was wondering, could you ask your daughter to pray for my sister?"

"Of course, Officer." Evelyn got up from the kitchen table and rummaged through a drawer for a pen and a small note pad.

"What's her name?" Evelyn asked.

"Laurie. Laurie Driscoll," the officer replied. "She's not married, and her boyfriend...well, I want my sister safe, and my niece born healthy."

Evelyn wrote Laurie's name on the small sheet of paper along with the prayer request. She tugged the page free from the notebook and stuck it to the refrigerator with a magnet.

"Thank you, Ma'am. I really appreciate it. I'll let my sister know," the officer said.

"Please do, Officer. It's always a comfort to know someone is praying for you," Tom said.

"You two be good to one another, and please thank your daughter for me."

They saw Driscoll to the front door. "Thanks, Officer. Sorry again for the disturbance."

Tom and Evelyn saw the news vans and the cameras pointed at the front door, recording the officer's departure. They didn't linger at the door, but they were certain the reporters would be asking Officer Driscoll for a quick interview before he went back to the station.

Tom shut the door and turned to find Evelyn waiting for him.

Evelyn grabbed him by the sleeve and dragged him into the living room. She didn't want to stay in the foyer and be heard by someone who might come up to the door, and she didn't want to go to their room where Madison would surely overhear them.

"What happened to you tonight?"

"Evelyn, I'm so sorry. I have no idea what happened." Tom pointed at the television, "I saw that Parker woman vibrant and alive, and I wondered, why not *my* mother? Instead of praising God for His mercy, I was jealous. Why did my mother have to die? Why was that Parker woman given a new opportunity at life? Instead of appreciating my daughter's faith, I blamed her for letting my mother die. I knew it was wrong, Evie, but I blamed her anyway."

An anguished Tom cried out, "My God, Evie, what have I done?"

Evelyn's anger began burning hot again, but not against her husband. Her husband's behavior was so uncharacteristic that she was convinced he'd been manipulated. "How did it feel, Tom? When you became angry?"

"It's hard to know now. I felt justified. Even as I told myself I was wrong, there was some part of me that said she had it coming. She deserved to be hurt, and maybe if I could make her hurt enough, then my own pain would stop," Tom sobbed. "That feeling came over me for a few minutes, and then it was gone."

"Dear God," Evelyn whispered. She was worried for her husband.

Tom shivered, "It was a dark feeling, Evie. It was evil." Then he stood up and said, "I have to apologize to Maddie."

"No. Not yet, Tom," Evelyn said as she stood to hold him back. "We have to pray first. Then I'll go up and see if she feels like talking."

"Thanks, Evie. Thanks for not giving up on me," Tom said. "Let's pray."

CHAPTER EIGHTEEN

If Chuck's hunch was right, and Madison truly had run away, he had to figure where she'd go next. The logical first choice was to Trisha's house.

With the rain and the late hour, the streets were empty of traffic. He could slip nice and easy down the quiet residential streets. But the rain also worked against him. The raindrops dotted his windshield, and the streetlights glared through the droplets, making it difficult to see in the dark. Chuck kicked the wipers up a notch.

He turned right and slowed to a crawl. This was Trisha's street. If Madison was hoofing it from the main road, then this is the way she'd come. He didn't want to miss seeing her.

He passed by the house. It appeared everyone had turned in for the evening. Still, Trisha may have slipped out of the house to meet her friend. He did a few passes through the neighborhood, but it proved to be a waste of time.

Maybe Madison really had decided to run away with her boyfriend. Chuck followed up on that possibility, but there seemed to be nothing of particular interest going on at the Warner household. Even so, he cruised the neighborhood longer than he felt was wise on the chance he'd see Madison walking toward Kenny's house.

His truck chimed and he glanced at the dashboard. Low fuel warning. That made up his mind. He'd abandon the hunt for Madison tonight. Besides, there was no chatter on his police scanner about a missing girl. Between the rain and the cold, she must have chickened out and gone home.

Chuck pulled into the station and cozied up to pump four.

Walking into the convenience store to pay for his gas, he was surprised to feel himself troubled over Madison's situation. He remembered how his world changed when his mom had first started seeing his stepdad. Sure, he was nice at first. Right up until his mom thought she couldn't live without him anymore. Then they got married.

His first instinct had been to get out and get as far away as he could. Easier said than done. How could he leave everything he'd ever known? His mom, his school, and his friends? So, he went back. And he kept going back.

Chuck pumped gas and thought about when life got ugly with his stepfather. He would run away from home for a few days and crash at a friend's house, but he always knew he'd be going home.

Sometimes he'd go over to his aunt's house. She knew the score, and she gave him a place to stay until the storm blew over. But that night when his stepdad got particularly violent, he decided he was done with life at home. He packed a few things and took the first road right out of town.

In this town, that meant State Route Three. North of the woods was an abandoned industrial park. There was a road, Industry Road, which separated the undeveloped land from the buildings and businesses.

During its heyday, they had trucks running up and down the highway eighteen hours a day. It was here that State Route Three changed from a four-lane through town, to a divided highway heading north toward Saint Louis.

These days the park sustained no commerce. No one manufactured there any longer, and no one opened businesses.

Oh, there was still business conducted on the property, but these entrepreneurs didn't offer their employees stock options, or 401k matches. There was a large contingent of homeless people living around the rear of the complex who stayed mostly out of sight, and they had developed their own shadow economy.

There were those who bought, and there were those who sold, and if a person wasn't too particular about how an item was acquired, they could discover some real bargains. Chuck had done some trading from time to time and had occasionally brought food to share with the community. It was a small gesture of goodwill.

***

As she emerged from the trees, Madison thanked the Lord. She was only a few minutes from leaving Oracle. With the industrial park ahead of her, and the State Route a half mile to the west, she should be on the road in no time.

Remaining alert, she watched for traffic, especially for the police. It had been more than two hours since she left home, and she was sure her parents would have called in a missing person report by now. She didn't want to have come this far only to be taken back home.

While she remained vigilant, she wasn't worried. She knew God's plans could not be thwarted, and the Holy Spirit was with her. She didn't know where she was going, but God had promised to provide all she needed. Right now, she needed transportation.

Madison crossed Industry Road and headed toward the highway. The abandoned offices and warehouses loomed in the dark. She didn't know what time it was, but it had to be after one.

She made her way west towards the highway. To avoid being seen, she hugged the shadows, but one of the shadows stepped out from the shrubbery.

Madison was startled and turned, ready to run, but her assailant grabbed her arm and spun her around to face him.

"What are you doing sneaking around in the dark at this hour?" he asked.

"Let go of me!" she demanded. Madison fought against him and finally managed to pull free of his grasp, only to be grabbed from behind by a second man.

He pinned Madison's arms behind her, and she hissed in pain.

The first man approached and yanked her beanie off. He took a good look at her in the feeble light. "You're young. Pretty." He ran a dirty hand through her blonde hair. "You don't belong here. What are you up to?"

"I was walking to the highway for a ride. Let me go." Madison tried to squirm away, but the man holding her was strong, and when he tightened his hold on her, she yelped.

The man holding Madison said, "Imagine our good fortune, Earl. Something to keep us nice and warm on a chilly night."

The two men shared a hearty laugh.

Madison took advantage of their momentary distraction to escape. She stomped down hard on the man's foot. He shouted in surprise and pain, and he lost his grip on her.

Madison tried to run, but he grabbed her by the strap of her pack and hauled her back. She saw stars as Earl delivered two vicious blows with the flat of his hand.

"This is going to be a long night for you," Earl growled as they dragged her away.

"Don't do this," she begged. "God will protect me!" Madison began to pray, "Lord, hear my cry. Deliver me from this evi–"

The second man clamped a gnarled hand over her mouth. "Save your breath. It's way past God's bedtime."

Madison kicked hard and Earl lost his grip. She dropped to the pavement just as a blinding light shone upon them, and a metal roar assailed their ears. The big truck ground to a screeching stop in front of them, tires sliding on wet pavement in a spray of water and gravel.

The door opened and Chuck shouted, "Back off. She's with me." He stepped forward and the truck's headlights cast his shadow. He was carrying a tire iron.

Madison was on the ground, watching as the second man made a move, as though he was going to dispute Chuck's claim on their prize.

"Really? You want to try your luck?" Chuck asked, brandishing the tire iron.

It didn't take long to figure the odds, and the man made his exit toward the rear of the complex.

Chuck turned his attention to Earl. "What am I going to do with you?"

Earl tried to explain, "How was I to know she was a friend of yours? If I'd known, I never would have–"

Chuck delivered a punch that laid Earl out on the ground.

"Don't ever hit a lady," Chuck warned.

Madison prayed aloud. "Thank you, Jesus. You are my shield. You are ever present. Thank you for sending your warrior."

Chuck was astounded at this unexpected opportunity. A couple of hours earlier he was cruising neighborhoods, searching, and wondering if he'd somehow missed her.

The next thing he knew, he had this crazy hunch that he'd find her here at the north end of town. Except, it wasn't an ordinary hunch. It was like he'd *known* where to find her. As soon as the idea came into his head, it consumed him. When he'd turned down this street between the buildings, he knew he'd find her exactly here.

Chuck shrugged it off. The mind is an amazing and mysterious thing. You pick up a little information here, notice something else over there, and the conscious mind doesn't make any connection. Yet the subconscious keeps chugging away in the background, trying to see how all the pieces fit together.

He approached Madison slowly, knowing she was scared. He didn't want to upset her any more than she was already. Chuck figured she was going to ask him to take her home. If she did, he'd take her back to her house and use the opportunity to build trust. She'd be absolutely no good to him taken under duress.

He bent down to offer her his hand, "Can I help you up?"

Madison shrieked with joy. "Chuck! Oh, my gosh, how did you know I needed you?" She took his hand and was on her feet in an instant, hugging him. "God sent you, didn't He?"

It was obvious she'd been crying. He could only imagine what had happened to her before he showed up. He didn't know how he was going to explain his presence here, but she'd provided him the perfect opening.

"Madison, I'm so glad to find you in time! Are you hurt?" Chuck asked.

"I'm okay. But I wouldn't be if you hadn't shown up." Madison looked into his eyes and smiled. "You truly are an answer to prayer."

"I don't know about that, but I think we'd better get going," Chuck advised. "Those guys have a lot of friends close by. If they hold a grudge, we could be in trouble. Give me your backpack. I'll put it in the backseat."

Madison shrugged off the pack and handed it over, then took off her wet jacket and draped it over her pack to dry.

"I really appreciate this, Chuck," Madison said, as she climbed into the passenger side of the big truck. "When God told me not to worry about a ride, I had no idea it would be you. I've never done this before, so I'm glad He sent a friendly face."

"Wait, you want to leave town?" he asked, feigning surprise.

"It's a long story, but God brought you here." Then Madison began to pray aloud. A prayer of thanks for God's generosity, and for sending Chuck to look after her.

Chuck was ashamed, knowing his heart didn't possess the good intent that Madison believed motivated him. Shame was an emotion he hadn't felt in years, and it troubled him.

He put the big machine in gear, and they were soon on the state route headed north.

"How did you know I needed help tonight? What were you doing out near those abandoned buildings?" Madison asked.

"Me? What were *you* doing there?" Chuck skirted the issue by asking her questions instead. "Shouldn't you be home in bed, fast asleep?"

He reached up and turned on the interior lights to look at her.

"Whoa, what happened to you?" He slowed down and pulled over on the side of the road. It was a quiet night with no traffic.

Chuck took her chin between his thumb and forefinger and turned her head to get a better look in the light. He'd seen her lip, when her face was brightly illuminated by the truck's headlights. He'd seen the mark on the side of her face, too. Those didn't happen just now. She'd had a fight with someone earlier.

"Tell me who did this, and I'll take care of them for you." Chuck wondered if her boyfriend had roughed her up. If he had, and her parents saw this, it was no wonder there was a big fight.

She pulled away. "There's nothing to take care of. This was my fault."

Chuck wasn't buying, "Your fault? How do you figure?"

"It just was. You'll have to take my word for it," Madison insisted. "Anyway, what were you doing out here in the middle of the night? Didn't you say you were going to Florida?"

Chuck figured he'd go for an outlandishly spiritual explanation. She'd believe it, for sure. "I was ready to leave for Florida tomorrow morning. I'd finished dinner and cleaned up. Before going to bed I sat down to pray about the trip and God spoke to my heart. He said you needed my help, but I had no idea where to find you."

"How did you know where to go?" Madison asked.

"I must have fallen asleep. I dreamed of that place you were at. In the dream I saw two wolves circling around you. It seemed so real. One of the wolves snarled and it woke me up. I had to come to see if the dream was real. You were really there!" He glanced over at her. Maybe he'd gone too far with the dream. He'd conceived it on the spot, and it was a little bit much.

"Will you take me with you?" asked Madison.

Chuck blinked in surprise. She believed his story. "To Florida?" he asked.

"Yes. Or wherever."

Chuck was silent for a long time. He simply couldn't believe it was going to be this easy. Still, he wanted to be sure the hook was set before he started reeling her in.

He made a great show of wrestling with his conscience.

"I don't know, Madison. I don't know what you're running from. I'm not worried about me, but I don't want you to get in trouble."

"God called you. When I was in urgent need, He sent you to help me." This girl was completely undeterred in her confidence. "You have to take me with you."

Chuck again spent some time considering her request. Finally, he nodded and said, "I think our meeting up again is too cosmic to be a coincidence. It appears that I've been assigned to be your driver, Ma'am."

"Thank you."

Madison was grateful it was Chuck with whom she'd travel. Having met him a couple times already, she felt like she was heading out on a road trip with a friend. For a moment there, she hadn't been sure that he'd agree to take her with him.

For the first time in hours, she felt she could relax. Basking in the flow of warm air from the truck's vents, Madison closed her eyes. Together they drove off into the wet and chilly night. Before long, Madison was fast asleep in the passenger seat.

CHAPTER NINETEEN

It was midnight, and Morris Abbott turned over in bed, sighing. He adjusted his pillow and tried without success to get comfortable.

He glanced over at his wife. She was sound asleep.

Tomorrow, Madison was leaving for New York for her interview with Sharon Sterling. He hoped the trip would go well, and that the interview would have a positive result.

Morris had watched the news before turning in for the night and had seen the special report on Andrea Parker. With this new, independent verification of another healing, it would be more difficult for anyone to discard Madison's testimony.

Morris reasoned that Mrs. Parker wouldn't be the only person to come forward and say Madison had healed them. Many of the stories would likely be false. He made a mental note to check with Madison whenever he heard of a new claim.

He turned over on his right side and, in spite of the chilly evening, shrugged the covers off his shoulders.

The girl had an undeniable gift. Morris wondered how many people she'd already prayed for, and how many had been healed. While the world was focused on Madison, Morris was more concerned about what these manifestations of spiritual power might mean for believers, and for mankind.

Why did God choose Madison, and what did He want to accomplish?

Morris snorted with irritation. Trying to figure out God's plan was an exercise in futility. He'd told Madison that the things of God could be discerned only through the spirit, yet here he was trying to unscrew the inscrutable.

Not wanting to wake his wife, Morris carefully eased out of bed and grabbed his robe from the closet. It was clear he wouldn't be getting any sleep. Something was nagging at him, making him restless, and he couldn't quite figure out what it could be.

Morris walked down the hall to his office where he had a red leather loveseat. It was his favorite piece of furniture in the house, and he'd spent a lot of time in front of it. Now, with his spirit restless and uneasy, he kneeled in front of it once again. He bent down with his elbows on the seat cushions and began to pray.

***

Tom and Evelyn found they had a lot to pray for.

Evelyn prayed that Madison wouldn't harden her heart against her father. She prayed for their marriage, that God would strengthen them as a couple, and that He would lead them through all the trials they would face together.

She asked God to help her understand her daughter. Evelyn recognized that what Madison experienced wasn't part of this world. She'd seen what happened when Madison prayed for Kenny.

When Madison spoke to God, she was more present with Him in spirit than in the flesh. It was this Evelyn longed to understand about her daughter, and she prayed that Madison would be open to talking to her after what happened tonight.

Tom's prayer was simple and direct, but no less sincere for its brevity. He begged God to forgive him for what he'd done and prayed he wouldn't lose his family.

Afterwards, Evelyn said, "I need to go upstairs and check on Maddie."

"It's late," Tom said.

"I know, but I don't want her to think we've abandoned her."

"I'm sure she heard us. Madison knows we were fighting, and she knows why. I'm sure she knows the police came. How could she miss the lights from her room? She's probably afraid to come out and see me," Tom said.

"Nonsense, Tom," Evelyn said, and immediately wished she sounded more convincing. "I'll talk to her."

Evelyn climbed the stairs, praying that God would give her words that would touch Maddie's heart. She didn't want to lose her daughter.

She gently rapped on the bedroom door. "Maddie?"

There was no answer.

She tried again, knocking harder this time. "Madison?"

Again, no answer. Evelyn tasted the corrosive, metal sting of fear.

She opened the door to find the bedroom lights were off. Evelyn was grateful to see the thin ribbon of light escaping from beneath Madison's bathroom door. She didn't know what she was going to say, but she prayed that God would open a door to understanding what her daughter must be going through.

Evelyn felt uneasy in her own daughter's bedroom. It was a strange sensation, to feel as though she didn't belong. She raised her child in this bedroom and knew it as well as she knew her own. But what once felt light and cheerful, now felt hostile and forbidding. She felt unwelcome. Evelyn shivered and turned on the light.

Evelyn cast a nervous glance over her shoulder, and then knocked on the bathroom door.

"Madison?"

There was no answer.

A helpless whimper escaped her lips. Evelyn turned to survey the room.

There was the suitcase Madison packed to go to New York. It was open, and her clothes spilled out in disarray, as though someone had pawed through it without regard. Then she saw Madison's bed was undisturbed. Madison hadn't slept there.

Evelyn threw open the bathroom door to find it empty.

"Tom!" she screamed. She felt a vicious resentment rise against Tom for his role in Madison's disappearance. It was a sharp-edged anger that took her breath away.

Tom was upstairs in an instant and found his wife on the floor, crying.

"Evie, what's wro–"

"She's gone, Tom,"

Tom looked around the room and then ran down the hall to their bedroom, just in case Madison had gone there, but it was empty.

"When could she have gone?" Tom was close to panic.

Evelyn snapped her reply. "How would I know? I'm not the one who drove her away!"

His wife's words hit him like a blow.

He had failed in the worst possible way. Tom had always been a positive influence in his daughter's life. He supported her in all that she did and encouraged her to try new things. Yet, when Madison wrestled with the biggest upheaval in her life, he had let his own pain spill over onto her. He'd accused her unjustly and shouted at her in anger.

And worse? He'd struck her. It was the ultimate betrayal of her trust.

His shame burned him like a brand. No wonder she ran.

What kind of father was he, anyway? But it wasn't as though he was a complete failure. He had a lapse, that's all. It wasn't like he was a monster. But you wouldn't know it to hear Evelyn talk.

You'd think his own wife would be supportive, or at least sympathetic. After all, he lost his mother. Doesn't that count for something? What about his feelings?

He already felt bad enough about what he'd done without Evelyn throwing it in his face. What gave her the right to point the finger and blame him? She'd be singing a different tune when he slapped that accusatory sneer off her stupi–

Tom gasped, and he reeled under the strength of his emotions. He'd never felt this way toward Evelyn. The inner dialog had run through his mind in a matter of seconds. It was God's own grace he hadn't succumbed to his feelings. Where had this anger come from?

Evelyn saw rage pass over Tom's features like a shadow, and then it was gone. She grabbed his hand and said, "Let's get out of this room. Now!"

Downstairs, Evelyn hugged her husband. "I'm so sorry, Tom. I didn't mean to say that. I promise, I really don't feel that way. Please forgive me. The anger swept over me, and I'm sorry for what I said."

A frightened Tom said, "You don't need to apologize, Evie. I understand."

"You felt it too, didn't you?" she asked.

Tom nodded. "Yes! But right now, our baby is missing."

Evelyn had her phone out and called her daughter. It went straight to voicemail.

She tried again with the same result.

"Give Lillian a call," Tom offered. "Madison probably went over to her friend's house."

Evelyn paced the living room floor as she listened to her phone. There was no answer, and the call went to voicemail. She swore and called again.

Finally, Lillian answered groggily.

"Hello, Lillian? It's Evelyn. I hate calling you at this hour. I was–"

"Evelyn, how is Maddie?" Lillian cut in.

"Well, that's the thing. Can you ask Trisha if she's heard from her?"

Lillian was quiet for a minute on the other end.

"Give me a minute," she finally said.

"Sure. I'll wait."

The minutes crawled by, and Evelyn continued to pace, raking the fingers of her free hand through her hair.

"Evelyn?" Lillian said. "Trisha got a text from Madison around eleven saying she wasn't going to New York after all. She sent a couple of texts to Madison after that, but she never got a reply."

"I appreciate it, Lillian," Evelyn said, sighing deeply. "Again, I apologize for calling so late. If you see Madison, or hear anything, please call me. Anytime."

"Did something happen?" Lillian asked.

Evelyn was hesitant to say anything, but she had to give some sort of explanation. "There was an argument and Madison left the house. I'm so worried about her. Thanks, Lillian."

"What did she say?" Tom asked as soon as the call ended.

Evelyn filled him in on the side of the conversation he hadn't heard.

"She must have turned off her phone," Tom surmised.

"If she's not at Trisha's house, where is she?" Evelyn wondered.

Tom frowned. "Could she have gone over to Kenny's?"

"I suppose so."

"Maybe we should call the police," Tom suggested.

"We've only known of her being gone for a few minutes. I don't think the police take reports unless the person is gone for at least twenty-four hours," Evelyn said.

"Are you sure about that?" Tom asked.

"Of course not," Evelyn answered. "I've never done this before. Besides, what are you going to tell them? You could end up being arrested, Tom. I need you here with me."

Tom was silent for a long moment. "We need to call Morris."

"I think so, too. We're way out of our depth he—"

The ringing doorbell cut Evelyn off like a switch. Frozen in place, they exchanged a look.

"Could that be Maddie?" Evelyn asked, hope rising in her heart.

He looked out the peephole. "Put on some coffee. It's Morris."

"Morris?"

Tom opened the door and Morris Abbott rushed in past him. He looked at Tom and Evelyn, his expression one of deep concern. "Where's Madison?"

CPSIA information can be obtained
at www.ICGtesting.com
Printed in the USA
LVHW090157090222
710669LV00004B/62